The Two Saras:
Coleridge in Cumbria

THE TWO SARAS: COLERIDGE IN CUMBRIA

BETHANY ASKEW

The Two Saras: Coleridge in Cumbria

Edited by Sarah Dawes

Cover by Oliver Tooley

Blue Poppy Publishing 2020

ISBN: 978-1-911438-72-4

Preface

This book is a sequel to my novel *Three Extraordinary Years: The Coleridges at Stowey* but can be read independently. It covers the years 1800 to 1804, when Samuel Taylor Coleridge lived in the Lake District and before he went away to Malta.

A few notes on the text:

Having two main characters called Sara was always going to be a challenge. To avoid confusion, I have spelled Sara Coleridge's name without the 'h' as she herself did, at Coleridge's request, and Sarah Hutchinson's name with the 'h' because she usually signed herself that way, despite Coleridge and the Wordsworths referring to her as Sara.

Many of the men have the same first names — William, Tom, George, Robert — so I have referred to them by their surnames throughout. Samuel Taylor Coleridge famously hated his first name. He preferred to be called Coleridge, STC or 'Col'. However, I have called him Samuel because it is what Sara called him.

Finally, I have referred to the county as Cumbria in deference to the modern reader, although it was known as Cumberland in Coleridge's time.

Chapter One

The house was better than Sara could ever have imagined: a large square building perched on a hill, its freshly painted white walls gleaming in the summer sunshine.

"Are we really going to live *here*?" Hartley asked excitedly.

"Yes, my sweet boy," Samuel said. "This is Greta Hall. We don't have all of it though, just the front part. Mr Jackson lives in the back."

Sara didn't mind. It looked like a palace compared with most of the places she had lived with Samuel. And, apart from when they lived in that dreadful little cottage in Somerset, they had always shared houses. For the last few months she had been living with her mother in Bristol while Samuel decided where they would settle. He had so many grand schemes; one moment he talked of living on the continent with his writer friends, the next moment he was talking about moving back to Somerset. Sara would have preferred to stay in the West Country, near her family. She hadn't wanted to come all the way up here to the north but Samuel wanted to be near the Wordsworths.

"We're going to work together again," he told her, "on a second edition of *Lyrical Ballads*. It's so exciting. I'll write some new poems and revise the old ones. I'll have everything I need: the company of people who inspire me and support me and somewhere quiet to work, with beautiful countryside around me."

'People who inspire me and support me' meant the Wordsworths: William and his sister Dorothy. Samuel was always looking for a family to attach himself to. At one time it had been *her* family. Her sister Edith had married his close friend Southey and her sister Mary had married his other friend Lovell: three sisters marrying three poets. It should have bound them together forever but Lovell had died and Samuel was always falling out with Southey about one thing or another. Wordsworth had taken his place in Samuel's affections.

The carriage had come to a stop and Samuel jumped out, rushing ahead as usual. He always rushed everywhere. She saw him speak to the plump middle-aged woman standing by the door before hurrying back again to help her and Hartley out.

"Wait Hartley," Sara told him. "Mama can't go as quickly as you can."

The woman bustled towards her. "Come in, come in," she said. "You must be tired." Her eyes fell to Sara's stomach. "And travelling in your condition! When is the baby due?"

Sara blushed. "Six weeks."

"And who's this little one?" She patted Hartley's dark head as he struggled to pull his hand away from Sara's firm grip.

"David Hartley," he replied clearly.

"Well, David…"

"We call him Hartley," Sara interrupted.

"Hartley." She laughed. "I'm Mrs Wilson, the housekeeper. Tell me now, how old are you?"

"Three," Hartley said, holding up three fingers proudly.

"Well, since you're such a big grown-up boy why don't I show you and Mama around the house while Papa unpacks the bags and boxes? I may have something in the kitchen for you to eat."

Sara felt herself relaxing already. This motherly woman was just the sort she needed to help her with Hartley and the new baby. They had been staying with the Wordsworths for the last month while Samuel recovered from a bad cold. It wasn't that Dorothy wasn't used to children. She had looked after her aunt's ever-increasing brood for years and when they were living in Dorset she and William had been paid to look after four-year-old Basil Montagu, but Dorothy's entire life centred on William. "When Basil cried we used to send him to his room," she told Sara, "and not let him out until he had stopped. William needs peace and quiet to work. Like Samuel does," she added pointedly.

Dorothy always made Sara feel that she wasn't good enough for Samuel. But what did Dorothy know about married life? She was a spinster and, with her looks and her strange ways, always destined to be so. Sister to a poet was nothing like being married to one, especially one like Samuel with his impulsive ideas.

"This is the parlour," Mrs Wilson was saying.

Sara was impressed. To save them transporting any furniture such a long way, Mr Jackson had arranged for the house to be furnished for them. The chairs and tables weren't exactly what she considered elegant but there was everything they could need. It was late July, an unusually hot day. The heat on the journey had been unbearable but the room felt cool and airy, the large windows wide open onto the beautiful view of the mountains.

"Mr Jackson had the house rebuilt, you know," Mrs Wilson went on. "It was originally an ob-serv-a-tory." She pronounced the word carefully. "To look at the stars, you know. I expect you'll meet Mr Jackson later." She turned to look at Sara. "Why, you look all in. Why don't you sit down for a while and put your feet up? I can show you round later. Let me fetch you some refreshment. Hartley can help me."

Hartley had been darting around the room, peering out of the windows, examining the furniture.

"You said you had something in the kitchen for me," he reminded her.

"Well, we'd better go and find it then," she laughed. "Come along while Mama has a little rest."

Sara sank down thankfully on the nearest chair and the kindly Mrs Wilson brought the footstool for her.

"There. Now we'll be back in a few moments..." Her voice receded as the door closed behind her. Sara closed her eyes. She could hear Samuel outside, his slow shuffle as he came into the house carrying a box or a package, his speedier walk back to the cart. Someone was helping him, a young lad by the sound of it, talking in that strange north country accent that Mrs Wilson had, a stronger version of William and Dorothy's accent, hard for Sara to get her mind round. The noises came and went, there was a cool breeze from the window, the pain in her back and legs began to ease.

She jumped as the door suddenly opened.

"Mama, Mama, Wilsy gave me some honey cake!"

"Mrs Wilson," Sara corrected him.

"Lord, I don't mind what he calls me," Mrs Wilson laughed. "Such a sweet lad. Here's some for Mama and a cup of tea."

"Oh, thank you."

"Tell me," Sara said as Mrs Wilson set the tea and cake next to her, "how far is it to the town?"

"Just a step. You can be there in a few minutes."

"It is such a relief for me to be near a town. My husband loves the countryside and nature but I was brought up in Bath and Bristol. I like to be near a town."

"You don't know this part of the world at all then?"

"Oh no. We lived in London for a little while and in Somerset before that. And Bristol and Clevedon when we were first married. My family all live in Bristol. But Samuel has friends up here."

"It's a long way from *your* family though."

"Three hundred miles." Sara sighed, remembering the long journey. "We stopped at Chester and then at Liverpool."

In Liverpool they had stayed for a week with the Cromptons, friends of Samuel's who had tried to help him several years ago when he was thinking of setting up a school. It was while they were staying with them that Samuel had caught a cold, which confined him to bed the moment he arrived at Grasmere, leaving Sara and Dorothy to sort out the unpacking.

"You'll soon make friends here," Mrs Wilson said kindly.

"Do we have neighbours nearby?" Sara asked.

"Well, let me see. There's Colonel Peachey who takes a house on one of the islands on Derwent Water in the summer; that's just about a mile away. Then there's Mr and Mrs Spedding, the Reverend Wilkinson of course, and Mr Losh. I daresay they'll all pay a visit once they know you're here."

"My husband will receive them," Sara said. "I shall of course wait until after my confinement."

"You'll be hoping for a girl this time I expect," Mrs Wilson said.

"Oh, I don't mind," Sara said quickly.

"Of course not. You never mind with the second one. Plenty of time for a girl later. And a little brother would be lovely for young Hartley. Someone for him to play with."

Sara's eyes filled with tears. "Oh, it's not my second. I had such a beautiful son." Her voice wobbled but she forged on. "Berkeley. He died."

"Oh, I'm so sorry," Mrs Wilson said. "Such a sad loss."

Hartley had stopped careering around the room at the sight and sound of his mother's tears and looked across at her worriedly. Sara caught Mrs Wilson's eye and shook her head slightly.

"Why don't we go and see how Papa is getting on?" Mrs Wilson said brightly. "And when Mama is a bit less tired she'll come and help."

Sara knew she should go with them but thoughts of Berkeley had brought back painful memories. She closed her eyes against the tears that trickled down her face, feeling the pain of hurt and loss cut deep in her chest. But rest was impossible now. She heard Samuel grumbling as he carried a box from the cart, Hartley shouting as he ran back and forth, the quieter voices of Mrs Wilson and the young lad. She had just heaved herself to her feet when Samuel burst into the room.

"Oh Sara! Just look at that view!" he said, rushing over to the window. "It's as though giants have pitched their tents there! Each mountain a giant's tent! And see how the light streams from them and look at the shadows on them!"

"Oh, Samuel, I'm far too tired to look at views!" The words were out of her mouth before she could bring them back. She saw the look of disappointment cross his face, the icy disdain that quickly followed. No doubt the saintly Dorothy Wordsworth would have agreed with him, hidden all her tiredness and enthused about the view. But Samuel had been saying things like this ever since the mountains came into view and Sara was heartily fed up with it. She had to admit to a passing excitement when she first saw the high mountains, the huge expanses of water, but the novelty had long since worn off.

"I've got so much to do," she went on. "The unpacking and sorting things out. Hartley will want feeding, so will you. Then I've got to put him to bed…"

"There's no rush, Sara. You can just unpack what's necessary and do the rest later can't you? And Hartley told me he'd just had a piece of honey cake, the lucky fellow. We should go out, explore the area."

"You go, Samuel," she snapped. "I just told you I'm tired. And I may as well get going on it all."

"I think I'll pop next door then and say hello to Mr Jackson. Such an interesting man. He has a library of five hundred books. He collects the modern writers: Gibbon, Hume, Johnson…"

"Yes, you go. Don't worry about me."

Her sarcasm was lost on him, or maybe he chose to ignore it. Sara sighed. They were back to bickering again. Coming up here was supposed to be a fresh start. Since he had been back from Germany the longest they had lived together was the ten weeks they had spent in London. That, too, was supposed to be a fresh start, a chance to heal the rift that had developed since Samuel had gone to Germany. When he first went abroad he had promised to send for her and the children once he was settled. But instead he stayed there for ten months, not even coming home when Berkeley fell ill and then died. She had felt abandoned, let down by her husband when she needed him most.

When they moved to London, Samuel wrote articles for a newspaper. It was a steady income. It all seemed so promising; Sara was pregnant again, she enjoyed city life, she and Samuel made new friends, they went out together. But the lodgings in Buckingham Street were cramped; Samuel needed peace and quiet to work in, as he was always telling her, and Hartley was a noisy little boy, full of mischief and high spirits. Sara was feeling sick most of the time. She couldn't keep taking Hartley out. They were constantly in Samuel's way and she could feel how much she annoyed him. The newspaper articles had to be in on set times. Samuel began to fall behind. Soon they were arguing again. Finally Samuel moved in with his friend Charles Lamb and Sara moved back to her mother's lodgings in Bristol.

But Bristol was three hundred miles from Keswick. No running home to Mama now. She had married Samuel for better or for worse, the vows she had made five years ago in St Mary Redcliffe in Bristol. And the baby that moved in her stomach now reminded her that there was, in fact, no choice. Samuel had to provide for her and her children. They were bound to each other.

When she stepped outside into the bright July sunshine, Mrs Wilson looked relieved to see her. "I'll have to be getting back to Mr Jackson now," she said. "You've got everything you need?"

"Yes, thank you," Sara said. "Come along Hartley, say goodbye to Mrs Wilson. You'll see her again soon."

Sara climbed the stairs, Hartley chattering next to her. *"Just like his father,"* she thought, *"always something to talk about."* Samuel had dumped his boxes of books just inside the doorway of the room which was obviously going to be his study, a large room with a big arched window overlooking the mountains. There were bookshelves and a writing desk as well as a bed so that he could sleep there rather than disturbing her at all hours of the night when he couldn't settle, or when he leapt out of bed with an idea for something he simply had to write down. And with the baby due so soon she didn't sleep well either. It made sense to sleep separately now that they had the room.

There were four other bedrooms and three more on the floor above that. It was far more than they needed. They wouldn't use most of them, unless they had people to stay. She couldn't imagine any of her family coming up but there were friends of Samuel's who would think nothing of making the journey. There were plenty of rooms to choose from, each one large, high ceilinged, the light flooding in, with views over the mountains that Samuel raved so much about. As she decided which ones she and Hartley would have, Sara's spirits began to lift.

For the last few weeks they had been staying with the Wordsworths in their tiny cottage. The Wordsworths' brother John was living there as well and, with their boxes and crates stacked in every available inch of space, it was a dreadful squash. But it couldn't be helped and Sara was grateful to the Wordsworths for letting them stay. Samuel's cold had deteriorated into what he called 'rheumatic fever'. He had always been prone to it, ever since he'd been a child. He ached all over, his eyes were bloodshot and swollen and he complained that the tiniest movement of his head on the pillow made the blood rush to and from his head like the tide raking over loose stones. He had dreadful nights; when he wasn't tossing and turning and grumbling he was having nightmares, waking Hartley and the rest of the household with his screams of terror. He'd never felt so ill, he said. With the baby due in six weeks, Sara herself slept badly, woken by indigestion or by the baby moving or settling painfully on her bladder.

The last time they had lived near the Wordsworths, two years ago in Somerset, it was William and Dorothy who had the big house, Alfoxton Park, a nine-bedroom mansion, while she and Samuel had lived in a tiny worker's cottage in Lime Street in

Stowey. They had been happy there to begin with, the first six months when it was just her and Samuel and Hartley, before Wordsworth and Dorothy turned up and took Samuel away from her. And here they were doing it again. She knew she wasn't the only one who thought they had too much influence on Samuel. Tom Poole, the only true friend she had had in the village, definitely agreed with her. He had tried so hard to find somewhere for them to live back near Stowey, rather than moving up here.

Charles Lamb, Samuel's London friend, wasn't afraid to speak out against the Wordsworths either, even if it meant upsetting Samuel. Then there was her sister Edith's husband, Robert Southey. He and Samuel were always falling out and he too felt Samuel was better off away from the Wordsworths. But at least here in Keswick they were a fourteen-mile walk from Grasmere. Of course, Samuel would think little of walking fourteen miles but he was unlikely to do it every day. When they were in Stowey he had walked the four miles over to Alfoxton nearly every day. But the cottage in Stowey had been tiny, like all the places they'd lived before, whereas Greta Hall was huge. Samuel could work uninterrupted, morning, noon or night. He didn't need to escape to somewhere quiet. It's what he'd always wanted. They would be happy here; things would be different, especially when the new baby was born and she could go out and pay visits. She would make friends, like she had in Stowey, other families with children whom Hartley could play with, women with babies whom she could talk to. She was sure that in Greta Hall (which she must remember to pronounce Greeta Hall, like a local) she and Samuel would be happy again.

Hartley was in bed by the time Samuel came home, full of talk about the collection of books Mr Jackson had and what an interesting man he was, how he had raised himself up from virtual poverty to financial independence, "by the severest economy."

She scarcely glanced at him as he spoke, except to notice that he looked more scruffy than usual, his breeches grubby, his stockings grimy with dust from the road. It was one of the first things she had noticed about him when she first met him: his long dark hair that needed cutting, his shabby clothes. She hadn't found him at all attractive with his flabby mouth, always hanging open slightly. But when he spoke, ah, then it was different. His whole face changed; a light came into those pale grey eyes, enthusiasm transformed him: he was irresistible. But that was six years ago. Things had changed since then. Now she scarcely listened to what he was saying. It was like Hartley's chatter, a constant background noise that was so boring she just shut it out. Then suddenly she heard him say, "D'you know what? Mr Jackson didn't want any rent! He said the house is barely finished. But I soon talked him out of it and we agreed a price."

"What?" Sara said incredulously. "Samuel, are you mad? You still owe the Wedgwoods money. Then there's Poole and Cottle and heaven alone knows who else."

"The Wedgwoods have so much money they don't know what to do with it! They don't mind me drawing on my annuity. Poole's my friend, he knows I'll pay him back sometime. And Cottle's my publisher, he needs me, he won't care when I let him have the money as long as I give him my work."

"There'll be things to pay for here," Sara went on unabated. "Food, clothes, fuel for the fire. If this Mr Jackson can afford for us to live rent free you should have agreed with it."

"But it wouldn't be right, Sara. In any case he says we don't need to pay for six months, he says the house is scarcely finished, there may be building problems that need sorting out."

Samuel was always like this when he met new people; he had a way of charming them, she had seen it again and again. Robert Southey, Tom Poole, Joseph Cottle, Dorothy and William Wordsworth, the Wedgwood brothers, all fell under his spell. She herself had been the same. Now she saw clearly through the charm to the needy person underneath. Maybe the others did too but they didn't live with him all the time. They didn't know how difficult he was. They didn't see him when he was bad-tempered and cantankerous.

Samuel was talking about something else now. "Once I've unpacked my stuff I must get on with writing *Christabel* for the second edition of *Lyrical Ballads.* Wordsworth has already written some beautiful poems for it. I don't want to be left behind."

Sara didn't pay much attention to what he was saying. She had long since given up any interest in

Samuel's work. She was only interested in the money it might bring in. Not that there seemed much chance with this *Christabel* poem. He'd been writing it for the last three years; it was supposed to go into the first edition but he hadn't finished it on time.

"Dorothy will transcribe it for me," Samuel went on enthusiastically, "along with the corrections I've made to *The Ancient Mariner*."

"Good old Dorothy," Sara thought, bitterly. She knew it would be like this once the three of them got together again. Oh, she was grateful to Dorothy for helping her when they had first arrived up here, especially when Samuel retreated to bed and left them to unpack and sort everything out. And she would need her again to look after Hartley when the new baby came. In fact, she couldn't possibly manage without her, so she had to keep up some sort of civil friendship.

At one time she had been quite jealous of Dorothy, the way Samuel spoke about her as though she were the most bewitching woman on earth. But that was before she met her. Once she had seen her, the small skinny frame, the gaunt brown face, scrawny arms and chest, the almost-toothless mouth, then she had changed her mind. If Dorothy were the last woman alive Samuel would have nothing to do with her. She'd been jealous of Wordsworth too, though he was equally strange looking, thin like his sister, the same dark hair and eyes but tall, wearing old-fashioned clothes. Neither he nor Dorothy cared what they looked like; they were only interested in nature and poetry. They had a way of making her feel shallow, left out of their intellectual, high-minded world. She thought she might have grown used to it over the years but it still rankled. She knew Dorothy thought she set too much store on domestic duties. But Dorothy didn't have children. She didn't understand that their needs had to come before all else.

"Sara!" Samuel exclaimed suddenly. "Just look at that view! I don't think I shall ever tire of looking out of these windows. Come for a walk with me."

"Samuel, I'm dead on my feet," Sara snapped. "I couldn't possibly take a walk."

He looked at her as though suddenly realising she was pregnant, even though it was hard to miss. "Well, I'm going anyway. It's such a beautiful evening."

The house was quiet once he'd gone. Sara cleared up the dinner dishes and sprinkled ashes over the fire to keep it going overnight. Then she climbed the stairs to bed. She glanced in at Hartley. She had thought he would take ages to settle in his new, big room but he was exhausted by the excitement and had fallen asleep almost immediately. It was still warm and she saw he had kicked off his blanket so she gently pulled it over him again.

Her own room seemed cavernous after the tiny bedroom at the cottage in Grasmere. Her trunk still lay partly unpacked but she was too tired to do anything more about it tonight. She undressed quickly and gratefully removed the tight brown wig from her head, running her hands through the thin wispy strands of hair on her scalp. She never looked in the mirror at this time of night. Her lustrous brown hair, of which she was so proud, had fallen out when Berkeley died and never grown back. Samuel had loved her hair; he used to run his fingers through it, spread it over her breasts and shoulders. He never said anything but she knew he found her bare head repulsive.

She pulled back the covers and sank back gratefully onto the pile of pillows she needed to prop herself up on at night now her stomach was so huge, feeling the pain in her back and legs beginning to recede. It was very quiet; there were no houses nearby, no sounds came through from next door, yet as she lay there she could hear odd creaks and groans as the house settled down for the night. Later, much later, she heard Samuel come in and make his way to his room. She thought she heard him call out once, a bad dream maybe, and she wondered if she should go to him in case he yelled again and woke Hartley. But after that all was quiet.

Chapter Two

At one time Samuel believed he could tell Sara everything. She would be the recipient of his innermost thoughts, the person he could turn to when things went wrong. Sally-Pally, his pet name for her, was his best and closest friend, the one person who would always be on his side. But that was a long time ago. The person he thought she was didn't exist. Sara wasn't always on his side. Quite the reverse; she was always criticising him, finding fault, telling him he could do things better. Now he kept secrets from her, secrets he confided only to his diary and to his closest friends.

He hadn't told her, for example, about Sarah Hutchinson.

He had met her last autumn. Word had reached him that Wordsworth had been taken ill while staying with his friends the Hutchinsons at their farm at Sockburn in County Durham. Samuel had dropped everything and rushed up to see him.

To his surprise Wordsworth was absolutely fine and was enjoying his stay at Gallow Hill with the Hutchinson family.

It was easy to see why. Mary Hutchinson, a childhood friend of Dorothy's, was absolutely charming. Tall and slim, quite reserved but not shy, she was interested in everything around her but especially nature, poetry and literature. Her younger sister Sarah was quite different: small, plump, full of fun. At first he wasn't sure which he preferred. They were like two halves of a coin, sisters so close that Mary called Sarah her 'second self'.

He only had to close his eyes to conjure up Sarah's face: the lovely eyes, the full curving lips, the beautiful auburn hair. She wasn't beautiful. Pretty maybe, despite her prominent square jaw, but not beautiful, not like his own Sara. Of the three Fricker sisters, Sara was known to be the beauty. Her sister Edith was the quiet one, her other sister Mary, who became an actress, the liveliest.

He had been so proud to be seen with Sara. She had the sort of figure he liked: full-bosomed and generous. He couldn't abide skinny women. But now Sara's lovely face wore a perpetual look of sadness. Her lovely blue eyes had lost the light of happiness. Her abundant brown hair that he had loved so much had gone. She had suffered of course, with the loss of Berkeley. But he had suffered too. They could have comforted each other. But Sara blamed him. She never said so but he knew it. She blamed him for going away, blamed him for not coming back. She didn't understand him, she would never understand him. She didn't smile when she saw him, the warmth had gone out of her voice when she spoke to him.

Sarah Hutchinson's voice was soft and gentle. She listened to him when he talked. Her eyes never left his face. She hung on his every word. Sara had been like that once. She had been keen on all his schemes. She had wanted to come to America with him, to help him set up a community of poets and writers and philosophers, people not afraid to try a new way of living. Equal rule for everyone, or Pantisocracy as he called it. That was one of the reasons he had married her; she wasn't afraid to speak out, to be seen as someone different from the rest. He thought she would always support him in everything he did. But she had changed.

He had loved his stay at the Hutchinsons'. The two girls had a younger sister, Joanna, and between them they kept house and worked on the farm with their brother Tom. Another brother, Jack, lived nearby and often came over. They all got on so well together and they liked the same things: long walks in the countryside, laughter and banter interspersed with serious talks on nature and philosophy.

It was so special to be included in this charmed circle. The Wordsworths, the Hutchinsons and him; it was like being part of a family.

He had a family of course: Sara and Hartley. But he and Sara had such different interests. She had no appreciation for nature, she wasn't interested in politics or theology, she never asked about his work, she didn't offer to transcribe his poems. Her whole life revolved around the home and the children.

Sarah Hutchinson was so different. She loved poetry, she wanted to be involved with everything he and Wordsworth were doing. He never saw her impatient, angry or upset. She was easy-going, strong and energetic. She was everything his Sara wasn't. He told himself it was just an innocent flirtation. What was wrong with an unhappily married man enjoying the company of a pretty young woman, one who enjoyed his company and made him happy? Sarah was everything Sara wasn't.

It was such a happy time last autumn at the Hutchinsons', with walks in the cold crisp sunshine, cosy evenings by the fire. One evening they were playing silly games together by the fireside, making jokes and laughing. Samuel's eyes kept meeting Sarah's. He contrived to move around the circle until he was standing next to her. He could feel the heat from her body, see the fire and candlelight light up her face. He knew she was aware of him. He could sense it. But she didn't move away. Emboldened, he reached his arm behind his back and took hold of her little hand, holding it so that no one else could see. He risked a glance at her face. She didn't look back but he saw her face had reddened.

It was an innocent flirtation, nothing more. Something to think about when his own Sara was being nasty to him: *someone* found him attractive, good company, fun to be with, even if his wife didn't.

She was always there at the back of his mind. Not just her but Mary as well, their brothers even. He would have liked to stay longer but he had had to go to London. He had been offered a six-month contract to write articles for the *Morning Post* and his situation was so desperate he had no choice but to accept it.

Sara had never enjoyed living in Stowey in the heart of the countryside. He thought she might like it in London. And to begin with she did. She was back in the heart of a city, with streets and shops and he took her out and introduced her to his London friends, important people like William Godwin.

Samuel was proud of his friendship with Godwin, a philosopher, journalist and novelist, a successful man who was not afraid to express his views publicly. His wife, the famous Mary Wollstonecraft, who had made her name as a writer and advocate for women's equality, had died in childbirth, and he was on his own looking after his young daughters.

Hartley liked going to see 'Mr Gobwin'.

"When can we go again?" he asked one day.

"I'm not sure he'll have us again," Sara said to Samuel. "When Godwin visited us the other day Hartley hit him on the leg with a skittle and he gave me a long lecture about Hartley's boisterousness."

Samuel laughed. "Nothing wrong with a bit of high spirits. Godwin's girls are so quiet. Positively catacomb-ish. I suppose it's because they lost their mother so tragically."

He saw Sara's hand go to the small swelling in her belly. "It's so dangerous, having a baby."

"Godwin has improved since I last saw him," Samuel said, changing the subject quickly. "Though I still think he made a mistake writing the memoir of his wife. All that about her living with a man, having an illegitimate baby, it's ruined her reputation."

Samuel spent a lot of time with Godwin, arguing politics and theology late into the night. He also dined regularly with his friend Charles Lamb and with Daniel Stuart, the editor of the *Morning Post.* Stuart tried to persuade him to take half-shares in the paper and his evening paper, *The Courier.*

"It would be a full-time editorial post," he urged, "worth £2,000 a year."

"But I've got so much else to do," Samuel replied. "My publisher has asked me to do a translation of Schiller's *Wallenstein* as well as a travel book on Germany. Then there's that series on Bonaparte you want... In any case I don't want to stay in London. I need the countryside and nature. I wouldn't give up the country for two thousand times two thousand pounds."

He saw the look of surprise on Stuart's face. Poole was the same; he thought Samuel should continue as a journalist and concentrate on the work he had planned from his time at university in Germany.

"If I were to live in London another six months I would dry up," he told them both. "I might be able to earn a lot of money but I'd have no time left for creative work. A writing career should be carefully divided between limited journeyman work for pay and self-publicity, and absolute literary work done in leisure and independence. There are two good ways of writing: one for immediate and wide impression, though transitory, the other for permanence. Newspaper articles for the first, books the second."

But that still left the question of exactly where to make his home. Poole was urging him to come back to Stowey, saying they might be able to rent nearby Alfoxton House where the Wordsworths had lived for a year.

"Maybe we could share it with Southey and Edith," Samuel told Sara. He knew she would like this idea and although he hadn't always got on with Southey, he liked the idea of living with another writer who would spur him on. Better still, he might be able to persuade the Wordsworths to come and live there, although Lady St Albyn had refused to renew their lease the last time they had rented it, all through some silly rumour about them being French spies.

But Wordsworth was settled in his cottage in the north and Southey had decided to go to Portugal. Edith had been suffering from depression for some time and it was making him ill too, sick and anxious, unable to settle at anything during the day and sleepless at night. He had been studying law in London but he and Edith both hated it there so he decided to give it up. His uncle in Portugal was always inviting him to stay and Southey thought that the sunshine and change of scene might do her good. Samuel wondered if he should go with them. He still hankered after the idea of setting up a colony of writers abroad but then his thoughts turned again to the Wordsworths and to that magical time he had spent in the north with them. While he was staying at Sockburn, Wordsworth had taken him on a walking tour of the area he had been brought up in. Samuel had been overwhelmed by the beauty of the countryside, the vast stretches of shining water, the magnificent towering mountains. Nothing had prepared him for such beauty. If Wordsworth and Dorothy were making this their home then he might seriously consider joining them. It was a long way to go for the company of two people but maybe he could persuade some of his other friends to join them: Godwin perhaps and Humphry Davy, who was a scientist at the Pneumatic Institute in Bristol. The greatest minds in the country would be gathered together.

But none of these schemes could come to anything until he had finished his contract with the *Morning Post.* He quite enjoyed his work as a journalist. There was something to be said for knowing that the words he wrote at midnight would be read by five or six thousand people twelve hours later. His poetry would never reach such a large audience. He was proud of his articles; he knew he could express himself well and had a good grasp of current affairs.

But he had never been very good at keeping to deadlines. When he knew he had to write an article his mind and his writing wandered. Then, at the last moment, he would dash off something, often late at night or early in the morning, and know it was good, brilliant even. But it was hard to work like that with a wife and a small child. Hartley woke up whenever Samuel did; Sara was exhausted and needed her sleep.

"I don't know why you have to disturb the whole household just because you want to write something down!" she would snap.

"If I didn't write it down we wouldn't get paid!" he would retaliate.

He found himself remembering fondly the way Sara used to be. When they were newlyweds in their cottage in Clevedon he used to write poems for her, they walked in the evening dusk, made love every night, slept in late, made love again. Bed was the one place they still seemed to get on; Sara had the same appetites as him and knew how to please him, even now. It was daily life together that they found difficult. He had long ago accepted that in so many ways they would never be suited.

He had been relieved when her mother suggested she and Hartley go and stay with her.

"I can move in with Lamb," Samuel said. "That will save money on the lodgings and it's only a few months. As soon as I'm finished here we'll find somewhere permanent to live."

Living with Lamb was much more successful; Lamb didn't care what hours he kept. The lifestyle suited Samuel. He could wear what he liked, do what he liked, go where he liked without anyone to criticise him. It was like being a bachelor again and he revelled in it. He worked hard and drank hard. Evenings out with Godwin and Lamb, filled with political and theological talk, were followed by feverish bursts of writing. Ideas poured from him. In one twenty-four hour period he wrote a 3,000 word profile of William Pitt, the prime minister, then went on to translate fifty lines of German poetry.

At the beginning of April he went up to Grasmere to visit Wordsworth and Dorothy in their new house. Lamb had tried to dissuade him. "You're constantly running after that man," he said. "He's not a god. You're better off without him."

Samuel had intended staying only a few days but ended up staying a month. Mary Hutchinson was staying with them and also William's brother John. Samuel had already met John: he had joined them on part of their walking tour to the Lakes in the autumn. John Wordsworth was a sailor, a quiet man, very shy, but Samuel, watching him with Mary, had a feeling that he had a fancy for her.

It was a glorious spring with blue skies and warm sunshine, the sort of weather that made you glad to be alive. Samuel walked every day, exploring the area, looking for somewhere that might be suitable for him and Sara to live. He hadn't altogether given up the idea of a house in the West Country but he thought he would keep his options open. One day he spotted a big white house, perched on a hill beneath Skiddaw, just north of Keswick. Asking around he was told it was Greta Hall.

When he returned to the cottage in Grasmere, Wordsworth told him he was thinking of publishing a second edition of the *Lyrical Ballads.*

"Cottle's first edition has sold out," he said. "We could do an enlarged version. I'd need your help, both as co-author and editor."

"*Christabel* could go in it," Samuel said excitedly. "It only needs a bit more work to finish it. I was thinking of publishing my ballads and conversation poems separately but I'll concentrate on that instead."

"I was going to work on *The Recluse*," Wordsworth said. "But that can wait too. As long as I know you're committed to it. I couldn't do it without you here with me."

"No..." Samuel said slowly. His heart, that had soared at the idea, now plummeted again. What would it mean to move three hundred miles away from his friends in the south: Poole, Lamb, Godwin, Davy? And how would Sara feel so far away from her family?

He travelled back to Bristol and made a last-ditch attempt to find a house in the West Country. But his heart wasn't in it and when it came to nothing he told himself that fate had intervened. The die was cast: he would move to the north and use his powers of persuasion to gather a group of writers, philosophers and scientists around him.

He went to see his friend Humphry Davy, head of research at the Pneumatic Institute, the new medical research unit that had been set up by Thomas Beddoes to study gases. Samuel had always been interested in science and he liked to keep up with new developments whenever he was in Bristol.

Davy loved poetry as well as science; he had written a sizeable body of verse himself, some of which had been published.

"I'm thinking of doing a translation of Blumenbach's *Natural History*," Samuel told him. "I'd need your scientific advice. And I need someone to proofread the second edition of *Lyrical Ballads* when we've done it."

"I'd love to do it," Davy said.

"It would be easier if you came up to live in the north of course. Godwin is keen to join us."

Davy had shown an interest in Pantisocracy before. If he could get them all to come up it would be a gathering of the intellectual elite of their time.

Leaving Davy to think about it, Samuel went next to his publisher, Cottle, to arrange for the printing of the book.

The most difficult task lay next: persuading Sara to agree to the move.

"It's a big house, Sara," he enthused. "Plenty of room for us and the children, a big garden, all the things I need. And near a town for you," he added, remembering he was supposed to be convincing *her* not himself.

"I'd rather have stayed in the south," Sara said mournfully. "It's such a long way away from my family."

"But they can come and visit."

She shook her head. "Mama will never come that far."

"Southey and Edith might," Samuel said, "when they come back from Portugal."

"But it would only be a visit. It's all right for you, you've got Wordsworth and Dorothy, but I'll have no one."

"You'll have *them*. They're your friends too." Even as he said it Samuel knew it wasn't true. Wordsworth and Dorothy were *his* friends. It wasn't the same when Sara was with them.

"Poole's right," Sara went on. "And Lamb. They both think the Wordsworths have too much influence on you."

"No they don't, Sara. There's room in my heart for everyone. It's just that Wordsworth and I are going to work together again, like we did at Stowey. It's exciting. It's what I need. It's for our future."

"I thought you said you could work anywhere as long as you had the space."

"I can but…"

"And you keep saying you've got plenty of work on hand."

"Yes, yes, but that's just mundane bread-and-butter stuff. *Lyrical Ballads* is creative."

Sometimes he worried he might have taken on more than he could manage. He had already received an advance from his London publisher, Longman, for the second part of the Schiller translation as well as the German travel book he had promised him. His patrons, the Wedgwood brothers, were expecting him to write the biography of Lessing that he had been saying he would write when he came back from Germany. And now he had committed himself to this second edition of *Lyrical Ballads*.

In the end Sara had to agree to the move of course. Her family were against it, but even her mother realised that with the baby due in four months she couldn't possibly stay with her any longer; her place was with her husband.

If he hadn't caught that cold on the way up things would have gone far more smoothly. As it was they had no choice but to stay with the Wordsworths until he had fully recovered. It wasn't the first time Sara and Dorothy had lived under the same roof. Wordsworth and Dorothy had stayed with them in Stowey when they had first lived there and he and Sara had stayed at Alfoxton House for a few weeks when she was expecting Berkeley. But Sara and Dorothy had a fragile relationship; they were friendly enough to each other but they would never be close, they were just too different. Dorothy loved the outdoors, walking and gardening; she didn't care a jot for her appearance and thought housework was something to be hurried through in order to get on with more important things. Sara liked to look neat and tidy, she still changed her dress for dinner, she prided herself on running an efficient, orderly household and was assiduous in the role of mother. Hartley, it turned out, was their one meeting point: Dorothy adored him. "He's such an original sprite," she told Samuel. "I can't wait to have him to stay when Sara is lying in."

Samuel couldn't help noticing how depressed and withdrawn Wordsworth seemed.

"Writing gives me a pain in my side," he complained. "I don't know how I'm ever going to be able to do this second edition of *Lyrical Ballads*."

"Oh, come on, we did it last time," Samuel said heartily. "You'll never get it done if you sit around grumbling about it. You've got me to help you. I tell you what, I'll do all the editorial work."

"Are you sure? With everything else you've got to do?"

"If it means having you back to your usual self, yes."

On their last evening in Grasmere they took a boat out to the island on Grasmere Lake for a picnic. They made a fire, hanging a kettle over a fir branch, and ate their picnic in a happy family circle.

Afterwards Samuel lay back on the ground, watching the clouds in the sky above him. He lifted his head. In front of him he saw the mountains and the lake, the surface shimmering in the smoke that rose from the fire.

"Let's make a bonfire!" he exclaimed suddenly, leaping up. "A huge bonfire to dance around. Like heathens."

They broke off branches from the alder bushes. The dry twigs caught the flames quickly, crackling like gun fire and sending great sparks shooting up into the evening sky. They stood for a while watching then danced around the bonfire, their laughing faces ruddy from the flickering flames. It was an evening Samuel knew he would never forget, a precious joyous time, the start of a new chapter in his life.

Chapter Three

While Sara dashed around the house like a whirlwind, unpacking trunks and boxes, putting things away in cupboards, getting everything ready for the new baby, Samuel set off from Greta Hall each morning to explore the area.

He had always loved walking, being out in the open air, at one with nature. Sara couldn't understand it. "Why don't you take a cart?" she used to say in Stowey, watching him set off to walk the forty-five miles to Bristol.

"I enjoy it, Sara. I like to see the countryside in all its glory. It inspires me."

Sometimes she agreed to a gentle stroll in the garden in the evening with Hartley running in front of them. Of course, she was heavily pregnant but, even if she hadn't been, she would never want to set off over the mountains like he did. Dorothy was the one for that. She thought nothing of clambering up the steep slopes, easily keeping up with his pace, hampered though she was by her long skirt and petticoat. Like him, she was tanned and fit. He was sure the walking did his joints good. He had suffered from rheumatism ever since he had been a child. He put it down to an incident when he was seven, when he had run away from home after an argument with one of his brothers and spent the night in a damp field. Ever since then he had been prone to bouts of rheumatic fever with extreme lethargy and desperate pain in all his joints. Laudanum eased it but he had to take more and more to make it work. The laudanum helped in other ways too: he found himself more relaxed, he wrote better when he had taken a dose, it helped his thoughts to flow more freely and he found it easier to cope with Sara and the pressures of work and family life. Now he often took it when he was feeling stressed.

The mountains Samuel saw every morning when he woke seemed to beckon him. He could see himself racing up those slopes, standing on top of the world, breathing in the fresh air like he had in the mountains in Germany, looking down at the lakes and valleys below him. It made him feel humble when he gazed at the huge vistas around and below him. His most pressing fears vanished like the mountain tops in the mist. He was such a small, insignificant part of this grand universe, what did his problems matter?

In the evenings he shut himself in his study and worked on *Lyrical Ballads.* All his other projects would have to wait for the time being. His partnership with Wordsworth, his career as a poet, these had to come first. He spent most of his time re-writing large sections of *The Ancient Mariner* and working on *Christabel* for

Lyrical Ballads. It was a real struggle. He had to force himself back to his writing desk, his pen in his hand, hovering over the paper, willing the words to come to him. Every single line was wrung from him with labour pains, he told Wordsworth. It was exhausting.

"We're all waiting for it," Wordsworth said impatiently. "Cottle keeps asking me how much longer."

"I know, I know," Samuel replied. "Let me read you the latest bit."

He often walked over to Grasmere, across the mountains. There was something about the steady pace of walking, the effort of the steep climbs, the exhilaration in battling the wind, walking through the clouds that clung to the mountain tops, that freed his mind. He filled his notebooks with descriptions of what he saw, phrases he could use or modify in future poems. When he arrived, Dorothy was often working in the garden that she loved so much. Sometimes Wordsworth was with her, digging over the soil or helping her with the planting, other times he was inside at his desk writing or in bed resting. Like him, the Wordsworths kept odd hours; they thought nothing of staying up until three in the morning then sleeping until midday.

By the end of August Samuel had finished a large chunk of part two of *Christabel* and he set out for Grasmere one afternoon feeling triumphant. It was a fine clear day, the blue skies promising a cloudless night ahead.

"How long will you be gone?" Sara asked as he was leaving, looking at him as though he were quite mad, although she should be used by now to his long walks. He had been doing them since they were married, after all.

"Oh, I don't know," he shrugged. "A few days maybe."

"I hope the baby doesn't come early." She patted the enormous bulge on her front.

"You can send word if he does," he said, "and I'll come straight back."

"You seem pretty certain it's a boy," she said. "It might be a girl, you know."

He shook his head. "It'll be a boy."

"Well, if you must go, I suppose you must. Though I wish you'd wait 'til morning, It'll be pitch black by the time you get there."

Samuel shook his head. "The moon is nearly full tonight. I'll able to see even when the sun goes down."

He set off with a feeling of freedom at the thought of the route he had planned: crossing the entire ridge of the Eastern Fells, Great Dod, White Side and Helvellyn.

It had begun to get dark by the time he reached Nethermost Pike and he stumbled the last part of the journey down to Dunmail Raise, feeling the stones tumbling under his feet. Every inch of the journey stuck in his mind and he would record it in his notebooks as soon as he could. But first he must tell Wordsworth and Dorothy the good news about

Christabel. He couldn't wait to read it to them and see their faces. All he needed was their encouragement and he would be able to finish it off.

It was nearly eleven o'clock when he reached Grasmere. The streets were deserted and the houses and cottages either side of him were in darkness. He left the village and walked on towards the tiny hamlet of Town End, just a cluster of cottages. There were no lights in the windows here either. He might be the only person alive in the world. The water on the lake shone like silver in the moonlight, the crags of the mountains behind the cottages were like huge towering black clouds. But he wasn't alone; as he approached Wordsworth's cottage he could distinctly hear the soft steps of someone moving around in the garden and when he got nearer he saw the small slight figure of Dorothy. She had heard his steps too in the clear night air and she hurried towards him.

"How lovely to see you!" she said softly. "William and John are both in bed. But stay with me a while." She put her hand on his arm. "Unless you are tired? You can go straight up to bed…"

"No, no. It's such a beautiful night. Just some tea maybe and a bite to eat."

"Of course. Then we can talk. You can tell me about your work. I'm looking forward to hearing all about it."

He had never had a relationship with a woman like the one he had with Dorothy: more than a sister, closer than a lover. He could tell her anything. She listened, sometimes she criticised, but she always understood.

The sound of their voices must have woken Wordsworth and he came out in his dressing gown. Nothing would disturb John. He worked for the East India Company and was used to life at sea: he could sleep through anything.

The three of them sat on a bench in the garden, the bright silver moon hanging over them in the inky sky. Unable to wait until morning, Samuel read them part of *Christabel,* his voice in the hush of the night heightening its mystique. He told them about his walk over the mountains and they promised to join him next time.

The chimes of the church clock marked the passing of the hours. "Half past three," Dorothy said finally. "We really should get to bed."

The next day again dawned bright and sunny. Samuel woke early, watching the motes of dust dancing in the sunshine that streamed through the window. He found Dorothy in the kitchen, writing her journal while the kettle came to the boil over the fire.

"I'm going to clear a bit more of the garden today," she told Samuel.

"I'll help you."

The garden had been their greatest project since they arrived at the cottage. Samuel was impressed at the transformation they had wrought. They had planted roses and honeysuckle against the cottage walls, and enclosed a few yards of the open ground at the front, roping it off, to separate them a little from the road. But their greatest achievement was the back garden, which had been nothing more than an overgrown slope of hillside and was now planted with wild mountain flowers, ferns and other plants. There was an area with a few old apple trees that Dorothy referred to as the orchard. This was where she set Samuel to work, clearing the knee-deep brambles and dense undergrowth from around the trees.

As he worked, fighting with the thorny bushes that scratched his arms and caught in his clothes, he stopped every so often to absorb the scene around him, imprinting it on his mind for his notebooks later. The fairy-like tufts of thistle and wispy dandelion heads floated in the air as though they were alive, skimming the lake like swallows or flying away on the breeze high up to the mountains. Hacking away at the undergrowth, he uncovered a rectangular mound of stone and as he pulled away the brambles he saw it was a small stone seat, set amongst the trees.

The next day they walked around Stickle Tarn, then went to the summer fair in Grasmere village, mingling with the crowds in their Sunday best, revelling in the festive atmosphere of the sunny summer afternoon. The festivities went on late into the night, with music and dancing. It was late when they walked back to Town End but another clear moonlit night. They sat and drank tea in the garden. There were still lights on in the village and the sounds of voices and laughter drifted across to them.

"I wish we lived together up on a mountain top," Samuel said.

"A house on Helvellyn," Dorothy said excitedly. "We should have one built. Just for us."

Samuel wasn't sure whether Sara and Hartley and the coming baby were included in the idyllic vision but for the moment it didn't matter. This was a dream world, just for him and William and Dorothy and John, who said nothing as usual just nodded his head shyly in agreement.

"A sturdy house to withstand the winds," Wordsworth went on, warming to the theme.

"And big enough to invite fellow academics: Davy, Godwin..." Samuel said.

"And the people we love," Dorothy broke in. "Mary, Sarah..."

Samuel knew she meant Sarah Hutchinson, not his Sara, and he felt himself reddening guiltily at the thought of her even as he imagined his own Sara laughing derisively at this conversation, asking where the money was coming from, who on earth would build a house on a mountain top and how they would obtain food and firewood.

But Dorothy and Wordsworth were enchanted by the idea. They went on discussing it, imagining the views and the walks and the landscape in all weathers, until finally John said he was going up to bed.

"I'm not at all tired," Dorothy said. "Shall we walk back to the village?"

They walked as far as the church. The fair was coming to an end, just a few stragglers sitting at tables with flagons of beer.

When they got back to the cottage Wordsworth went up to bed but Dorothy stayed talking with Samuel in the garden, sharing their last evening together for a while.

The next day Samuel walked back over Helvellyn to Keswick. Wordsworth accompanied him as far as the ridge and Samuel walked the rest of the way home feeing exhilarated. He had made the right decision moving up here. With Wordsworth and Dorothy and the stunning scenery that surrounded him, he had everything he needed.

Chapter Four

Sara was sure Samuel would be away from home when she had the baby. When Hartley had arrived two weeks early, Samuel had been up in Birmingham. It had all happened so quickly that she had delivered the baby on her own, the nurse only arriving in time to deal with the afterbirth. And when Berkeley was born in Stowey two years later, Samuel had been preaching in Taunton. Again, it was a quick labour and by the time he came home she had been sitting up in bed feeding their new baby son.

But miraculously this time Samuel was at home. The baby, a boy as Samuel had predicted, was born at half past ten on the evening of 14th September. Sara again had a quick and easy labour even though the baby was very big and, although most women lay in for a month after giving birth, she felt well enough to get up and come down to the parlour after three days.

Samuel looked up at her and smiled as she eased herself gingerly onto the chair. "How are you feeling, Sally-Pally?"

Sara loved it when he called her by their special name. It reminded her of when they were first together. She had been his best and closest friend in those halcyon honeymoon days. But the birth of the baby had brought them close again, this perfect being that was part of her, part of him, binding them together like no other. Samuel was so proud of her for giving him another son. He had written to all his family and friends telling them the news.

He had told Sara they would call the baby Bracy, after the minstrel in *Christabel*. If it had been a girl she would have been called Greta. Sara was used to Samuel choosing unusual names for their children. Both Hartley and Berkeley had been named after philosophers.

Sara thrived on motherhood. She couldn't imagine life without children; they made her world complete. Her milk came quickly and the baby fed greedily. Most women of her class had a wet nurse but she had breast-fed both Hartley and Berkeley until they were sixteen months old. It was less expensive for a start but she loved the feeling of nurturing her own babies, the closeness it brought to her.

When the baby caught a cold she didn't worry too much; the runny nose and sniffles didn't seem to bother him. Then she woke up one night and heard him coughing. Her blood ran cold. Memories of Berkeley's hacking cough came flooding back.

"It's nothing," Samuel reassured her. "Just a cough. He'll soon be better."

But the cough grew worse. When he breathed it sounded like a creaking door. The doctor was called.

"It's just a bad cough," he said as well. He left some medicine. It looked like the one Berkeley had been prescribed. Sara was beside herself with worry. To lose another child would be more than she could bear.

The baby's cough seemed to improve and Sara allowed herself to hope but in early October he started having convulsions. Samuel sometimes sat up all night with Sara, watching the baby hopelessly as he had fit after fit, neither of them knowing what to do to help him.

Sara knew Samuel was worried. The baby's illness seemed to have spurred him on to work harder, or maybe it was just his way of coping. Either way, when he wasn't with her, doing his best to comfort her, he was in his study working, sometimes all through the night.

"I need to finish some of this work I promised Stuart," he told her. "And I've still got work to do for *Lyrical Ballads*."

None of these things seemed important to Sara but Samuel had to earn money of course; there was the doctor's bill to pay on top of all their other debts. Things were getting desperate.

Mrs Wilson came in every day, offering support and good practical advice. Sometimes Mr Jackson came with her.

"I think you should have him baptised," Mrs Wilson said one morning.

"Oh no," Samuel said quickly. Sara knew he didn't believe in infant baptism. "I agree with Mrs Wilson, " said Mr Jackson.

That decided Sara. If the childless Mr Jackson, who knew nothing about babies or their ailments, thought it should be done then it should.

"We'll call him Derwent, after the river," Samuel said decisively, pronouncing it Darwent like the locals did. "It seems appropriate. And it's poetic and novel."

Sara didn't mind what her baby was called. She was just relieved to know he wouldn't die without a Christian baptism. She was sure now that he *would* die. Everyone thought so. She scarcely slept and woke from the few hours she did get with a feeling of dread in her heart. She couldn't stop crying. Tears ran down her face the whole time.

"George says Derwent is a heathenish name," Samuel told her, waving his brother's letter in his hand. "I shall tell him it's his fault for using all the good Christian names for *his* children."

One morning, after another sleepless night with the baby, Samuel announced he was off to Grasmere. "I've finally finished part two of *Christabel*," he said. "I need to let Wordsworth have it as soon as possible. It's been such a struggle, Sara. I'll never be the poet that Wordsworth is. He finds depths and heights I simply can't. I can't even do what Southey does, the popular, dignified stuff. Maybe I should just stick to journalism."

Sara wasn't really listening. She was more worried about how she would cope on her own with Hartley, a sick baby and only the servants to help her.

"Do you really have to go?" she asked.

"It's work, Sara." Samuel said in the voice that she knew brooked no argument. "I haven't even been able to write to them because of all that's been going on. And Wordsworth has been so ill. I'm worried about him."

"Your son's ill, too," she snapped.

"Yes, but if Wordsworth can't complete his work the book won't be finished. And he has to hear *Christabel* as well."

"Well, how long do you think you'll be gone?" Sara asked, wearily.

He shrugged. "A couple of days. It depends on what Wordsworth makes of it. It might need a few revisions."

"What if..." Her voice broke. "What if something happens?" she managed to say.

"Send word," he said, "and I'll get a cart back."

Watching him walking off jauntily, savouring his freedom, looking forward to seeing his friends, Sara went from loving him to hating him. He had been so sweet to her recently, so loving and supportive, sitting with her, holding her hand, comforting her. How could he think of leaving her on her own after a night like they'd just had, knowing she had another sleepless night ahead of her? Surely he could have found a way to deliver the work to Wordsworth without having to leave her when she needed him most. Resentment burned in her chest, all the feelings from when Berkeley was ill resurfaced, feelings she knew were detrimental to her marriage, but feelings she couldn't suppress. Samuel was so thoughtless, so uncaring. She was so unimportant in his life. He preferred his work and his friends to her.

The big house felt empty, once he had gone, with just her, Hartley and the baby. There were the servants, of course, but she couldn't confide in them. She had Mrs Wilson next door. "You can come to me whenever you want," she had said. But really Sara wanted her family, her mother and Edith, people who understood her and would help her cope with this dreadful situation.

Samuel was gone four days. She looked for him every morning, keen to tell him the latest news about the baby, rehearsing the words in her mind. *"He wasn't too bad the first night you were gone, but worse the next. He had another fit this morning but his cough seems better today."*

When she finally saw him toiling up the hill her heart lifted. Strange how he irritated her when he hung around at home yet she missed him when he was gone.

"Papa! Papa!" Hartley cried excitedly. Sara opened the door and Hartley ran out to meet him. Samuel swooped him up in his arms and carried him on his shoulders to where Sara waited in the doorway. She lifted her cheek for his welcome kiss.

"How's the baby?" he asked, setting Hartley down on the floor.

"Papa, Papa! Come and see what I've done with my soldiers," Hartley cried.

"In a moment," Samuel said. "When Mama has told me about your baby brother. Now run along."

"We had a pretty good night last night," Sara said when Hartley had trotted obediently out of the room. "His cough seems a lot better. He still won't feed much though…" She had been going to say more but she noticed Samuel seemed distracted. "Did the Wordsworths like your poem?"

"Yes." His face brightened, then clouded over again. "But there might be a hitch to do with the publication."

"What sort of hitch?"

"It doesn't matter," he said quickly. "No need for you to worry. It'll all be sorted out soon."

"It's because you haven't finished it yet," Sara said. "They can't wait any longer."

"No, it's not that. It's just it's a bit long."

"Well, can't you shorten it?"

He looked at her as if she were completely mad.

"I thought the whole point of moving here was to write your poem for Wordsworth's book," she said briskly.

"*Our* book," he corrected her.

"Well, it'll be *his* now, won't it? With all his poems in it."

"No, there'll still be some of mine. And I'll still help him, putting it together."

"Well, as long as the money comes in," she snapped. "I can't go on putting off the tradespeople forever."

"No need to worry. I've got plenty of work in hand. It's not as easy as you think, Sara."

"So you're always telling me."

"Well, I'll go and get on with it then," he said.

Sara sighed as he disappeared to his room. For all she saw of him he may as well go and live with the Wordsworths.

Chapter Five

Samuel had been so pleased when he finished part two of *Christabel.* He had been working under such pressure, with worrying about money and Derwent and then hearing from Wordsworth how ill he had been. Everything seemed to be going wrong but at least he had finished the second part of the poem. It would cheer Wordsworth up, the fact that their book could be published. It would be a great success and Samuel could pay off some of his debts.

It had rained hard on his walk over and he arrived, wet through, just as the Wordsworths were eating dinner. He should have been exhausted after the long walk and having had no sleep the night before, sitting up with Derwent, but he was dying to read *Christabel* to them. As he read he glanced up every so often, gauging their reaction. He could tell they liked it.

"It's delightful," Dorothy said.

"Absolutely," Wordsworth agreed. "Truly splendid. Most impressive."

Buoyed up by their praise, Samuel's tiredness vanished and they sat and talked until midnight. With no ill baby and sorrowing wife to disturb him, Samuel fell instantly into a long, deep, dreamless sleep and woke feeling totally refreshed. The sun was shining. It was a lovely morning.

"We'd love to hear part two of *Christabel* again," Wordsworth said.

When he'd finished they both said it was superb.

"We need to work on an addition to the preface," Wordsworth said.

"I can help if you like," Samuel offered.

"No, no," Dorothy said quickly. "You go out. We'll be fine on our own."

Samuel had already agreed that the book, in two volumes, should be published under Wordsworth's name alone and the first draft of the preface would say: For the sake of variety I have again requested the assistance of a friend who contributed largely to the first volume, and who has now furnished me with the long and beautiful poem *Christabel*, without which I would not yet have ventured to present a second volume to the public.

He had also agreed to *The Ancient Mariner* being moved from the front of the first volume to the back.

He left them alone to work and went out for a walk. When he came back Wordsworth looked very ill. "He's often like this when he's been working," Dorothy said. After dinner Wordsworth sat down again to write but finally he said, "I feel too bad. I'll have to go to bed."

"Samuel and I will go for a walk," Dorothy said. "Then we won't disturb you at all."

They walked past Grasmere Lake and Rydal Water to Ambleside. It was a clear cool evening; the mountain of Silver How was reflected in both lakes. When they returned Wordsworth was still in bed so they talked in hushed voices while Dorothy made tea, reusing the dried leaves she had kept from the day before. Tea was the Wordsworths' one extravagance. It was dreadfully expensive. They ordered it from Bristol and reused the leaves over and over until they were almost tasteless. Dorothy added plenty of sugar to hers, the only other luxury they allowed themselves.

Anxious not to disturb Wordsworth they went to bed soon after. Samuel wrote for a while, then extinguished his candle and slid between the cool sheets, listening to the night sounds of the owl and the distant church clock, making the most of his last undisturbed night's sleep.

He had intended leaving the next day. He didn't want to leave Sara and the baby any longer than necessary and he was looking forward to his own room with his own bed, his books and writing materials nearby, his little family and Sara's cooking. The Wordsworths ate so frugally; porridge was their most regular offering. Dorothy's teeth were bad so they rarely had meat, maybe the odd piece of boiled mutton now and again, and occasionally Dorothy made pies from the fruit and vegetables in the garden.

He woke to the sound of rain pattering against the windowpane.

"It may brighten up," Dorothy said hopefully. But by late afternoon it was still pouring down.

"I'll go tomorrow instead," Samuel said.

After dinner it eased off enough for them to walk to Rydal. When they returned, Wordsworth read his poem *The Pedlar* to them.

"I've been thinking," Wordsworth said when he had laid the manuscript to one side. "*Christabel.* It's a beautiful poem. We're so impressed. But it's very long."

"Much longer than I intended," Samuel agreed.

"And it's so different from the other poems that I've written."

"Yes, but *The Mariner* is different too."

Wordsworth hesitated. "Yes, as you know I still have reservations about *The Mariner.* But I've explained them in the preface."

"It explores preternatural rather than rural life," Samuel said. "Like *Christabel.*"

"It's just too long for an anthology of poems," Wordsworth said decisively. "I think we should omit it altogether. You can publish it separately under your own name when it's finished. I can put my poem *Michael* in its place. It's just the right length."

"But you've sent part one to the printers already haven't you? And written the preface."

"We can change it. It doesn't matter."

Disappointment surged through Samuel. So much hard work had gone into part two. Every line had been a struggle. And now it wasn't to be published. Yet he could see the logic of what Wordsworth was saying. Dorothy, in the background, was nodding her head in agreement but watching his face closely to make sure he wasn't hurt or angry. There was a moment's more silence then Samuel said, "You're right. It's too long for *Lyrical Ballads*. I'll get on with my work for Stuart and the Wedgwoods and go back to part three when I'm ready. There's no rush to publish it."

"Oh, but you must publish it soon," Dorothy said. "It's so splendid. Everyone must read it."

Wordsworth nodded, held out his hand for Samuel to shake.

That night in bed Samuel thought it over. Wordsworth was right: *Christabel* belonged in a separate category from Wordsworth's poems. It was too long, too different in style and too good to go into an anthology that didn't even bear his name. He would finish it and publish it when he had done some of his other work first. After all, Wordsworth was solely a poet, albeit a brilliant one, but Samuel was more than that: a journalist, a philosopher, a translator, a German scholar. He had many projects on hand. Wordsworth had only the next book of poems. He fell asleep thinking of the work he would throw himself into when he returned.

Chapter Six

No one had warned Sara how cold it would be in the north. As the fine summer and crisp autumn turned only too quickly into a damp dismal winter, the defects of the hastily-built house suddenly became all too apparent with the cold wind whistling through the cracks in the poorly fitted doors and windows and penetrating every room. She thought it had been cold in the damp little cottage in Nether Stowey but it was nothing to the cold she felt here. The high-ceilinged rooms, so cool and airy in the summer, were now glacial, the small fires they could afford to keep going barely taking the chill off the air.

Samuel still went regularly to Grasmere but the cold weather had set off his rheumatism.

"I don't know why you go at all in this weather," Sara said. "It's ridiculous. All that way in this cold, then you're worse when you get back."

"We need to get *Lyrical Ballads* sorted out. It's not something I can do by post."

He went down with a bad cold and cough and complained of pain in his knees.

"I'm not surprised," Sara said, "with all that traipsing up and down the mountains. What do you expect? You're making yourself ill. And what about the work you're supposed to be doing for the paper? You can't just ditch everything else for *Lyrical Ballads*. It's not even *your* book."

"You don't understand, Sara."

"No, I don't. You should stay here. Do your work, think of me and the children for a change."

But he wouldn't listen. There were days when he was in so much pain he couldn't get out of bed. Laudanum was the only thing that helped but it made him sleep all the time and Sara was worried about how much he was taking. And although he slept deeply he woke with dreadful nightmares, calling out and disturbing the whole household.

At least Derwent was getting better and she was beginning to establish some sort of routine; he fed more regularly and slept better at night. He was putting on weight. The worst was over. She let herself hope he would be fine now.

Then it was Hartley who became ill. When he didn't come hurtling into her room as usual one morning she went to find him. He was lying in his bed. "I've got a tummy ache, Mama. And I feel sick…"

She took up some porridge for him. "Try to eat a little," she coaxed. "It may help settle your tummy." He swallowed a mouthful then turned his head away and was violently sick.

"Children often get these little upsets," Mrs Wilson said when she went round to ask her advice. "He'll be fine tomorrow."

Samuel had an upset stomach too and had stayed in bed. With two of them calling her, needing her, and Derwent to feed in between times, Sara was exhausted.

The next morning Hartley was much worse. Putting her hand to his forehead Sara found he was burning up and when she drew back the curtains she saw his skin was a sickly yellow. Frightened, she sent for Dr Edmondson. "Keep him in bed and warm, away from draughts," he said, looking meaningfully at the empty grate in Hartley's room. "I'll leave you some medicine and come back tomorrow."

Sara rushed around lighting the fire, getting a warming pan, while Hartley lay moaning and listless in bed.

Samuel's stomach upset was better but he was still in bed. His rheumatism was bad again and his eyes had become so inflamed, so red with blood, that he looked like a murderer. Looking after him was like looking after a small boy. He was only happy when she was hanging around his sick bed.

"My eyes are too sore to read," he said plaintively. "Stuart has sent me all these." He gestured to the pile of *Morning Post*s lying next to him.

"Maybe he's trying to encourage you to finish some of that work you promised him," she said as she picked up one of the papers.

"I'm working on a piece about Bonaparte," he said confidently. "It's all in hand, Sara. Stuart knows I'll send it when I'm ready. Anyway I'm too ill to work now."

"You can still write to your friends," she pointed out. There was always a pile of letters to post.

"Only my closest ones," he said. "I'm way behind with any meaningful correspondence. When I'm better I shall write an essay on pain." He went on, "I shall send it to Davy; he's interested in such subjects."

Sara took no notice. Sometimes she wondered if all these ailments were all in Samuel's mind. The Wordsworths were the same, always complaining of stomach pains, chest pains, headache and toothache. Yet they all seemed fit enough to walk miles when the mood suited them.

As for Samuel's grand plans to write this, that and the other, he'd do better getting on with it rather than talking about it. What she needed was a man to support her, financially and emotionally.

Sara had made very few friends, confined to the house as she had been, first with her pregnancy, then Derwent's illness, then the cold weather, which had precluded all but the most daring or foolhardy (like Samuel) to venture out of doors. Her closest acquaintances were the Misses Spedding, two chatty ladies who reminded her of the sort of society she'd had in Bristol before she met Samuel. Other than that the only female society she had was Mrs Wilson. Snug in their rooms at the back of the house, away from the prevailing winds, Mrs Wilson always welcomed Sara. She adored Hartley, who persisted in calling her Wilsy, and Mr Jackson was fond of him too, listening patiently to his constant prattling and playing with the toys he brought in, while Sara talked to Mrs Wilson. But Mrs Wilson didn't count as proper society, not the sort she was used to.

It was at times like this that she wished herself back in Bristol, where she knew so many people, or at least in Stowey. She had been lonely there to begin with, and homesick. It was the first time she had lived away from Bristol and everyone she knew. But she had soon made a circle of female friends, women with young children who had helped her with Hartley and supported her through Berkeley's dreadful illness. And she had Tom Poole and his mother just a short step away. Poole was Samuel's friend of course but he had been a good friend to her, too, when Samuel was away. And he agreed that the Wordsworths were a bad influence on Samuel, keeping him from his real work as he trotted around like a faithful servant to Wordsworth.

But what she really wanted here was female society. So when Samuel said that one of Dorothy's friends was coming to stay for the winter she found herself looking forward to meeting her. "She's the sister of an old schoolfriend of Dorothy's," Samuel explained. "Miss Sarah Hutchinson. You'll like her, Sara, I know you will. She's quite enchanting. She has the most lustrous auburn hair."

Sara's hand flew involuntarily to the stiff wig on her head and tears smarted in her eyes. Did Samuel really have no idea how hurtful it was to hear him praise another woman's beautiful hair the way he used to praise hers?

"I only hope I live long enough to see her," Samuel went on mournfully. "I'm so ill. I'm sure I'm dying."

November brought snow and Sara wondered if Miss Hutchinson would travel in this weather. If she did come she would invite them all over. Hartley was getting better. He was a lot thinner than before and his skin still had something of the yellowish hue but his appetite had come back and some of his liveliness had returned, enough for Samuel to rebuke him for making too much noise when he was trying to rest.

When she heard a knock at the door one evening she knew it had to be the Wordsworths. It was pitch black and an icy cold wind was whistling around the house. No one else would venture out so late in winter.

Wordsworth was on his own. "I would have come sooner," he said, "but the weather has been so bad."

Sara looked at him blankly.

"Samuel said he was so ill," Wordsworth explained.

"Well, he's in bed," Sara said carefully. She didn't want him to think he'd made a wasted journey; it was a five-hour walk at the best of times, much longer when it was icy and snowy like today. "But he'll be pleased to see you," she went on. "I'll bring you some refreshments then I'll go and find him."

She left Hartley chattering to him by the meagre fire that she had managed to stir into some sort of life. Samuel was in his dressing gown, a weird creation covered in hieroglyphics that made him look like some sort of wizard as he crouched over his desk, his pen scratching on the paper in front of him. He waved his hand behind his back when she went in, as a signal not to interrupt him, finished the sentence he was writing then turned round.

"Wordsworth is here," she said.

His face lit up.

"Splendid," he said. "I was just writing to him."

Her heart sank. She'd hoped he was doing some work, not just writing a letter.

"He seems to think you're dying," she said, acidly.

"I think I am, Sara. I have a pain here." He gestured to the region of his heart. "And a dry cough. And I ache all over." He leapt to his feet. "But I shall go down and say hello to him now he has come to see me."

"You don't want to dress first?" she asked, looking at his gaping dressing gown, the short nightshirt exposing his white legs. "Oh no, no. I've seen Wordsworth often enough in his nightshirt."

"Dorothy has had a letter from Sarah," Wordsworth told them. "She will arrive on the 17th."

"In three days!" Samuel exclaimed. "You must all stay here. There's more room."

"Well, we'd certainly welcome a few days here," Wordsworth said, "to break the journey for Miss Hutchinson. I will write to Dorothy. She can come over the day before."

So Wordsworth was staying here, Dorothy would be coming too and then Miss Hutchinson. No one bothered to consult Sara but actually she didn't mind. It would mean extra work but it would make a change to have someone new to talk to. This Miss Hutchinson obviously wouldn't be as unconventional as the Wordsworths, who thought nothing of staying up half the night and sleeping until noon the next day.

With Wordsworth there, Samuel's mood improved dramatically. He said he felt better and the two men sat in his room talking and writing late into the night.

Dorothy arrived on the 17th and the next day Wordsworth set off for Threlkeld to meet Miss Hutchinson. Samuel walked with him part of the way.

As Sara changed her dress to receive her visitor she saw, in her mind's eye, the young lady Samuel had described: charming, cultured, beautiful and with that stunning auburn hair that Samuel loved so much. Jealousy trickled through her. Dorothy didn't change of course; she never did. She met their guest in the same homely workaday dress that she'd worn all day. Miss Hutchinson had been travelling of course and probably didn't look her best but, even allowing for that, Sarah couldn't believe that the young lady in front of her was the same one Samuel had described. Oh, there was no doubting she had lovely hair, but really she was very ordinary, small and dumpy with a square determined-looking jaw. She was an outspoken little thing, confident in herself and her opinions, brimming over with enthusiasm. Sara found herself warming to her, although it was hard to see what Samuel found so fascinating about her. And he *was* fascinated, she could see he was. His eyes followed her every move, he hurried to make sure she was comfortable, asked if she needed anything. Just like he used to for her. She looked about the same age as Sara was when she met Samuel, around her mid-twenties. Sara was nearly thirty now, a mother with two children. Obviously she couldn't compete with this young, fresh-faced, as yet unmarried lady.

"I'm helping out on my brother's farm at present," she told Sara. "It's so good to be back with my family. I was brought up by a relative but he gave me a good education and encouraged me to read the right sort of literature and discuss it with him afterwards."

"I was separated from my sisters when I was young too," Sara said. "It makes you appreciate them more when you're older. It was the same with the Wordsworths."

Samuel came over to them. "You're warm enough over here are you? You don't want to come closer to the fire?"

The remark was addressed to both of them but clearly meant for Sarah and she saw the young woman redden, flattered by his attentions. '*You know nothing,*' Sara thought bitterly. *'You have no idea what he's really like:*

he may seem charming but he can be crotchety, impatient, bad-tempered, needy. It's easy for him to put on an act for you. But I'm his wife. I know him for what he really is...'

Conversation at dinner centred on literature and Wordsworth's and Samuel's poetry. Miss Hutchinson joined in with gusto, her face animated and glowing in the candlelight. Sara noticed the way Samuel frequently asked her opinion on his work. Clearly she hero-worshipped him and Wordsworth. Sara felt out of her depth. She had been to literary dinners before, with Godwin and Lamb when they lived in London, and she wasn't averse to discussing poetry and literature but there were usually enough people there who didn't want to talk endlessly about their own work like Wordsworth and Samuel did. Sara had never understood Samuel's poetry; she preferred Southey's. She had told Samuel this once, not to hurt him but to show him that she had her own critical opinion, but instead he had taken it as a personal insult and accused her of being swayed by public opinion. When *Lyrical Ballads* was first published it was lambasted by critics. She couldn't understand why they were even considering bringing out a second edition with even more of the same style of poems.

When they weren't discussing their poetry the conversation moved on to the walks the four of them would go on, the moonlight on the lake, the snow on the tops of the mountains, the sharp frosty air. Sara felt excluded. She knew nothing of the places they talked about. She'd been up in the night with Derwent. She hadn't sat down all day. The conversation drifted above her. They were a happy little foursome. They didn't need her.

"I think I'll go on up to bed," she said when she had cleared the dishes.

"Yes, my love," Samuel said vaguely, taking her hand and kissing it as she leant over him. "We'll be up later."

She had no idea how long they stayed up talking but luckily the house was large enough that she didn't hear any of them coming to bed.

There was no sign of them the next morning either, when she went down to get Hartley's breakfast. She herself had been up at five feeding Derwent. She had taken him back to bed with her and dozed fitfully but it wasn't long before Hartley had come in, leaping onto the bed as well and jumping around. After that any more rest was impossible.

It was midday before first Dorothy, then Sarah and finally the two men staggered down into the parlour. By then Sara was busying herself with Hartley's lunch but she stopped to offer them breakfast.

"It's a fine day," Samuel said. "We can walk out. Where shall we go?"

Sara had thought of going out herself, into the large garden, through the shrubberies and down to the shaded walk along the river. But no one asked her what she was going to do. She told herself it was silly to be jealous. She wouldn't have wanted to go with them even if they asked her. But it would have been nice to have been asked.

Chapter Seven

Samuel had never stopped thinking about Sarah Hutchinson. In her absence she had become even more perfect. He had always known, deep inside, that he would see her again.

The Wordsworths, the Hutchinsons and him: they belonged together. They were more than a family; they didn't need other people. When guests arrived they were impatient for them to leave. They didn't even need to be all together at the same time. John Wordsworth had been staying at Grasmere since January, just after the Wordsworths moved into the cottage, and only left in October to go back to sea. Mary had stayed for six weeks from the middle of February until April and now Sarah was here, the group shifting and changing but the bond never breaking.

It was Wordsworth who had started calling some of their favourite places after individual members of the group. "It's a way of keeping us together even when we're separated," he said.

Samuel had noticed how up here every brook, every crag, almost every field had a name. He had scribbled many of them down in his notebook on his walks with Wordsworth and Dorothy.

They took to calling a little spit of land at the foot of Grasmere Lake 'Mary's Point'. One of their favourite walks was up to a copse that they called 'John's Grove'. Samuel himself had 'Coleridge's Seat', a small indentation in the ground on a hillside, just right for admiring the beautiful view below. Now that Sarah was here they would have to find a special place for her.

It had been almost a year since Samuel had seen her. He had heard about her of course, through Dorothy, so he knew what she was doing. The Hutchinsons were a large family. As well as Mary, Sarah had two sisters: Joanna, whom he had met, and Betsy. Then there were four brothers: Henry, Tom, George and Jack. At present Sarah and Mary were living with their brother Tom, who had moved from his farm in Sockburn to one in Stockton-on-Tees in Yorkshire, and Joanna and Betsy were living with an aunt in Penrith.

When the time had come to see Sarah again he was half afraid. Maybe she would be different from the image of her he had built up in his mind. He might be disappointed. But the moment he laid eyes on her he knew for certain: this was love, love in its purest form. The girl in front of him with the shining auburn hair, the merry welcoming smile, the perfect face, she was the one, the only one for him. Whatever it took, whatever the cost, he had to see her, again and again.

In many ways he had dreaded introducing Sarah to Sara. His wife knew him well; she would know he had taken a fancy to her. And yet it seemed important that they did meet. And he wanted Sarah to meet Hartley and Derwent. He was proud of them. They would love her too. Everyone must get on together and be friends. Sara would understand. She would love Sarah like he did once she met her.

Their stay wasn't altogether a success. Sara, as he expected, had noticed his preference, had felt left out. If only she could keep her feelings to herself. He could have put up with sulks, quiet resentment. But she had never been one to keep quiet.

"You never even asked me what I wanted to do!" she stormed afterwards. "I cooked and cleared up for everyone, made the beds. And you all just went off without a backward glance. I'm not your slave, I'm your wife! I deserve to be treated as your equal. That's what we always said we'd do."

"And as my equal you should love the people I love, make them feel welcome."

"I did make them welcome!"

And so it went on. Samuel was heartily fed up with the idea of female equality. He yearned for a wife who wanted only to please him, who would greet him with a sunny smile when he returned, welcome him, not remonstrate with him about how long he'd been away and remind him they still owed money to the butcher or tailor or whomever it happened to be.

He was only happy when he could escape to Grasmere, to people who appreciated him, made him feel welcome, loved the same things he loved. Now that Sarah Hutchinson was here the winter that had seemed dull and dreary, the dark days racked with pain and misery, was transformed. At last he had something to look forward to. He hadn't really recovered from his last bout of rheumatic fever — his knees were still swollen and big boils had come up on his neck — but as soon as he felt well enough he set off for Grasmere, ignoring Sara's parting grumbles.

The thought of seeing Sarah again was enough to dispel the discomfort of the biting wind in his face, the slippery ground under his feet, his numb hands and the pain in his knees. But the mental strength required in getting there wasn't enough to overcome his body's weakness. All the way over he had pictured their happiness at seeing him, the days they would spend together, but by the time he arrived he was exhausted, in so much pain from his knees, his eyes red and streaming from the cold wind, his neck stiff and throbbing from the huge boils. The welcome smiles on their faces faded as he staggered across the threshold and Dorothy helped him wordlessly to the bedroom where he collapsed onto the bed.

She was the perfect nurse: she knew when to make a fuss and when to leave him alone. He could see he was disrupting the household. "I'll go back home," he said, "if you order me a carriage."

"No, no," Dorothy insisted. "We'll look after you. You'll be better here with us."

Household life went on around him as he lay in his bed, unable to move, his eyes so dry they felt like sandpaper, the boils in his neck so swollen and throbbing that he couldn't find a comfortable position for his head on the pillow. It was reassuring to hear Dorothy and Sarah in the kitchen, Wordsworth's deeper voice joining them every so often.

The three of them went out for walks almost daily. He was so envious when he heard the door slam, their voices retreat up the road. He pictured them walking in the places he loved so much. He made Dorothy describe them later when she brought him tea. He couldn't eat anything but, in any case, Dorothy assured him that not eating was the best thing to cure the boils. He listened out especially for Sarah's cheery voice, her ready laugh. He pictured her in the kitchen helping Dorothy with the baking or cooking or washing. He longed to be better so he could go out with them on those long wintry walks.

Mornings were his worst time but some afternoons he felt able to stagger into the sitting room and sit by the fire.

"I'll stay with you," Sarah said one day when Wordsworth and Dorothy were getting ready to go out. She brought in some books. "We can look at these together. This looks good: *British Plants* by William Withering."

"Ah yes," Samuel said. "Wordsworth ordered that so we could study nature indoors over the winter. He ordered two microscopes as well but we haven't used them yet."

It was cosy by the fire with this lovely woman next to him, her head close to his as they looked through the books together.

"Wordsworth says these are called forget-me-not up here," Sarah said, pointing to the little blue flowers. "Isn't that a lovely name?"

"I'd like a record of some of these names," Samuel said. "My eyes are too sore to write at the moment but when I'm better I'll copy them down."

"If you let me have your notebook I'll do it for you now," Sarah said.

Samuel hesitated. No one looked at his private notebook. There were too many intimate thoughts in there, not to be shared with anyone, which is why he wrote much of it in Latin, in case his wife chose to take a peek; she would love to know what he was scribbling down all the time. But Sarah wasn't the type to snoop. He trusted her. So he handed the book to her.

After four days he began to feel better. A few more days, he thought, and he'd probably be able to go out for a walk. But he had to get back to Sara; she'd be worried if he stayed any longer.

The moment he was back at Greta Hall he wished he had stayed in Grasmere. Sara didn't look after him like Dorothy had. She was hardly ever ill herself and had no sympathy for anyone who was, unless it was one of the children. But Dorothy suffered with dreadful headaches, raging toothaches, stomach upsets; she understood what it was like.

After two days at home he was desperate to go over again. Sara looked at him sceptically as he shouldered his bag. "Are you sure about this?" she asked. "You don't want to collapse again like you did last time."

"I'm better Sara," he said cheerfully. "I'll only stay one night. I'd just like to see them."

He arrived just as they were finishing dinner.

"Will you have some?" Dorothy asked. "It's pork that the Simpsons gave us. Very good. Nice and tender."

Samuel shook his head. "I don't think I should," he said. "My boils are just beginning to improve."

When the plates were cleared they sat and talked, the conversation flowing easily between the four of them. Samuel's eyes rested frequently on Sarah sitting by the fireside. It seemed so natural to be partnered with her. Dorothy and Wordsworth had that special bond and he had the same with Sarah, the perfect woman.

"There's a beautiful moon tonight," Dorothy said, drawing back the curtain. "Shall we go out and look at the snow on the mountains?"

The cold hit them the moment they stepped out of doors, taking their breath away. The ground was glassy with ice, their feet sliding with every step. Dorothy leant on Wordsworth's arm, Sarah took Samuel's, her small hand firm on his forearm.

Langdale Pikes had very little snow but the more distant peaks looked magnificent with their sparkling canopies of ice.

"It's beautiful," Sarah said, squeezing Samuel's arm. "I feel like we're the only people alive. You, me, Dorothy, William."

"Our own world," Dorothy agreed. "Magical, spiritual…"

They fell silent, a communion of spirits so close, so intimate. Nothing could compare with these special moments, there was no one else Samuel could share them with.

They were absolutely frozen by the time they returned. Wordsworth stirred the fire into life while Dorothy made tea and they sat and talked until half past one.

The next morning was bitterly cold with heavy driving rain.

"I promised Sara I'd be back," Samuel said.

"I'll walk with you," Wordsworth offered.

The wind was biting and they hadn't walked far when Samuel's eyes began to smart and sting, then stream with tears. "It's no good," he said to Wordsworth after they had stopped several times for him to wipe his eyes. "I can't keep my eyes open long enough to find my way. We'll have to go back."

They returned to find the house smelling deliciously of cooking: Dorothy and Sarah were busy baking bread and cakes. It was a cosy day, by the fireside with Wordsworth, the women's voices floating from the kitchen.

In the evening Sarah sat down to write to her sister Mary.

"I hoped your brother might bring her over to stay," Dorothy said. "I haven't seen her for such a long time."

"He needs her on the farm." Sarah defended her brother loyally. "Joanna is too young to run the house on her own."

Samuel moved to stand next to her, watched her sign her name at the foot of the letter.

"Don't you think your name would be better without the 'h' on the end?" he asked.

"I do leave it off sometimes," she laughed. "But I was christened Sarah. It's my proper name."

"I prefer Sara," he persisted. "It's so much more refined."

"I'm not changing it just for you," she said playfully.

He picked up his pen, wrote both names on a piece of paper. "See," he said, "Sara looks so much neater. It's symmetrical with its four letters. You don't need the 'h'."

Samuel loved words and word puzzles, puns and anagrams. He wrote 'Sarah' out several times on the paper, mixing up the letters.

"Haras…" he mumbled. "Ahsra… I know! Asahara: that's what I'll call you. It sounds Arabian, like the Arabian nights, an exotic princess, a mystical Moorish maiden…"

"Don't be silly!" she laughed.

He saw Dorothy watching them. He knew she and Wordsworth approved of their friendship. He had no idea what future he saw for himself and Sarah. His mind darted away from any complicated intricacies. At present this loving, uplifting, innocent intimacy was enough, a balm for his wounded heart, a refuge from the pressures of home life with Sara, where he had to be responsible for everything.

What could be wrong with an unhappily married man finding solace in the company of a young unattached woman? Because he had to accept now that he was unhappy in his marriage. He and Sara were just too different to be happy together. Sara blamed everything on him. She didn't stop for one moment to consider her own faults: her lack of understanding about his work, the hasty hurtful words she flung at him, her obvious dislike and disapproval of his friends and the time he spent with them. She no longer made him happy. Oh, there were times when the old happiness came back, like when Derwent was born, the worrying and grieving when he fell ill even, that brought them close again. But mostly they were as distant as two remote planets, each in their own little world that the other couldn't reach and didn't want to.

He had a theory about being in love: each person should strive to *be* the other, and both together make one whole. They should support that person and they too would be supported. If he and Sara had once had that, they certainly didn't have it now. She had withdrawn her support years ago. It was rare now for them to share anything, except their love for the children.

The next morning dawned bright and sunny and he knew he must go home.

"We'll all come with you," Dorothy said. "At least part of the way."

They fell into a natural foursome, Samuel sometimes striding ahead with Wordsworth, the two women coming along behind, at other times Dorothy holding on to Wordsworth's arm, with Samuel and Sarah behind, her little head tilted up to him when he spoke, her cheeks reddened by the wind, wisps of her hair escaping her bonnet. She was tiny, less than five feet tall, but like Dorothy she was strong and energetic. She could walk miles on terrain that most women wouldn't dream of venturing onto, uncaring about muddying her skirt and petticoats or ruining her boots.

Walking was a good time for confidences: the natural rhythm of their strides, the open countryside, walking side by side instead of sitting opposite each other, it invited intimate talk.

Samuel found himself confiding his disappointment in his marriage. A small part of him felt disloyal but mostly it felt liberating to unburden himself.

"I simply can't work when I'm in the same house as her," he said. "Whatever I do, wherever I go, I can feel her presence, her constant demands on me. Why am I not working? Where is the money coming from? Why do I spend all my time with you? I tell her why: because *you* all love me and support me. You make me feel welcome. You don't run me down and nag me all the time. You understand what it is to love nature and the great outdoors, you inspire me…"

He'd run out of breath and Dorothy, next to him, pressed his arm sympathetically. "We're always here for you, Samuel. If you're too ill to come to us, we will come to you."

"She is in many ways an excellent wife," he said, feeling suddenly he should make amends for what he had just said. "She runs the household well. She's a good mother…"

"She certainly spends a lot of time with the children," Dorothy said acidly. "It took her two and a half hours one morning just to dress herself and two small boys. I can't imagine why it takes so long.

"She never has time to listen to me," Samuel went on. "She's always darting around doing something that she considers more important. She's not interested in the same things as I am: walking, nature, literature, science…"

His glance fell on the diminutive figure in front of him, listening to every word he spoke. He knew Dorothy was thinking the same thing.

About halfway there the two women turned back. Samuel watched them go with a sinking heart. All his happiness lay in the company of these two women.

But he still had Wordsworth, who walked on a bit further with him before he too turned back.

Samuel's spirits sank lower as he approached Greta Hall. Every step made his stiff knees ache, his eyes were sore from the cold wind, the boils on his neck chafing against his scarf. As the house came in sight he found himself dreading the thought of going in, the scenes that would ensue, his wife's cold welcome, the resentments and recriminations she would hurl at him. For one crazy moment he thought of turning round and walking back to Grasmere. Only the thought of seeing Hartley and Derwent again kept him going. But already he was consoling himself with the thought of his next visit to the Wordsworths.

The first thing Samuel was aware of when woke up the following morning was pain. Every joint and muscle was seized up. His limbs felt like they were made of glass: one tiny movement and they would shatter into a thousand pieces. He ached all over, his knees wouldn't bend, his shoulders were like lead weights, his hands like claws. When he tried to open his eyes he could feel his eyelids scraping painfully over his eyeballs. The tiniest movement of his arms and legs took a superhuman effort and even the weight of the bedclothes was too much for them.

"Sara, Sara!" he called. "Help me. I can't move."

His voice echoed into the corridor. He knew she was upstairs somewhere; he could hear her voice and Hartley's high-pitched, childish replies. He yelled again. It seemed an age before she finally came bustling in, a look of irritation on her face.

"You were a long time," he snapped.

"I was feeding Derwent," she said. "Whatever's the matter?"

"It's my rheumatism, Sara. It's so bad."

"I've got no sympathy with you, Samuel. If you insist on walking miles in this awful cold and damp in this godforsaken place you must accept the consequences."

"For pity's sake, Sara, can't you see I'm ill? At least bring me a little breakfast. And pass me my medicine. I can't move."

"You take too much of this," she said, passing him the bottle on the table.

"No, not that one," he said. "That's no good. The Kendal Black Drop. The chemist in Keswick recommended it. It's much stronger."

"I think we should call for Dr Edmondson, see what he can recommend," she said, looking doubtfully at the bottle.

"He'll only say it's rheumatism, Sara. Or gout. It's all the same."

"He might advise you to stay inside rather than gallivanting out in the cold and damp."

"Or live in a warmer climate," Samuel said, dreamily. "We could all go. Wordsworth, Dorothy… We could set up a commune." He closed his eyes, seeing blue skies and sunshine.

When he opened them he found Sara gone. If only Dorothy and Wordsworth and Sarah were here with him now. They would make him feel better immediately. They would come anytime, Dorothy had said. The next day he struggled to his desk and wrote to them.

They arrived two days later. His heart leapt when he saw them walking up to the house: Wordsworth, flanked on either side by Dorothy and Sarah.

"I can't believe it," he heard Sara mutter. "They've walked all this way in the snow."

"They're my friends, Sara. They'll do anything to see me."

He heard Sara sigh. "Well, I'd better go and get them some food. They'll be famished."

"But you're better!" Wordsworth exclaimed when Samuel opened the door to him.

"It's my first day up," Samuel said. "I'm still in a lot of pain. But your presence will cure me."

They stayed four days, the four of them falling easily into their usual intimacy. The weather was fine and Samuel felt well enough to go out for walks with them, ignoring Sara's disapproving looks.

"Don't you think we should ask your wife to join us?" Sarah said a couple of times.

"No, no," he said quickly. "She won't want to come."

If it was cold and wet they sat by the fire reading and talking. Sara joined them sometimes but she was busy with the children and the cooking. She excused herself, saying, “I’m trying to build up Derwent’s strength now that he’s beginning to feed properly.”

Dorothy and Sarah’s offers of help in the kitchen were accepted but they usually came back as quickly as they could, saying Sara was managing without them.

“You must all come to us for Christmas,” Dorothy said one evening. “Stay as long as you like.”

When they’d left Samuel wondered what he could he give Sarah Hutchinson for Christmas. It had to be something special, something she would really appreciate. In the end he decided on a book of poetry, Anna Seward’s *Original Sonnets.* Inside he wrote, ‘To Asahara, the Moorish Maid’.

Chapter Eight

Sara had no choice but to accept the Wordsworth's offer of spending Christmas with them. Quite apart from the fact that Samuel was so keen to go, they had very little food and firewood, and no money to buy more, so it seemed logical to live with someone else for a while. She didn't know exactly what their financial situation was but they owed money to nearly every business in Keswick.

"I'll write to Poole," Samuel said confidently when she told him.

"But you already owe him money."

"He won't mind. He's my friend."

"What about the Wedgwoods? Would they let you have some of next year's annuity?"

She saw him hesitate.

"You still owe them from last time, I suppose," she said. "It's *this* that costs the money, Samuel." She picked up the bottle of Kendal Black Drop from the table.

"I need it, Sara. You know how much pain I'm in. I can't work when I'm in pain or when you go on at me all the time. Can't you just leave me in peace?"

Sara and the children travelled to Grasmere in a carriage. Samuel insisted on walking but it poured with rain all the way and he arrived wet through and scarcely able to walk. The following morning he was feverish and ached all over.

Sara had hoped that she would at least have Samuel as a buffer between her and the Wordsworths but she had to leave him in bed and face them on her own.

She had noticed a growing distance between herself and Dorothy. At one time she had considered her to be a friend. Not a close friend, like her sister Edith or the friends she had had in Stowey whom she could confide in, but at least someone who understood what it was like to be a woman, someone to talk to about the house and cooking and children. Dorothy had helped her in the past; when they were living in Stowey she had invited them to stay at Alfoxton for a week when Samuel had toothache and the cottage chimney was smoking so badly. And she didn't know how they would have managed without Dorothy looking after Hartley when she had Berkeley. When they didn't see each other Dorothy wrote to her, lively, newsy letters, telling her of people they had seen, places they had visited. It was a small piece of contact with the outside world. Sara didn't have as much time for correspondence as Dorothy did but she replied to her as often as she could. She was still her closest female friend up here and women had to stick together; despite the best efforts of Mary Wollstonecraft it was still essentially a man's world.

So Dorothy's antipathy was hurtful. Even Sarah Hutchinson, who had seemed so friendly when she first met her, now seemed awkward around her. As for Wordsworth, well, he had never spoken to her much anyway and now he spoke even less. She couldn't believe that Samuel would talk about her behind her back and yet it seemed the only explanation.

There was no escape from each other. The cottage was tiny. The toys and the cradle and all the other paraphernalia needed to look after a three-month-old baby and a four-year-old child took over much of the parlour and the kitchen was filled with the baby's nappies and nightdresses hanging on racks above the fire to dry.

They had gone there to be in the company of others but Sara, who used to hate it when they all went out without her, was now only too pleased when they bundled themselves up in coats, hats and scarves and hurried out into the freezing air. The cottage seemed to heave a sigh of relief as it fell silent except for Hartley's little voice and the baby crying. Occasionally Samuel would call out plaintively, "Has everyone gone out, Sara? Can you bring me some water?" or something to eat or whatever it was he suddenly needed.

On Christmas Day Samuel felt well enough to stagger into the sitting room and open presents with them. Hartley was excitedly showing off his new toys to all the adults in turn. In the general hubbub Sara didn't take much notice when she saw Samuel pass Sarah a small parcel. She heard the young woman exclaim excitedly when she opened it but she had done the same with all her presents. But then she saw her look inside and burst out laughing, glancing across at Samuel who looked pleased at her reaction. Later on Sara idly picked up the book, opened it and read, "To Asahara, the Moorish Maid." It seemed like complete nonsense to her, one of Samuel's foolish jokes, the sort of nonsense she used to find so appealing and now irked her beyond reason.

She took the children back after Christmas but Samuel stayed on, saying he had work to do for Wordsworth. "I've promised to copy out his *Michael* poem for the printers," he told Sara.

"Can't he do that himself?'

"Well, I can't do much else at the moment so I said I'd do it."

"Well, don't go out walking in the cold and make yourself worse," she said.

"Just the occasional short walk, that's all," he promised.

In the new year they all descended on Greta Hall. The Wordsworths and Sarah had arranged to go and stay with their friends the Clarksons, who lived at Pooley Bridge, and Keswick was a good stop-off point. While they were there William Calvert, an old friend of Wordsworth's, came to visit.

"I'm rebuilding my house at Windy Brow," he said to Wordsworth. "There would be plenty of room for you and Dorothy to come and share it when I've finished."

"Oh, you should!" Samuel enthused. "You'd be closer to us."

Sara's heart sank. The last thing she wanted was the Wordsworths practically next door. Samuel would be there the whole time. Although at least it would stop him tramping the fourteen miles over to Grasmere several times a week.

"It's certainly an idea," Wordsworth said slowly. "There would be a lot more room for us, Dorothy."

"But all the work I've done on the garden..." Dorothy said wistfully.

"If you *do* come," Calvert went on, "I was thinking of building a laboratory as well. I know you're both interested in science."

Sara saw Samuel's face light up. "What a marvellous idea. Davy will definitely come up here then. We can study chemistry, biology, physics. It would give you some background knowledge for your epic poem, Wordsworth."

"Well, I don't know," Wordsworth said slowly. "I'm not a scientist."

"But think of it," Samuel said excitedly. "All the experiments we could do if we had the equipment. Other people would join us. Keswick would be a seat of learning."

Sara was relieved when everyone left, Calvert to his project at Windy Brow and the Wordsworths and Sarah Hutchinson to stay with their friends.

"We'll be gone several weeks I should think," Dorothy said.

Once they had left, Samuel retired to his bedroom. He had been struggling for some time, a painful swelling on one of his testicles having added to his other symptoms of rheumatism, fever, stomach upsets and headaches.

"You really should call for Dr Edmondson," Sara said.

"But it's so embarrassing," he said.

"I'm quite sure he's used to things like that," she said. "And you can ask him about all your other ailments at the same time."

Dr Edmondson prescribed a course of leeches to take down the inflammation, vinegar poultices for the swelling and a sal ammoniac rub and a brimstone paste together with bark infusions for his rheumatism.

"So no laudanum?" Sara asked, looking at the small pile of medications.

"Oh, he knows I'm taking it, Sara," Samuel replied confidently. "I told him it helps for the pain."

"But does he know how much you're taking?" she went on. "And about your dreadful nightmares?"

"A small price to pay, Sara. I couldn't manage without it."

"It's where all the money goes, Samuel, I've told you. I don't know how we're going to manage."

"I've got to take it. I can't work if I'm ill. And if you go on at me all the time…"

"If I don't tell you, who will? I'm the only one who knows how much you're taking and what it does to you."

"Leave me alone for God's sake, Sara!" he yelled. "You just can't let anything go can you? I've told you why I take it. So I can work and earn some money."

"Which will go on more laudanum or this Black Drop stuff; it's all the same thing." She grabbed the bottle from beside him and for one mad moment she thought of hurling it onto the floor until she remembered how much it cost. "The children and I will be in the poorhouse at the rate you're going on," she yelled instead. "If you don't think of me at least think of them! They need to be clothed and fed. You want them to have a good education, like you did, don't you? Where's the money coming from, Samuel?"

It was hopeless. They were going round in circles. Arguing day after day about the same thing. Sometimes she hated him, really hated him, for what he was doing to her and the family. It was hard to remember a time when they had been happy, when she had looked forward to him coming home, when he had hated being away from her, when he had been proud of her. In the early days perhaps, when she first knew him. Even then there were things he wanted to change about her. She had been Sarah with an 'h' but Samuel had persuaded her to drop the 'h' from the end. Sara was so much more elegant, he told her. And she had been brought up to admire elegance and good manners, good speech and good conversation, a good education and female equality. None of these things meant anything to her now. Samuel was happier with people who didn't care about fine possessions and fine manners. All they cared about was nature and poetry. Everything had to revolve around that. They weren't allowed to upset the great poets in any way. They had to be their acolytes, Dorothy and the Hutchinson sisters toadying around Wordsworth and Samuel like they were their servants, spending hours writing out their work, pandering to their every need with no thought of themselves, too afraid to speak their mind. Well, she wasn't like that. If Samuel didn't like it then he'd married the wrong woman.

Yet there were times, when she was lying in bed alone at night or when Samuel cried with another one of his dreadful nightmares, that pity welled up in her chest. Pity for what they had been together. Pity for Samuel as she comforted him like a child. Pity wasn't love but it was close to it. And she could feel some of her love creeping back into her heart as she comforted him, her arm around his shaking shoulders. *"I'll be better,"* she told herself. *"Kinder to Samuel, more understanding; I won't mention money again."* And for a day or so it worked. But then Samuel would snap at her for something or grumble because she hadn't come when he called her and they'd be back to arguing again.

The damp weather and the draughty house affected Sara too. She went down with a series of heavy colds and sore throats, recovering from one only to find herself coughing and sniffing again a few days later. She couldn't stay in bed like Samuel did, as she had the children to look after. The small amount of sympathy she had for Samuel evaporated altogether.

By the end of January she was beginning to feel a little better and when Samuel told her Miss Hutchinson was going to pay a visit she found herself looking forward to it. Sara had been too ill, the weather too bad, Samuel too demanding, to think of going out. It would be nice to talk to someone and she quite liked Sarah; she seemed a sensible little thing with a childlike enthusiasm for everything. It would be good to hear about her visit to the Clarksons with the Wordsworths. And it would put Samuel in a better mood. He certainly seemed to be looking forward to it; he was up and dressed and down in the parlour by the fire long before she was due to arrive.

Hartley flung himself at Sarah the moment she stepped through the front door. Anyone visiting made a welcome change to his routine and Sarah had written to him several times during her stay, simple letters that Sara read out loud to Hartley.

Leaving the three of them talking, Sara went to find refreshments. When she came into the room they were gathered in a cosy threesome by the fire. Sarah was in the middle of a lengthy description of a walk she had been on with the Wordsworths. No one had heard Sara come in. Samuel was leaning forward in his chair, his head cupped in his hands as he listened. The look on his face told her everything.

Samuel's relationship with Miss Hutchinson wasn't just a friendship, it wasn't even an innocent flirtation. This young woman was a rival: Samuel was in love with her.

Chapter Nine

It had been a monumental struggle but *Lyrical Ballads with Other Poems, In Two Volumes,* finally came out on 25th January 1801. The reviews in the papers were disappointing. Some critics didn't even see the point of writing a review for a new edition of the same work. But although volume one only contained one new poem that Samuel had written, volume two was completely new. Samuel had offered to write a collection of poems on the naming of places for volume two but he hadn't felt well enough to do it.

One day when they were out walking Sarah had stopped at a gate to admire the view.

"Pass me your knife," she said suddenly. They watched as she carved her initials into one of the wooden bars of the gate. "This is *my* gate," she laughed.

Sarah's Gate, Mary's Eminence, John's Grove, Coleridge's Seat: special places for the special people in Samuel's life. He didn't know what he would do without them. They were the only ones who listened to him, who understood him.

"I can't do any work," he told them one day.

"When you're better…" Dorothy began.

He shook his head. "It isn't just my illness. I'm so miserable at home. I can't concentrate on anything in such an atmosphere. And I've got no money."

His financial situation was much worse than he could ever admit to anyone, especially Sara. He had been paid in advance by publishers for work which he hadn't even started, let alone finished, he owed £25 to various Keswick tradesmen, £13 to Charles Lamb, he had overspent again on his annuity from the Wedgwoods and he had just borrowed another £18 from Poole, when he didn't dare ask how much he already owed him. On top off all this he had no money to pay Sara's mother her annual allowance and one of his creditors was threatening to sue.

"I can lend you £30," Wordsworth said, "if it will ease your mind. And I think you should write to Longman to ask him if he'll publish *Christabel* when you've finished it."

"*Christabel: A Legend in Five Books*," Samuel said enthusiastically.

"Five?" Wordsworth said. "I thought you said there'd be three."

"I'm going to add two essays," Samuel explained. "I thought about it while I was ill. I get some of my best ideas then, when I'm half-dreaming. There's something about that state of mind, almost like a trance; it frees the creative part of my brain."

"Two essays?" Wordsworth prompted him.

"Oh, yes. One about the preternatural and one about metre."

"That's just the sort of thing you should concentrate on," Wordsworth said. "Not all your German metaphysics."

"But my imagination is dead. I can't think of anything to write. I'll never be the poet you are. I should just give it up."

Even if he'd been a good enough poet, he couldn't abandon all his other interests and concentrate solely on poetry. There were so many other things that fascinated him, so much still to learn and discover. There were new scientific discoveries all the time. And so many aspects he hadn't even started on. Quite apart from the articles he enjoyed writing on current affairs and theology, there was the travel book he planned to write about Germany, and the biography of Lessing that he had researched while he was over there.

He never tired of wondering about the world around him: the plants that grew on the ground, the rocks that towered above him, the clouds that poured rain; the sun, the moon, the planets. He took Hartley out one night to look at the moon, a tradition he had started when they lived at Stowey. As they gazed at it the moon disappeared behind a cloud. Shortly afterwards several stars were also obscured. "Pretty creatures," Hartley said. "They are going in to see after their mother moon."

Alone in his bed, trying to find a position where nothing ached too much, Samuel thought of the things Hartley said. There was a childish simplicity to his enquiring mind that Samuel recognised. Like him, Hartley wasn't content just to accept the world. He wanted to question it, to explore it, to find out why things reacted as they did.

When his eyes weren't too sore Samuel read books on philosophy. He saw himself as a poet-philosopher. Humphry Davy was a scientist who wrote poetry. Why shouldn't he be a poet who wrote philosophy? And he was interested in every branch of science. Dr Edmondson had lent him some medical journals and he read up on rheumatism, finding an article in which a patient had found considerable relief from pain by rubbing laudanum oil into the swollen joints as well as taking it orally. So he tried it himself and it definitely helped.

The study of optics also fascinated him and he studied Newton's experiments, deciding it would be interesting to do some of his own. He ordered a prism and coaxed the cat into his room one night so that he could rub its fur to produce sparks. Grabbing the prism from his desk he tried to see if he could refract the light from the sparks but the cat, angry at being manhandled, hissed and scratched his arms and hands so badly that he could hardly hold his pen the next day.

He always found it hard to settle after these night-time experiments, his mind active and restless. The Kendal Black Drop that had once helped him to sleep no longer seemed to work. As he lay there he thought of how little work he was doing and was filled with self-loathing. He was lazy; he had lots of ideas but couldn't galvanise himself. He must get some sleep, then he could do some work tomorrow. But sleep brought dreams and those dreadful nightmares with visions of evil and terrifying she-monsters who tormented him. When he did finally manage to get to sleep he found it hard to get up the next morning. What was there to get up for? He would have to heave his stiff and aching body out of bed, he couldn't face the idea of applying himself to any work, the house was cold, Sara colder still, no welcoming smile when she saw him, a constant brooding, accusing presence.

But there were Hartley and Derwent of course. Hartley's voice filled the whole house. He whirled around like a manic spirit and had an incredible imagination. Samuel heard him talking to himself as he played, his building bricks becoming, in his mind, a real house: one brick a chimney, another a fire. And Derwent was growing and changing, his personality beginning to show. He was a chubby, healthy little thing now, with no sign of the illness that nearly took him from them. If only he and Sara loved each other half as much as they loved their children their marriage would be a happy one.

As it was, he was love-starved. If he didn't see the Wordsworths or Sarah his life wasn't worth living. But he was too ill to go to them, he had to wait for them to come to him. When Sarah offered to visit his heart leapt. She was the one person who would make him feel better.

When she had left Sara came to his room. "You care for her."

It was such an unexpected statement coming from her lips that just for a moment he was taken aback. But he saw no reason to prevaricate. "Yes."

The naked pain showed in her face. "Why Samuel? What have I done?"

"You can't pretend we're happy together, Sara."

"But you're my husband. You made your vows. To be faithful to me."

"I *am* faithful. She's a friend. A friend I have tender brotherly feelings for. That's all."

Sara shook her head. "You love her. I can tell."

"Just because I'm your husband does it mean I can't love anyone else? I have a right to love as many people as I like."

"*I* have rights too. I should come first in your life, me and the children; you should support us, look after us, consider our feelings and be loyal to us."

"I do. All those things. But none of that means I can't love anyone else. You're saying that because I'm married to you I must never have any feelings for anyone other than you? No one can live like that. No one would marry at all if it were in the contract that his wife would be his only friend, the only person he could ever love, that all the rest of mankind, however amiable, can only be distant acquaintances."

"But it's not fair. You care *more* for her and the Wordsworths than you do for me."

"They don't grumble at me."

"That's because *you* don't grumble at them. You're nicer to them than you are to me."

"That's childish, Sara."

"No, it's true. If you loved me you wouldn't want to be with them all the time."

"Don't be silly," Samuel said. "You're with them too some of the time, like at Christmas and when they come here."

"They don't like me," Sara said.

"You make it so obvious that *you* don't like them. You're jealous because I love them. What do you want me to do? Dismiss them from my heart because *you* don't happen to like them?"

"I'm your equal, Samuel. I deserve better treatment."

"This is hopeless Sara, we'll never agree. I'm not going to give up my friends for you. And that's final. If you don't like it, well… "

"Well, what? What are you going to do? Throw me out of the house, me and Hartley and Derwent? You promised, when you married me, to support me. I don't deserve the way you're treating me. I won't stand for it!"

"I'm not giving up my friends, Sara."

But she'd gone, slamming the door behind her. She always had to have the last word. She didn't love him. She couldn't possibly love him if she made his life so miserable. That wasn't love. Love was generous. There was plenty to go round. Jealousy, wounded pride, they had no place in real love. She should be happy that he had such close, loving friends who loved him. Not jealous and twisted and bitter.

He could hear Sara slamming doors as she went through the house — the parlour door, the kitchen door — then Hartley's high-pitched voice querying something, her gentle voice in reply. She used to be gentle with him once, gentle and kind and loving. *She* was the one who had changed, not him. At home here with her he felt like great hooks were holding him down, preventing him from doing any work, reminding him of his duties. He longed to be free, away from this dark prison, in the company of people he loved and who loved him, who appreciated him. He reached for the bottle of Kendal Black Drop on his desk. It would settle him down, clear his mind.

He nursed a forlorn hope that Sarah Hutchinson might stay in Grasmere. She could be his secretary, transcribe his work, support and inspire him. Wordsworth had Dorothy. He could have Sarah. No one could possibly question such a relationship; it wouldn't bring any disrespect on Sarah. He would see her every day. She would be his closest companion. But part of him had always known it would never happen and when he heard she would soon be leaving he accepted it with equanimity.

He was half-dozing in bed one afternoon when he heard Wordsworth's voice downstairs in the hallway, then his hurried steps on the stairs before he knocked gently on the bedroom door.

"Come in," Samuel said feebly.

"You're still ill," Wordsworth said in a worried voice.

"I'm dying, I'm sure of it," Samuel said. "I feel so bad. You'll make sure Sara and the children are provided for when I'm gone won't you? I have nothing to leave them…"

"It won't come to that," Wordsworth said briskly.

"Please. Just promise me."

"I promise," Wordsworth said. "It's *my* fault you're so ill," he went on. "I should never have brought you up here. It's this climate, the cold and damp. I'm sure you'd be better somewhere warm."

"Yes," said Samuel. His eyes wandered from Wordsworth's face, so out of focus in the background, to the glass on his bedside table with Kendal Black Drop mixed with water. The colours of the liquid in the weak sunshine melded into blue and orange, which fascinated him.

"I'll talk to my brother John," Wordsworth went on. "See where he can recommend that would be best for you."

"But I have no money to finance it. And I won't go without you and Dorothy." *"And Sarah,"* he added in his mind. "A colony of writers," he said excitedly. "Southey can join us, Godwin…"

"We'll raise the money somehow," Wordsworth said.

"I can always ask a publisher for an advance on some of my work," Samuel said enthusiastically, "if you would be my guarantor. *Christabel*, maybe, or something else. I can start as soon as I'm better."

Wordsworth shook this head. "You're not well enough to work. But I'm sure your friends will rally round when they know how urgent it is. Oh, I brought someone with me who might cheer you up," he went on. "She wants to say farewell."

"Sarah?" His heart leapt. "But I can't see her like this. Tomorrow maybe. You're staying of course?"

"If that's what you'd like."

The effort of getting up the next morning, washing and dressing, was made easier by the thought of seeing Sarah. He shaved in his mirror by the window, distracted as usual by the view of the mountains, the peaks and crags ever changing in the different light and different weathers. He was always cutting himself shaving because he was sidetracked by the ever-changing scenery.

He had seen Hartley gazing out of the window a few weeks ago. "Will those mountains always be there?" he had asked. It was just as well he had asked Samuel and not Sara, who would probably have replied briskly, "Yes of course they will. Don't be silly. Go and play with your toys."

As it was, Samuel fetched a mirror and held it up above his head so that Hartley could see the entire range of mountains in it. He could see the little boy struggling to get his mind round the difference between looking at a small portion of the mountains from the windows and seeing an image that gave him a wider view. Samuel had never seen anyone make such an effort to reconcile it in their mind, the process of actually thinking about something as opposed to having transient thoughts.

When Samuel had washed and dressed he went down to see Sarah. He could tell immediately that she wasn't happy. "My brother George has just taken on his first farm," she said. "He needs someone to look after the house so I have to go. The farm is called Middleham Hall," she went on. "It sounds impressive but George says it's in a bit of a state. The village, Bishop Middleham, is pretty though, he says. But not very big. I shall be lonely without my sisters. But it's only ten miles from Stockton-on-Tees, so maybe I'll be able to see Mary sometimes. Joanna has moved to Penrith with Betsy, to live with my aunt. I'm hoping to pop in and visit them on my way up to George's farm."

She had told Samuel before about Betsy. There was something slightly wrong with her; she was prone to moods of depression and temper and she needed to be looked after carefully.

"I've so enjoyed it here," Sarah went on wistfully. "I wish I could stay."

"You'll be able to come for visits I'm sure," Samuel said. "Or maybe I can visit you when I'm better."

"I thought you were going abroad," Sarah said, "for your health."

"It would be best for me," Samuel said. "But I'm not sure how I can manage it. And I don't want to leave my *friends*." He looked at her meaningfully and she reddened.

"We could look at *Bartram's Travels* together," he said, reaching for the book he had ordered. ("I see there's always money for books," Sara had said acidly when it arrived.)

"It's the nearest I'll ever get to travelling," Sarah said wistfully. "I need to go where I'm needed most."

"It must be nice to be needed," Samuel tried to reassure her.

The book, with its long, detailed descriptions of the natural features of an area, suddenly made him think of the way in which Wordsworth's creative energy was inspired. "The harsh rock-like earth produces gigantic trees," he said excitedly to Sarah. "Like Wordsworth producing poems, like trees, out of what appears to be barren soil." It was the sort of comment that his own Sara would have found mystifying but Sarah Hutchinson nodded and he knew she had understood.

She left at the end of March, leaving a vacuum in his heart that no one, not even the Wordsworths, could fill. The cold winter lingered on and his spirits sank lower with every dark and dismal day. Ignoring Wordsworth's advice, he threw himself into the metaphysics that interested him so much, in particular the German philosophers like Kant, and he began to form his own theory of idealism. Stretching his mental capacities like this excited him but it left him nervous, on edge and unable to sleep, his mind going over and over strands of thought, chasing them as they escaped from him, having to get out of bed and check a reference in a book or write something down while it was on his mind.

He wrote four long letters about his philosophical conclusions to Josiah Wedgwood, hoping that it would make him realise that he was still working despite his illness.

April at last brought warm weather and Samuel began to feel a bit better, though he knew that it would only take another cold spell to set everything off again. The financial situation improved slightly as well, when Wordsworth paid him the money he had promised to him from *Lyrical Ballads*.

If only his marital problems could be solved so easily. He and Sara scarcely spoke to each other now except to bicker and the atmosphere was so bad that even the Wordsworths noticed it.

"William was right; you really do need to get away from everything for a while," Dorothy said. "It doesn't need to be far. Portugal or the South of France, maybe, somewhere with a milder climate. So you can recover your strength and regain your creative powers."

"I'd love to go somewhere warm, with blue skies and sunshine," Samuel said longingly. *"With no Sara and no responsibilities,"* he added in his mind. "It would cure me," he said out loud.

But at the moment he was far too ill to travel so instead he threw himself into ideas for when he was better. He had been reading about Herschel's work on the thermometric spectrum and he wrote to Humphry Davy for more information about it, reminding him that he could come up to Calvert's house at Windy Brow to set up a chemistry laboratory. And having heard that Southey had returned from Portugal he wrote inviting him and Edith to come and stay at Greta Hall. There was plenty of room, he told him, so they could live with them indefinitely if they wanted. It would make life easier all round: they would share the rent and Sara would have constant company. Edith and Southey were very close to Sara, they had supported her when Berkeley died while he was away in Germany. With them living here he would have much more freedom. Or they could all go abroad. He still clung to his old Pantisocracy scheme; he would persuade the Wordsworths to come and whoever else wanted to join them. They could emigrate to America, like he had planned all those years ago, to live and work off the land and be free to study nature and write. It didn't have to be America of course; anywhere warm would do. John Wordsworth had recommended the Azores for a climate that would suit his rheumatism. Or there was John Pinney's estate in the West Indies.

His recovery was slow. There were still days when he woke as stiff as a board, scarcely able to drag himself out of bed. He never knew which was best: to stay in the one position in bed where nothing ached but get stiffer and stiffer or to force himself to get up, every movement making him cry out in pain and move around slowly until some of the stiffness eased.

On good days he walked outside, using a stick. Sometimes he took Hartley with him. He had decided to start educating him in natural history so they crawled around the vegetable gardens of Greta Hall together, examining leaves and plants, insects and bugs. Hartley's fascination for anything new, any learning, was inspiring and infectious. If Samuel went abroad, even for the winter, he wouldn't have this. He loved his children. He had missed nearly a year of Hartley's growing up when he had been studying in Germany and he didn't want to miss any more. His children made him happy and he couldn't imagine being parted from them but his wife made him miserable and he couldn't bear living with her. It was an impossible situation.

He gradually extended his walks until by June he could tackle the steep mountain paths again, revelling in the freedom, the fresh air, the beauty of nature. He could walk for miles and not see a soul, the countryside beckoning him on.

He paid for these exertions by a day in bed the following day, sometimes more, with swollen joints and aching muscles. But it was worth it. And as soon as the pain eased he was off again.

He wasn't doing any meaningful work though, except reading, but at the end of the month he felt well enough to correct the draft of a tragedy that Godwin had sent him. He still hoped Godwin would consider coming up to the Keswick area. He missed their long conversations. If he and Southey and Davy came,

Samuel would have the intellectual stimulation he needed.

In early July he had a surprise: Josiah Wedgwood sent him £50, an advance on his annuity, which was the answer to his immediate financial problems. He paid off the rent arrears and all his household bills. He had already decided what to do with the rest. "I need to do some research at the cathedral library in Durham," he told Sara. "They have the works of Duns Scotus, Leibniz and some other important philosophers. I can stay at George Hutchinson's farm while I'm doing it. That will save on accommodation expense."

He had no idea if she guessed his real reason for going and frankly he didn't care. All he knew was that he was going to see Sarah Hutchinson again.

Middleham Hall looked very imposing from a distance; it was a large square house with a shallow roof and big windows. But as he drew closer Samuel could see it had fallen into disrepair, the rendering falling off in patches and the paint on the window frames chipped and peeling.

The Hutchinsons greeted him with the warmth he had expected, Sarah smiling up at him prettily, George giving him a hearty handshake. He was pleased to find Joanna and Betsy there as well. He knew Sarah would be lonely without at least one of her sisters with her.

"Betsy couldn't stay in Penrith any longer," Sarah told him quietly. "Her condition has deteriorated so much that she needs to be kept away from people."

"So they'll be living with you permanently?" Samuel asked.

"It looks like it," she said. "Poor Joanna. She loves it in Penrith. Maybe she'll be able to go back one day."

The two women had made the interior of the house as comfortable as possible. It was a warm summer and the big sash windows were open to the cool breeze, but it was easy to see that in the bitter northern winter it would be just as cold and draughty as Greta Hall.

Samuel went to the library at Durham Cathedral but there was only one work by Duns Scotus and the librarian had no idea what he meant when he asked if they had any books by Leibniz. It didn't matter; he was really only there to be with Sarah and to enjoy being included in the Hutchinson family. George Hutchinson had a great sense of humour. He made up funny rhymes in the local northern dialect in the same metre as Robert Burns. The results were hilarious and tears would run down their faces as they laughed, holding their stomachs to stop them hurting.

Samuel stayed two weeks and was wondering how he could find a way to stay longer when he woke one morning with one of his knees stiff, swollen and painful to move or walk on. George called a local doctor in to see him.

"Bathing in seawater is the best cure for this," the doctor said. "It brings down the swelling. And horse-riding, to strengthen the muscles."

"The nearest seaside town is Scarborough," George told him. "It's not far from Tom's farm. You could stay there."

"You could come with me," Samuel suggested to Sarah, doing his best to keep his voice casual, "if George can spare you. You would see Mary," he added as an extra incentive.

"Of course you can go," George said enthusiastically. "You haven't seen Mary for a while. It will be good for you both. And I have Joanna here now."

"We could ride there," Samuel said. "The doctor said it's good for the rheumatism."

It was sixty miles but he knew Sarah liked riding. She was so different from his own Sara, who wouldn't have dreamt of getting on a horse.

He was told there were enclosed seawater baths at Scarborough but the crashing grey waves of the North Sea looked more exciting and he threw himself in every day, floating on his back as the waves rocked him, gazing up at the blue sky, feeling glad to be alive, knowing Sarah would be waiting for him when he returned. Not just Sarah but Mary, the two of them helping him to the sofa in front of the fire in the big farmhouse kitchen, a stool placed for his swollen knee, food and drink brought to him whenever he needed. Every evening the two women sat either side of him on the sofa with Tom on his big chair opposite. He could feel the warmth of Sarah's leg pressed on one side of him and Mary's on the other. Each had an arm close to his. Sarah's generous breasts rose and fell when she laughed. It was exquisite agony to be so close yet unable to touch her beautiful body.

Samuel craved affection. When he first knew Sara she couldn't pass him without touching his arm. Sometimes she would go over to him wherever he was sitting and stroke his hair and he would lean his head against her. She would put her arms round him and hold his head against her breast when he was feeling low. "It will all be all right," she used to say. "I love you." She was kind to him in those days. She didn't mind when he went away. She understood it was work. She saw him off with a lingering kiss that made him long to come back to her, welcomed him back home with a smile. He could be friends with whomever he liked as long as he came back to her. But now she had become jealous and spiteful. The kindness and warmth had gone; he no longer felt loved and cherished. Hartley was the only one he could rely on for physical affection, with his warm little body, sturdy little arms, warm wet kisses. Sara seldom kissed him. No long, lingering kisses anyway. How he longed to feel the touch of a warm responsive woman…

Mary and Sarah had no idea what they were doing to him. Their simple physical affection was so innocent. On warm days they would stretch out on the ground with him in the shade of a willow tree, looking up at the sunlight slanting through the dappled leaves over their heads. Sometimes Mary sat with his head and Sarah's cradled in her lap. He could feel the heat from Sarah's head against his skull, smell the sweet scent of her hair. The three of them carved their initials on the trunk of the tree as they had done on rocks, tree trunks and gateposts in the Lakes.

In the evenings when Samuel lay on the sofa Mary sometimes came over and lifted his head so she could sit down, putting it down gently on her lap and stroking his hair.

These things meant nothing to them but, alone in his room at night, he found himself picturing Sarah's naked body, her beautiful hair falling over her plump white shoulders, her lovely pendulous breasts, the big nipples pointed with desire, her ample hips, the dark mound of pubic hair. At this point he was aroused beyond control. Later he would lie in bed disgusted with himself. Sarah was an innocent maiden, he reminded himself, and he was a married man. He couldn't possibly seduce her, debase her, turn her into an object of sexual desire. It was sweet torment to be with her and yet he couldn't keep away from her.

He prolonged his stay at the farmhouse as long as possible but in the end he knew he had to go. He didn't know where or when he would see his sweet Sarah again, he only knew he would find a way.

When he arrived home a letter from Poole awaited him. It seemed that Wordsworth had been so concerned about Samuel's health that he had written asking Poole to find a way to finance a six-month stay in the Azores for him. Poole's letter began by telling him that he had put his name forward to Tom Wedgwood, who had been ill for some time and was looking for a travelling companion for his trip to Sicily for the winter. If nothing came of that, Poole went on in the same sort of scolding big brother tone, he could lend him £20 to help pay for a stay overseas and he was sure there were other friends who would do the same. He pointed out, however, that Samuel already owed him £52, far more than Samuel had realised.

"It seems to me impossible to imagine that you would not be well if you could find a mind freely at ease," he wrote. "Make yourself that mind. Take from it its two weak parts — its tendency to restlessness and its tendency to torpor — and it would make you great and happy."

Samuel knew that there was some truth in what Poole said. If he was happy at home he would be able to settle down to proper work. But that wouldn't cure his stiff and swollen joints, his aching back, his bad stomach and bowels. Even Sarah Hutchinson's company couldn't do that.

Although he missed Sarah and Mary, it was good to be back in his own beloved study with his view of the mountains. Sara had greeted him coolly – he had been gone far longer than she had expected – but Hartley was there to throw his arms around him and hold him tightly and prattle about what he had been doing.

"Uncle Southey is coming to stay," he told him.

"I know," Samuel said. He had had a letter from Southey telling him he was coming up. "And Aunt Southey," he told Hartley. "You will be able to play with them and show them all your favourite places."

He was looking forward to seeing Southey. Despite several disagreements and estrangements over the years, he was still one of Samuel's closest friends. When they first knew each other they had worked together on a play, *The Fall of Robespierre*, and Southey had been one of Samuel's strongest supporters in the Pantisocracy scheme. Being brothers-in-law strengthened their ties. Edith was Sara's favourite sister, although Samuel found it hard to understand why. Edith was a nervous, highly strung woman, weak and needy, often depressed and anxious. But it was touching to see their reunion, Sara rushing to greet Edith, both women so happy to see each other, with so much to talk about. And he had Southey to talk to, a man he had known so long, shared so much with.

It was high summer. Day after day they woke to blue skies and sunshine, the open windows of the house letting in the cool breeze, birdsong in the air. In the holiday atmosphere engendered by having Southey and Edith to stay, Samuel felt kinder to Sara. They went on the sort of short walks that the two city-born women enjoyed, taking a picnic with them and sitting in the shade of a tree while Hartley raced around getting hot and sweaty and fat little Derwent crawled around on a rug next to them. Sometimes they took a boat out on the lake and in the evenings they strolled in the gardens of Greta Hall and Southey talked to Samuel about Portugal.

"You would love it," he told Samuel. "The climate would suit you. It made such a difference to Edith. Cured her completely of her depression. We had some incredible adventures. We spent three weeks travelling right into the heart of the country with a group of friends. You wouldn't believe the hardship Edith put up with: mosquitos, sleeping on rough, lumpy mattresses. One night my bed was made of a heap of salted fish! By the end of the three weeks Edith was as brown as a squaw!"

"I'm still deciding where to go," Samuel said. "If you and Edith and the Wordsworths could join us…"

"It's not as easy as that," Southey laughed. "That's the trouble with you, Samuel. You spawn plans like a herring but you never see any of them through."

"That's not true!" Samuel said indignantly. "I went to Germany, didn't I? I came up here. If I had the money I'd be off abroad as soon as I could."

"Aye, there's the rub," Southey said. "If we all had the money we could do what we liked. But money has to be earned."

Southey was always so practical and so right. Samuel often felt they got on better at a distance, where he could ignore his hectoring lectures like he ignored Poole's. Thinking of Poole reminded him. "Poole has suggested I go to Sicily for the winter with Tom Wedgwood," he said. "He's looking for a travelling companion."

"Well, why don't you?" Southey asked delightedly. "That would be perfect wouldn't it? He'd be financing the trip. It's the answer to everything. Except you couldn't take Sara and the children."

Southey *would* say that of course. He was always on Sara's side. Like the Wordsworths were on his. Not that it should come to sides. "It's not just that," Samuel said quickly, as though leaving Sara were the last thing on his mind. "Tom Wedgwood and I have nothing in common. And two invalids travelling and living together, it would be impossible. He needs someone fit to go with him."

Wordsworth had gone away. He had been invited to a wedding in Scotland. "I wouldn't have bothered to go," he told Samuel, "but I didn't want to miss out on the chance to travel to Scotland."

Samuel missed him. He thought of him constantly, dreaming up scenarios where they were all together — Wordsworth and Dorothy, the Hutchinson sisters and him — the charmed circle, living in some distant country where the skies were always as blue and the wind always as warm as it was in these late summer weeks in England.

Everywhere he went reminded him of them. All their special places, the places they had named after themselves. Climbing over the fells one day he saw a pool of spring water bubbling up from the springy turf. To him it seemed to sum up the Wordsworths and Hutchinsons: so loyal, so certain, so forever bound up in each other. In his notebook he wrote, "The spring with the little tiny cone of loose sand ever rising and sinking at the bottom, but its surface without a wrinkle: W.W. M.H. D.W. S.H."

But, as the days grew shorter and the nights cooler, it became obvious that neither the Southeys nor the Wordsworths would go abroad with him for the winter and there had never been any question of the Hutchinson sisters coming. Everyone had their duties, their responsibilities, their livings to earn, even him.

Wordsworth came back at the end of September and Samuel rushed straight over to visit.

"I can't face another winter up here," he told Wordsworth and Dorothy. "I have to get away."

"On your own?" Dorothy asked perceptively.

"Sara wouldn't thank me for dragging her and the children down south again just as she's settled," he said. "In any case I need to get away on my own to think about my future."

"Where will you go?" Wordsworth asked anxiously.

"There's not much choice. I can go and stay with Poole in Stowey. I'd love to be back in the Quantock Hills. I can write, walk, find my muse again. Though without you two that's unlikely…"

"Or?" Dorothy prompted him.

"Or London. I'm sure Stuart will take me on for the *Morning Post* again. I can earn a bit of money."

Much as he hated the thought of living in a city again it did make more sense.

Before he returned to Greta Hall he walked up to White Moss Common with them to put the finishing touches to 'Sarah's Seat', a rocky little outcrop that they had lined with stones and moss. Sarah had chosen it herself and laid the first stone. Now it was complete as a memorial to her forever.

With the harvest over, Sarah's brother Tom arrived at the cottage in Grasmere for a long-promised visit. A week later Mary Hutchinson came too, staying the night at Greta Hall before going on to Grasmere. He could see Sara liked Mary, but Mary was such a quiet charming woman, not wanting to be any trouble, keen to help Sara in the kitchen, it was hard not to like her.

It was Samuel's twenty-ninth birthday on 21st October. The first snow fell and, like the birds that migrate south in the winter, it seemed a good time for Samuel to be moving too. He stayed long enough to see Hartley's breeching ceremony, his heart contracting at the sight of the little boy out of his baby petticoats and into his big boy breeches. Hartley was ecstatic. He strutted around, jingling the coins that had been put in his pockets, as if he were too grown-up now to roll around the floor like he did in his long skirts.

Samuel spent his last few days with the Wordsworths in Grasmere. Wordsworth shook his hand and wished him well but Dorothy's eyes were full of tears. "I'll soon be back," he said. "In the spring."

Parting from them, like parting from the Hutchinsons, was like a physical pain in his chest. Parting from his children had been the same. Parting from Sara, however, was like a weight lifted from his mind and he felt as free as air as he set forth on the long journey back to London.

Chapter Ten

As Hartley grew older it became harder to hide things from him. He noticed Samuel's bad moods, heard Sara shouting at him, sensed the antipathy between them. Other children may not have noticed but Hartley was a sensitive little boy.

"Why are you crying, Mama?" he asked her one day in the kitchen.

"Oh, it's nothing," Sara said quickly. "I banged my elbow."

"Shall I kiss it better?"

She didn't know what she would do without the children. Hartley's warm little body to hug, Derwent's constant need of her. Which was better, she wondered, to be unhappily married and have children or to be happily married and not have any? She had seen how Edith had gazed wistfully at chubby little Derwent when she came to stay. There was still no sign of a baby for her and Southey after six years of marriage.

"You're so thin, Edith," Sara told her.

"You should have seen me before we went to Portugal," Edith said. "I was far worse. It made all the difference, going abroad, getting away."

You only had to look at Edith to see how highly strung she was. She was quite a pretty woman with brown hair and blue eyes like Sara, but her thin face had a perpetually anxious look, as though she were expecting something bad to happen all the time, and she hardly ever smiled. She couldn't sit still and even when she did her hands fidgeted in her lap or she pulled at her cap or hair or chewed at her nails. Eating made her feel sick, she said, her stomach felt bloated, she had bowel problems. But at least she had a supportive husband, one prepared to do anything, go anywhere, just to make her happy.

Sara had known Robert Southey for many years. She used to see him at his aunt's house in Bristol when she was working as a seamstress. Brought up mostly by this maiden aunt, he was dressed in girlish clothes and not allowed to play outside in case he got dirty. He grew up to be a fastidious young man with high standards of dress and behaviour. Private matters should remain private, he said, and passionate feelings kept under control. He was good-looking, tall and slim with black curly hair, hazel eyes, a straight nose and very pale skin.

Although Sarah was four years older than he, they had become good friends and when he went to university he wrote to her. By then he had become something of a rebel: he had been expelled from Westminster School for writing an article on flogging in a radical newspaper. Like Samuel, he was deeply affected by the French Revolution and it was this that really drew them together. But it was hard to understand how they remained friends. They were so very different: Southey was neat, tidy, punctilious, with a strong sense of responsibility and a caring nature whereas Samuel was untidy, unpredictable, disorganised, irresponsible and selfish. Just look at the way he had dragged her all the way up here, away from her family and friends, all for the friendship of the Wordsworths.

How naive she had been to think of it as a fresh start. The house that she had admired so much last summer had turned into a prison. Edith had raved about it when she arrived. "Why Sara, it's like a palace. You should see the places we've been living in in Portugal. But this is wonderful: so spacious, so light and airy. It reminds me of our house in Westbury. Do you remember? It had big square rooms like this and huge windows…"

Sara remembered it well. In those far off days of her youth, her family had divided their life between a smart town house in Bath and a villa in Westbury near Bristol. She and her sisters were sent to the Hannah More School in Bristol, where they had learned French, Latin, Greek and maths. They were brought up to believe in female equality. Not that it seemed to have made any difference to their lives now.

"And you're close to town," Edith was saying.

"I can't go at all in the bad weather," Sara said. *"There I go again,"* she thought, *"whining all the time, just like Samuel says.*" "The winters are so bad here." she went on, trying to justify herself. "The house is bitterly cold. You have no idea. It starts snowing in October and doesn't let up until late March. No one can go out except crazy people like Samuel and the Wordsworths."

"He still sees as much of them?" Edith dropped her voice conspiratorially. "Robert thinks they're a bad influence on him."

"Nothing's changed," Sara said, keeping her voice down, too. "If anything it's worse."

Oh, how she would have loved to tell Edith everything. She had always been closer to her than any of her other sisters. But Edith would tell Southey and that would start off another argument between him and Samuel just when they were back on good terms again. And Samuel would blame her. It would be one more thing for them to argue about.

They were magical, those late summer weeks that Edith and Southey came to stay: the picnics, the boat trips, the walks in the garden. In their company Samuel had been kinder to her and she found herself responding, taking his arm, laughing at his constant ridiculous jokes. It was almost like the old days in Bristol, before they were married, when the four of them went round together.

"I do wish you could live here all the time," she said to Edith, taking her arm as the men strolled ahead.

She felt Edith stiffen slightly. "I can't imagine *living* here," she said. "It's too remote, Sara. We like to be near civilisation. Maybe not London, we didn't like it there much, but somewhere there's a bit of life and society. There was so much to do in Portugal, Sara. The religious festivals are so colourful and exciting. And we made a lot of friends. There were parties and outings, always something going on." She made it sound wonderful compared with Sara's dreary, daily routine. "Anyway," Edith went on, "Robert needs to be somewhere he can get paid work. He can't make enough from writing."

So she wasn't surprised when Edith wrote in October to tell her that Southey had accepted a position in Dublin, as secretary to the Irish chancellor, with a salary of £200.

"Why can't you do something like that?" she asked Samuel, waving Edith's letter in his face.

"Of course it's a great opportunity," he said airily. "Men of talent are in great demand by the ministry. I could do the same if I wanted but I would rather achieve greatness in my own way and in my own time."

"In the meantime you're happy to see your family starve."

"Oh, come on, Sara. We're not starving. We have enough until Christmas. I'll find something before then, I always do."

"By scrounging off your friends," she snapped.

Sometimes Sara wondered why she hadn't married Southey instead of Samuel. They had always got on well. But Southey was so cold and prissy, where

Samuel was full of fire and excitement. She had been seduced by that fire, literally and metaphorically, led along on a wave of enthusiasm, as others had been and still were. Meanwhile Southey had met the quiet, reserved Edith and decided she was far better suited to him. She probably was, but Southey was still Sara's closest male friend and her staunchest ally.

She had hoped he might be able to talk some sense into Samuel in the summer, in the evenings, maybe, when they were closeted in his study together. What Samuel needed was someone to tell him to knuckle down and work. Of course Samuel would say he'd been ill and it was true, he had. It wasn't put on; she had seen the swollen joints in his knees and hands, helped him out of bed when he could hardly move. But the moment he was better he was rushing around the countryside on flimsy excuses when she knew very well he was just off having fun with his friends.

Of course she was jealous. Who wouldn't be? Samuel was only happy when he was away from her, with the Wordsworths or the Hutchinsons. Every fibre of her being burned with the injustice of it. *She* should come first in Samuel's life. They had made their vows, *forsaking all others.* She knew Samuel had strong religious views. He had studied theology at Cambridge and preached at Unitarian chapels in the north and in Somerset. He believed in the sanctity of marriage. No one could say Sara didn't keep to her vows: there was always a meal on the table; the children and Samuel never wanted for clean, well-mended clothes; the house was spotless. And all this with far fewer servants than most women in her station would expect to manage on. Sometimes she felt like a skivvy, doing all the work while Samuel sat around reading or travelled all over the countryside to visit his friends, friends who didn't like her, didn't want to be with her, clearly thought she wasn't good enough for Samuel.

All she wanted was a husband who wanted to be with her, who looked after her and cherished her like Southey did with Edith. But when she tried to explain this to Samuel it always came out like an accusation. He would leap to defend himself, then come up with some high-blown philosophical arguments about love that tied her up in knots so that she ended up screaming in frustration. Not only did he think he was superior to her in every way, he seemed to think he was above all the mundane rules of society, free to come and go as he wanted without regard to his wife and family.

He was the same with money. It was as though having to earn a living was for ordinary mortals, not brilliant men like him. He thought nothing of borrowing from his friends, assuming they would support him in any venture he had. "I'll pay them back," he would say, loftily. Sara hated owing money. Her father had been declared bankrupt when she was sixteen and she had never forgotten the shame of it, losing their two houses, their furniture, their social standing. The family had been broken up, her mother and the two younger children to live with a friend, her sisters Mary and Edith, only fourteen and twelve at the time, to another, while Sara and her father moved in with yet another. She had learned to make do with very little but the fear of losing everything again was always there.

When Edith and Southey had left, the summer seemed to come to an abrupt end. The mornings were cold and misty. Sara drew the curtains earlier and earlier every evening. The brief truce between her and Samuel had come to an end too. He began talking again of travelling, of going away somewhere warm for his health.

She had never taken any notice when he said he was going abroad for the winter. There was no money to pay for it for a start and no one to travel with him. It was pathetic the way he clung to the idea of the Wordsworths going as well. It was obvious to anyone with any sense that they were settled in Grasmere. Dorothy's letters were full of what she had done in the garden and her plans for the future. Samuel was the only one who didn't seem to realise the cottage was their home for life.

She was surprised that Dorothy still wrote to her at all actually. Some kindred female spirit still seemed to hold them together despite their differences. When they were face-to-face however, Dorothy couldn't hide her antipathy. Everyone up here was on Samuel's side: Dorothy, Wordsworth, Sarah Hutchinson. Sara didn't blame her namesake; she quite liked the woman. Sarah was no seductive siren and, although she couldn't have been oblivious to Samuel's feelings, she didn't seem to do anything to encourage him. No, it was the Wordsworths who were to blame, for persuading Samuel to come up here in the first place and for encouraging his friendship with the Hutchinsons. They probably enjoyed Sara's humiliation.

With Edith and Southey gone, Sara was more alone than ever. The very sight of Samuel sitting there, hunched over his books, while she rushed around and did everything from morning to night was enough to drive her to distraction. She would find herself muttering aloud in the empty kitchen. "Stupid lazy good-for-nothing man. I do everything around here while he sits around and expects meals to be ready, clothes to be put out for him. He's lazy, that's what he is. Why can't he get up and help me now and again. I'm sure Wordsworth helps Dorothy…" And so she would go on. It made her feel better to voice her feelings even if there was no one to listen.

She didn't know which annoyed her more: his days of indolence in bed or by the fire or his excursions to the Wordsworths and Hutchinsons on the flimsiest of excuses. What did they actually *do* there all the time? As far as she could tell all this so-called work consisted of little else than talking, talking, talking. Samuel liked nothing more than the sound of his own voice.

She was losing respect for him. And he had lost any for her. But she had right on her side. All he had were some half-baked arguments about love and the marriage contract that he turned to his advantage. She deserved to be treated better. And she needed to be provided for. But she had no power really, no woman did, and when Samuel told her he was going to London she had to accept it.

"How long will you be gone?" She didn't know why she was asking. He never told her how long he would be anywhere. When he went to Germany he had said it was only for "a few months," and he'd been away for nearly a year.

"Oh, I don't know. Three months maybe. Until it gets warmer," he said vaguely.

"You don't need a wife," she snapped, "or a family. You spend more time away from us than you do with us."

"And whose fault is that? If you made my home more tolerable I would stay here more."

"You wouldn't stay here whatever I did. You're only happy when you're away from me. And please don't tell me it's for your health. You should never have brought us up here. You should have known it would make you ill."

"I think another winter here would be the end of me," he said melodramatically, ignoring what she'd said. "But *actually* I'm going to work on the *Morning Post.* A proper job. I thought that might make you happy."

"Nothing will make me happy," she snapped. "I don't know why I agreed to come up to this godforsaken place. What am I supposed to do while you're gone? I see no one; I know no one."

"It's not *my* fault you've got no friends. Maybe you should ask yourself why?"

Spiteful words. Sara bit back the tears. She wasn't going to let him see he'd won.

The night before he left he came to her room. "Sara, my love," he murmured, sliding into bed next to her. What could she do? She was his wife. Her duties entailed more than cooking and housework. No one would ever be able to say she had reneged on them. But she wasn't going to be his whore as well as his skivvy. And she hadn't forgotten his hurtful words or his devotion to Sarah Hutchinson.

She turned her face from the kisses she used to revel in and lay like a statue while he took what meagre satisfaction he could from her.

Chapter Eleven

Thrown back into the heart of the city, Samuel suddenly realised how isolated he had become up in the north with only the Wordsworths for company. Stuart found him lodgings at 10 King Street, between Covent Garden and Fleet Street, and Samuel threw himself back into the thick of the London intelligentsia, seeing old friends like Godwin, Lamb and Davy and meeting new people with exciting new ideas.

There was so much going on, so much to fire up his articles for the *Morning Post.* Henry Addington had just been appointed prime minister and Samuel wrote three long articles on his new cabinet. Everyone was talking about the peace treaty with Bonaparte.

"You know what we should do," Samuel said excitedly to Davy. "Pop over to France and observe the new regime at first hand so I can write an article on it."

"You're crazy," Davy laughed.

"Well, if you don't want to I'll go on my own."

But in the end he didn't. He had missed Tom Poole as much, if not more, than his other friends and he longed to get out of the city and back to Somerset and the freedom of the Quantock Hills.

"I need you here," Stuart protested, but Samuel took no notice. He deserved a holiday. He left London on Boxing Day, his heart feeling lighter and lighter as the crowded houses and dirty streets, the noise and the stench, gradually fell away and he headed out into the countryside.

When he walked into Nether Stowey it was as though he had never been away. Lime Street still rang to the sound of weavers' looms clacking and people talking as they sat outside their cottages, sewing gloves and saddles. When he walked past Gilbards, the cottage he had rented for three years, he could almost imagine Sara was waiting inside for him. Not the Sara he knew now, shrewish and bad-tempered, but the one he knew then, sweet and pretty and smiling, welcoming him with warm soft arms, Hartley tottering around at her feet, Berkeley sleeping in his cradle. His heart contracted nostalgically at the thought.

But someone else was living in Gilbards now of course. "A minister," Tom Poole told him later. "Parson Cave, a very serious man, doesn't have much to do with anyone."

People still stared as Samuel walked past. Strangers were unusual in the village, especially those so obviously gentry, despite the mud-spattered clothes. But some people remembered him and nodded politely but coolly. They probably remembered also the reputation Samuel and his friends had of being radical, revolutionaries maybe, who had come to the village to set up a network of spies in preparation for the French invasion, false rumours that grew and spread until Poole began to rue the day he had invited Samuel and his friends to Nether Stowey. Now, though, with talk of peace with France, Poole had no reason to worry about his friendship with Samuel.

Poole was still at work in his tannery when Samuel arrived at his fine house in Castle Street but his mother greeted him like a long-lost son. Older, a bit frailer, and a lot deafer, she fussed around him, bringing him food and drink and shooing the cat off what used to be his favourite chair.

Tom Poole was only six years older than Samuel but he had been working in his father's tannery for many years and he seemed a lot more mature. Like Mr Jackson of Greta Hall, he was a self-educated man. He would have loved to have gone to university, to be properly educated, but he had always known he would have to take over the family business when his father died. It hadn't stopped him spending all his spare time studying though, reading widely and building up a substantial library, which Samuel used when he lived in Stowey. Poole also had a keen interest in politics, both local and national, and as a wealthy and influential man he liked to help his village and the villagers. He set up the Stowey Book Club, which stocked books by Paine, Franklin and Mary Wollstonecraft. And he had followed the events of the French Revolution closely, earning himself something of a reputation as a radical. He often dreamt of emigrating to America. However, when Samuel had approached him seven years ago with his scheme for Pantisocracy his reaction was, "I fear human nature is not yet perfect enough to exist long under the regulations of such a system. Particularly when the executors of the plan are taken from a society in a high degree civilised and corrupted."

They had remained friends, however. It was Poole who encouraged Samuel to come and live in Nether Stowey, Poole who supported him financially and emotionally, through Samuel's ups and downs. Quite simply, the man was his rock. They had very few disagreements; Poole believed in him, lectured him and harangued him now and again but never doubted his abilities.

Samuel's patrons, Josiah and Tom Wedgwood, were down in Somerset too. Tom hadn't found anyone to go to Sicily with him and, despite Samuel's insistence that they had nothing in common, they did, in fact, share an interest in science, particularly optics and light. Tom had been experimenting with trying to capture photographic images.

"I coat a piece of paper or leather with silver nitrate," he explained excitedly to Samuel, "then expose it to light. Solid objects or light passing through a painting on glass leaves an image on the paper or leather. The image darkens and you get a kind of silhouette. The problem is it goes on getting darker. I can't work out how to stop it. I've been talking to James Watt about it."

"What does Davy think?" Samuel asked.

"He's extremely interested. He wants to write a paper on it when I've done some more experiments."

"I've promised him I'll get back to London for his lectures at the Royal Institute," Samuel said.

But in the meantime the snow had thawed and, although the roads were still muddy, Samuel set off to revisit the places he loved so much, places inextricably linked in his mind with Wordsworth and Dorothy and the magical summer of 1797 when everything was new and young and fresh. It all seemed so different now, in the depths of winter: the walk up to Alfoxton Park, through the dark, damp dripping leaves; the house empty and shuttered; the deer melting into the woods when they heard his approach. If only he could go back to those halcyon days! Nothing could compare with them: the long rambles on the Quantock Hills, listening to the nightingales in the dusk, walking by moonlight.

He had been happy then. Happy with Sara as well. She didn't come with them on their walks of course, she had Hartley and Berkeley to look after, but she was always there waiting for him. How had it all gone so wrong? Was there a way to make it right again? Maybe, if they went away, far away, somewhere warm so he wouldn't be ill all the time, maybe they could rekindle their love and their life together. But he would still need his friends. He had to have people he could talk to, who understood him.

"What do you say to a two years' residence at Montpellier?" he wrote to Sara. "Under blue skies and in rainless air? We would go from Liverpool to Bordeaux by sea. Southey would go that way to Lisbon," he went on. "and spend some months with us."

This time he was sure it would all go ahead. Southey had already said he was thinking of going to Portugal again. And when Wordsworth announced he was going to marry Mary Hutchinson it seemed perfect. They would all go: the three Wordsworths, Southey and Edith, Sara and the boys. It was falling into place just as he had always hoped.

Wordsworth's news hadn't come as a complete surprise to him. There was something about Wordsworth's reaction when he saw Mary last time that had alerted Samuel to the change in their feelings for each other. Somewhere along the way the brotherly love of a long-standing friend had deepened to romantic love. They were both thirty-one, they didn't need to ask anyone's permission, but Samuel wondered how Dorothy must feel. Her life had revolved around Wordsworth for so long and she was not used to sharing him with anyone on a daily basis. And how Mary would feel, knowing that Dorothy and Wordsworth shared such a special bond?

He told himself he was pleased for Wordsworth, of course he was, but he couldn't help a pang of envy. Wordsworth would have a happy marriage. He had everything he wanted. He was surrounded by women who loved him, looked after him, would do anything for him. Samuel didn't want to be left out. He had to find a way to keep them together.

He understood the wedding would be in March, so he would need to get back to Keswick before then to organise their respective travel arrangements.

In the back of his mind he had another plan just in case there was any delay in going abroad: William, Mary and Dorothy could move in to Greta Hall. It made so much sense: the cottage at Grasmere was tiny and was very much Dorothy's domain. Mary and William would want more space as they were sure to have children in due course. At Greta Hall there were rooms to spare and they would all be together.

But before he made any arrangements he needed to earn some money. Back in the city, he wrote a fourth article on the new cabinet for the *Morning Post* but all his other work had stalled. If he wanted enough money to go abroad he would need to get some work published.

"You may be assured that in a very short time the first sheet of my metaphysical work will go to the press…" he wrote to Poole. In truth, he hadn't even written the first word. He knew he was lazy but he went on procrastinating. There was always something else to do; he just didn't have the self-discipline he needed to be a writer. Instead he spent his time writing letters and dreaming of his trip abroad.

The only real obstacle to going away was that it would mean a complete break from Sarah Hutchinson. When was the moment he fell in love with her? He had always found her attractive but there were many women he was attracted to and he didn't fall in love with them. He traced it back to last winter, when they sat and talked together, their walks with Wordsworth and Dorothy, his visits to her brothers' farms, those cosy evenings with her and Mary by the fireside, the night he held her hand behind her back. Yes, that was it. That was when fancy turned to love. And now? Now it was too late. He would love her until the day he died.

He wrote to her regularly, very different letters from the ones he wrote to Sara. Sarah Hutchinson wasn't interested in his social success or the money he might make from his newspaper work, she cared about him as a person, she believed in him. He lived for her letters. If she didn't reply straight away, if she didn't write the words of love and support he needed, he was desperate. His other Sarah, his Asahara maid; he didn't like to think of her with the same name as his wife. She was so very different. He played around with the letters of her name in his notebook, finally settling on Asra, his special name for the woman he knew he would always love, however impossible it was.

At this distance from her, his confidence grew. It was so much easier to express his feelings in writing than it was in person and in one letter he poured out everything to her, told her she was the only woman for him. But he had gone too far; the letter she wrote back broke his heart. He had made her ill, she wrote, she was distraught. He must stop writing to her, stop seeing her. Suddenly everything else in his life paled into insignificance. He must go to her. He would explain everything. They could go back to where they were before, just as long as he could go on seeing her.

Sarah and Mary were both staying with their brother Tom at his farm at Gallow Hill in Stockton-on-Tees. He had to think of a way to see her. It was 21st February and he had told Sara he would be back in early March for Wordsworth's wedding. If he left now he could go and see Sarah first. He just needed to think of an excuse. Then it came to him: the wedding. He could tell Sara that Miss Hutchinson might be going over to Grasmere to help with the preparations. "If it is decided that Sarah is to come to Grasmere," he wrote as vaguely as possible. "I shall return by York, which will be but a few miles out of the way, and accompany her back."

But he had to cover his tracks. Dorothy sometimes wrote to Sara. She might say she knew nothing about a visit from Sarah. He wasn't even sure when the wedding was taking place. So he wrote to the Wordsworths saying he would be bringing Sarah for the visit that she had arranged. He knew it would confuse them but it was a necessary lie. And maybe not even a lie at all; he might be able to persuade her to come with him.

Next he had to tackle Daniel Stuart. He told him there was urgent family business he needed to get back home for.

"Can you stay another week?" Stuart asked. "Just until I can find someone to replace you."

He had no choice. The week dragged by but finally he was on his way. He would need to think of a reason why he had had to make a further detour to Stockton-on-Tees rather than meeting Sarah in York but that seemed unimportant. All that mattered was that he would see her.

As Samuel approached the farmhouse at Gallow Hill, he could see it was nothing like the one the Hutchinsons had been living in at Sockburn. That had been a large, elegant, red brick house, standing in the loop of the River Tees, almost as though it were on an island, and surrounded by beautiful woods and meadows. It must have been a wrench to leave it for the ugly square farmhouse he saw in front of him, situated on a small rise overlooking the dull, flat Vale of

Pickering, a collection of barns and outhouses enclosing the farmyard, and the busy main Pickering to Scarborough road only a few hundred yards away. But the rent at Sockburn had gone up to nearly £400, Sarah said in her letters, whereas the farm at Gallow Hill was only £120 a year and had more land.

Samuel's heart sank when Mary opened the door to him. Usually she greeted him with a welcoming smile. Instead she looked so worried. Sarah must be worse than he thought. She took his hand absent-mindedly. Tom appeared in the hallway behind her. "Oh, it's you," he said gruffly. "Come to cause more trouble, have you?"

It was so unlike Tom that Samuel was quite taken aback. Was it a joke? But no, there was no smile.

"He doesn't mean it," Mary said quickly. "It's just…"

"What?" Samuel said. "What have I done?"

"Your letters," Mary said, her face reddening. "They've upset Sarah. Upset all of us. That's what's made her ill."

"I didn't mean to," Samuel said, bewildered. "I care for her."

Mary's blush deepened. "That's just it. You must see the position it's put her in, an unmarried woman and you a married man."

"But I love her," Samuel burst out. "I'd do anything for her."

"She's worried that people will think you're separating from your wife," Mary went on, "and that she will be your… "

"No, no," Samuel said quickly. "I wouldn't dream of it."

He could see that Mary believed him.

"You'll let me see her at least?" he asked. "I can help you look after her. As a friend. I won't breathe a word to upset her."

"Well, I suppose so," Mary said but the reluctance showed in her face. "Now you're here you must stay, of course." Her good manners wouldn't allow her to turn him away after the distance he had travelled. "Sarah can tell you herself how she feels. It's not up to me."

Sarah was sitting in a chair by the fire. She looked up at him anxiously when he went in. He could sense her awkwardness.

"Sarah, my love," he said, hurrying over to her.

"No." Her voice was surprisingly firm. "Don't call me that," she said.

He had been so looking forward to seeing her, to see her face light up like it always did when she saw him, but now she wouldn't even meet his eyes. He reached out his hands to take hers, as he had done many times before, but she shrank back in her chair.

"You must go," she said. "People will say…" Her voice broke and she started crying. "They'll say… Oh, the most awful things."

Mary must have been listening outside the door because she was by her side in a moment. "Sarah, my sweet. You mustn't. We've talked about this. It's only words. They can't hurt you. We all know it's not true."

"But they think… they think…" she sobbed.

"Come, let me take you back to bed. I'll bring you something to settle you."

It was the same the whole time he was there. Even when Sarah seemed better she wouldn't spend more than five minutes in his company before she was fidgeting to get away. Gone was their easy camaraderie, the touch of her hand, the flirtatious banter. She wouldn't even sit next to him.

"There's no one to see us," he reassured her. "And even if there were, we're not doing anything wrong. We never have done."

"You don't understand," she said briskly. "It's not right for you to be with me. I see that now. I was foolish. I should have realised before."

He couldn't tear himself away, however agonising it was. It was enough to be in the same house. He went to sleep at night thinking of her, woke in the morning with the same thought on his mind. It was more than love. She was his life, his reason for living. His whole happiness lay with her: to see her and be with her. That was enough; he didn't want more. But now she shunned him. It cut like a knife. If only she would let him explain that he meant her no harm. But she had put a huge distance between them.

After ten days he knew he couldn't stay any longer. He was already late back and Sara would be worried. He would have to tell her he'd been here in due course. If he didn't, the Wordsworths would. Dorothy wrote to everybody: Mary, Sarah, his wife. It was bound to come out. He couldn't ask them to keep his visit a secret.

He was still hoping to persuade Sarah to come to Grasmere. "It would do you good," he said. "The fresh air, the walks we all love, the company…" But she wouldn't go with him. "I'm too ill," she said. "I'll go when I'm better."

"The wedding's not for months anyway," Mary told him. "I don't know why you thought it was in March."

It was a wild day when he left, an icy wind blowing hard shards of stinging snow in his face as he walked to the mail coach. It was lucky no one else got on when he did; wrapped in his greatcoat, huddled in the corner of the draughty coach, Samuel found tears rolling down his face at the thought of leaving Sarah. He tried to force himself to stop but the tears turned into huge sobs that rasped at his throat and chest until he gave way to a storm of weeping that would have put Hartley to shame. His heart was breaking, he was sure of it. Every moment that took him further away from Sarah broke it a bit more. But he had to go home. His other Sara was waiting for him. His duty lay with her and the two little boys he had missed so much.

Chapter Twelve

It had been a long, cold, lonely winter for Sara. Samuel's letters were her only respite. They always got on better at a distance. He called her his Sally-Pally and signed off lovingly. Maybe she was clutching at straws but there might be some hope in their relationship, even if it was just for the sake of the children. She knew he missed them and they missed him.

It was just over eighteen months since they moved here but she knew very few people and there was no one she could call a close friend. She wouldn't mind if Samuel wanted to move again, back south, where the climate would be better for him and she could see her mother and sisters again. But when he spoke of going abroad, well, that was a different matter altogether. Especially with only the Wordsworths for company. And there was the danger of travel and disease for the children. She really wouldn't want to do it. Edith had assured her there was no question of her and Southey going with them. "Robert says he is just too different from Samuel to think of living together," Edith wrote.

That was the trouble with Samuel: he always took so much for granted. He had written to tell her that Wordsworth was marrying Mary Hutchinson in March and that they would all travel together afterwards but Dorothy had written to say the wedding wasn't for months yet. And she said nothing about moving abroad.

Sara would just have to wait for Samuel's return to find out what was happening. Wherever he went, she would have to go too. And if they did go overseas at least it would separate him once and for all from Miss Sarah Hutchinson. But it was a high price to pay. Bad enough to have moved hundreds of miles from her family, how much worse to go so many more.

She was busy in the kitchen one morning when she heard Hartley's cry of delight. "Papa! It's Papa! Come quickly!"

Despite herself, her heart quickened. It was partly nerves; she hadn't seen him for so long. She was lonely. It would be lovely to talk to someone else, to have someone there every day rather than just her and the children. She dried her hands quickly and rushed to the looking glass but, really, what could she do to make herself look better? The wig was firmly in place, her face was flushed, her eyes bright with excitement. It would have to do.

"Can I go out, Mama?" Hartley was begging. "Please, let me go to him."

"Well, put your coat on first. And be careful, it's slippery out there. No, not you Derwent, you stay with Mama." She held the chubby little boy's hand.

At least the children took the edge off any awkwardness but Samuel seemed genuinely pleased to see her, pulling her towards him and holding her as though he would never let go.

"Miss Hutchinson isn't with you?" she asked, looking past him. She had made a bed up especially. Visitors to the Wordworths usually stayed at Greta Hall the night they arrived in the area, saving the extra fourteen-mile journey to Grasmere until the next day when they were more rested.

"Oh, she's ill unfortunately," Samuel said.

"Oh, what a shame." She did her best to sound sincere, though the last thing she had wanted was Miss Hutchinson here on Samuel's first night back.

"The wedding's not for a few months anyway," Samuel said. "It seems I was mistaken."

So many other questions crowded into her mind: were they all still going abroad? And if so, when? But Samuel looked so tired and bedraggled and the children were making such a racket that it was impossible to talk.

The evening went well. The children were excited to have Papa back and Samuel looked up often at Sara with love and pride in his eyes. After she had settled the boys for the night, Samuel told her about his life in London. "You would have been proud of me, Sara. I was so popular everywhere. Everyone wanted me to dine with them. The famous poet and fine speaker."

Part of Sara, the mean, spiteful part, laughed at him for his hubris but part of her felt sorry for him. These things were so important to him. He really didn't know her at all if he thought they meant so much to her. She would trade all his celebrity as a writer and fine speaker for a man who loved his home and family and supported them in every way.

But it was hard to resist him when he was like this. It was why she had fallen for him in the first place, why other people went on falling for him, why he still had so many friends despite all his foibles. He was enraptured by his own enthusiasm; his eyes sparkled, he threw his head back and laughed. His stories were genuinely amusing, so that she found herself laughing with him. The fact of the matter was she had missed him. There had been times when she wondered if he would come home at all. The letters he wrote, making sure she knew she was included in his future, had been her lifeline.

There was so much still to discuss but she could see Samuel was tired and it would wait. When they went up to bed she didn't question it when he followed her into the room. It wasn't the best lovemaking they had ever had — she still couldn't quite give herself to the man who had told her he loved someone else — but he was her husband and he wanted her; it was something. More than anything else, she needed to be needed.

It was at breakfast the next morning that he said, ever so casually, "I stayed at Gallow Hill for a few days on my way home."

"What?" She stopped in the middle of cutting a piece of bread for Hartley.

"Tom Hutchinson's farm," he said.

"Yes, I know," she said sharply. "But I thought you were collecting Miss Hutchinson in York."

"She was ill," he said.

"But if you knew she was ill and couldn't come, why did you go and see her?"

How foolish she had been. Why hadn't she seen it before? The woman obviously wasn't ill at all. And she had never intended visiting Grasmere. It was all a ruse dreamt up to dupe her. Everyone was in on it: the Hutchinsons, the Wordsworths, all laughing at her. All those stories he had spun her about a new life together, all lies.

But he had chosen a good time to tell her. He knew she wouldn't make a scene in front of the children. Already Hartley was looking at them both anxiously and she didn't want him to think his parents argued all the time. She finished cutting the slice of bread, wishing she could cut Samuel's throat instead, and waited until after breakfast when the children were both playing with their toys. By then her anger had grown in strength. She could feel it pulsing through her body even as she spoke gently to both children. "I'm just going up to talk to Papa," she said. "I won't be long."

Hartley gave her a quick, perceptive look but Derwent had taken hold of one of his toy soldiers and as he snatched it back and went to hide it somewhere, Sara escaped from the room.

Samuel was in his study, at his desk, writing, She didn't knock. She didn't wait until he had finished.

"So what's the matter with your mistress?" she hissed. "An attack of the vapours maybe? Or a guilty conscience for what she's doing to our marriage?"

He leapt up from his chair, flew across the room towards her, his face contorted with rage, spit flying from his mouth as he spoke. "How dare you call her my mistress? She's the sweetest, most innocent…"

"Huh!" she snorted. "That's not what everyone is saying. Didn't you get what you wanted from her when you visited? Is that why you used me instead? You're vile!"

"Sara!" he groaned. "How low can you sink? You're degrading yourself and our marriage."

"*You're* the one degrading our marriage!" she yelled. "*I'm* the one making all the sacrifices. You don't need us. You don't want us…"

She was crying now, great sobs heaving from her chest.

"Oh, for God's sake!" Samuel snapped. "I can't stand this. Do you wonder why I don't stay at home more, woman? I come home to *this,*" he gestured towards her, "when all I want is peace and quiet, a wife who welcomes me, provides a happy home."

"I *did* welcome you, didn't I?" she spat out. "I wish I hadn't."

Downstairs she heard a crash and a yell. "Mama! Mama! Derwent has fallen over!"

"How am I supposed to work like this?" Samuel said. "It's impossible."

"Well, go back to Miss Sarah Hutchinson then. *If* she'll have you. More fool her. Or your precious friends the Wordsworths. But they may not want you once Wordsworth is married."

"They'll *always* want me. Not like you."

"Well, *go* to them for God's sake. I don't want you anymore!"

She didn't have time to think about what she had said. Downstairs she had to pick up the sobbing, yelling Derwent from the floor.

"'Artley push me!" he screamed, pointing furiously at his brother.

"I didn't! It was an accident!" Hartley protested.

Later on, in the kitchen, Sara regretted her quick words. He'd be over to Grasmere now the moment he could. Luckily the snow still lay thick on the ground and there was no question of anyone going anywhere.

They circled each other in the house like two caged animals. Sara prepared meals that Samuel ate silently before going straight up to his study. If they passed each other on the stairs they kept their distance. If they spoke at all it quickly degenerated into an argument. Hartley, who had been looking forward so much to seeing his papa, now viewed him suspiciously, scared of this cold, severe man who spoke only to snap at him.

They were back where they started all those months ago. Nothing had changed.

Four days later, when the snow had begun to thaw, Samuel came down with his bag in his hand.

"I'm off to Grasmere for a few days," he said.

"As you say," Sara said tersely.

She offered him her cheek and his lips brushed it briefly. She watched him go. He'd be better with them. What a trap she had walked into when she married him. Unable to leave, with day after day of loneliness stretching endlessly in front of her.

Chapter Thirteen

"The woman is impossible!" Samuel burst out.

"Who?" Dorothy asked, though she must know.

"Mrs Coleridge," he said. "Oh, how proud I once was to call her that. But she's changed, Dorothy, changed beyond all recognition." He could still see her face, contorted into an ugly snarl when she said Sarah's name. "She shouldn't even utter it," he mumbled.

"What?" Dorothy looked confused.

"Sarah's name. Asra…"

"Samuel, you mustn't," Dorothy said. "You don't know what it's doing to her, this… affection." She reddened.

"I can't stop," Samuel said. "I can't stop loving her, Dorothy. You might just as well ask the sun not to rise, the moon not to shine…"

"Yes, yes," Dorothy said impatiently. "But people are talking. It's making Sarah ill."

"Who's talking? I don't understand. Sarah wouldn't tell me. Or Mary. Who knows about our friendship? We've done nothing wrong."

"You don't understand, Samuel. A woman's reputation, it's very fragile. You must stop seeing Sarah, promise me."

"I can't."

Dorothy put her head in her hands. "I have such a headache," she said. "With you and Sarah, and then there's the wedding…" She broke off as if she'd said too much, then she went on, "It will be such a change."

"But it's all still going ahead?" Samuel asked.

"Yes, yes, of course," she said quickly.

"I wish you'd reconsider my suggestion," Samuel said.

Dorothy shook her head. "It would never work, Samuel."

"But it makes sense," Samuel persisted. "The house is far too big for us. We've got all those empty rooms. This cottage is tiny."

"It's our home," Dorothy said firmly. "We love it. And Mary loves it too. And you know it would never work, Samuel: your wife, me and Mary, all sharing the same house."

Later, after Dorothy had gone to bed, Wordsworth said, "There's something I need to tell you."

Samuel put his finger in the book he was reading and looked up in surprise. He had never heard his friend sound so serious.

"When I was in France," Wordsworth went on, "I…" He seemed to be searching for the right words.

"I contracted a relationship with a young woman," he finished in a rush.

It was such a startling revelation that Samuel didn't know what to say. All the time he had known Wordsworth he had never known him to be romantically involved with anyone.

"But that was a long time ago," Samuel said carefully. He thought of his first love, Mary Evans, the innocent courtship, the shy smiles. "Why does it matter now?" he went on. "You didn't promise to marry her, did you?"

"No. Well… Yes… The thing is, she had a child."

"What?" Gone was his vision of an innocent flirtation, two young inexperienced lovers. In its place a passionate liaison, secret meetings, amorous embraces. But Wordsworth wasn't the type; he was a steady, steadfast man.

"A little girl," Wordsworth went on, gathering confidence and sounding quite proud now. "Caroline." He paused. "I thought… " he went on. "I mean, I assumed…"

"That you'd go back and marry her," Samuel finished quickly. "Of course."

"But I couldn't. The political situation…"

Samuel nodded. There had been so much upheaval and violence in France. Wordsworth couldn't possibly have gone back.

"And now she's like a stranger to me," Wordsworth said. "And the baby, well, she's no longer a baby, she's nine years old."

"So you're free to marry Mary."

"But am I?" Wordsworth sighed. "Morally, Annette is my wife."

"Annette," Samuel repeated, trying to conjure up an image of the twenty-two-year-old Wordsworth with a young French girl. She would be pretty, bewitching, a minx, a seductress. Wordsworth would have been swept along by the romance and drama of the revolution…

"And there's little Caroline," Wordsworth said.

A nine-year-old girl. Four years older than Hartley. Wordsworth had been a father all this time and Samuel didn't know. But not really a father. He hadn't held his baby in his arms, seen her at her mother's breast, watched while she took her first steps.

"How is Annette managing?" he asked Wordsworth. "It must have been difficult for her, on her own."

"Well, her parents have helped. And in all the chaos she has managed to pass herself off as a widow. I don't know what to do, Samuel. My heart tells me to marry Mary but my head tells me I have a duty to Annette."

"But it's impossible," Samuel said. "You'd really go back to France and marry this Annette woman? Does she expect you to?"

"It's what she's always assumed."

"And you've been writing to her all this time?"

"Off and on. Oh, it's hard to explain. It all seems so long ago, it's like a dream. I never really knew her. Not like I know Mary. I think of Mary all the time. I never think of Annette. I can't see a life with Annette. I can't see my life without Mary."

Samuel thought of his loveless marriage. He couldn't condemn his closest friend to the same fate. "You must marry Mary," he said decisively. "Annette will understand. She's been living without you for ten years."

Wordsworth shook his head. "I've tried to tell her. But in a letter, it's so hard to find the words."

Samuel hesitated. "It *is* possible to travel to France now," he said. "Or at least it will be once the peace treaty is signed."

Wordsworth nodded. "I've thought about it," he said. "I could go and see them. I could talk to Annette; explain how I feel. And I could see my daughter. Dorothy would come with me, of course."

"You're sure she would want to go?" Samuel asked. When they had gone to Germany with him Dorothy had been dreadfully seasick and she had never enjoyed being abroad. "Everywhere is so dirty," she had complained. "And the locals take advantage of us not knowing the language or the currency." Samuel thought she and Wordsworth hadn't tried hard enough to integrate. Cooped up together in their lodgings through a cold, hard winter, they learned very little of the language and didn't experience the German way of life like he did.

"She will want to meet Annette," Wordsworth said. "She has been writing to her. And she'll want to see Caroline. Of course she would come with me. Yes, I think it's what we must do. It's my duty."

"You don't think Annette will try to persuade you to marry her if you actually see her?"

Wordsworth looked uncomfortable. "Of course it's what she wants," he said. "And morally it is right, Samuel. How can I marry Mary when I have a child with Annette?"

To Samuel it was obvious. Wordsworth and Dorothy, Mary and Sarah. Neither could be separated from the other. They were just being regrouped: William, Dorothy and Mary. Everyone knew that Sarah was Mary's 'other self'. She would come too; not always, maybe, but whenever she could. This French woman, a distant stranger from the past, a past none of them, not even Dorothy, had shared, she was an outsider, a usurper. She wasn't needed.

"You won't tell anyone will you?" Wordsworth said suddenly.

"My wife, you mean? Of course not." Sara was the last one to be trusted with such information. She would love nothing more than the opportunity to denigrate the Wordsworths as unworthy people with no morals.

"Who else knows?" Samuel asked. "Have you told Mary?"

"Not yet," Wordsworth looked embarrassed. "But I will have to. I will go and see her."

Samuel couldn't stay long with the Wordsworths. He dreaded going home to Sara but she would grumble even more if he stayed away.

"You'll come to visit me soon?" he asked when he left.

"As soon as we can," Dorothy promised.

Samuel walked home with a heavy heart. Everything seemed to be going wrong. He could no longer turn to Sarah Hutchinson for consolation and this French woman seemed intent on taking Wordsworth away from all the things he loved. The more he heard of Annette, the more determined Samuel was that Wordsworth should marry Mary. No one, least of all his best friend, should be trapped in an unhappy marriage like he was.

Sara was nowhere to be seen when he returned but he could smell the sharp, hot smell of laundry and hear her voice from the wash house at the back of the house as she rebuked the maid about something. It must be the 'big wash', a marathon procedure that went on for several days. He could hear the rhythmic flick and snap of the damp linen as she shook it out to hang it up on the airing rack. She wouldn't want to be interrupted, he decided, so he called out, "I'm home!" in the general direction of the wash house. He didn't wait to hear her reply. There was no sign of the boys. Maybe Mrs Wilson had taken them next door, he thought, so Sara could get on with her chores. She and

Mr Jackson were very fond of them and they loved going there.

He hurried up to his study. He had an idea for a new poem. It would be based on what he was going through, his emotions, his struggles, his relationship with Wordsworth and Dorothy, his happiness with Mary and Sarah Hutchinson, his unhappiness at home, his long walks on the mountains, his lonely sleepless nights at Greta Hall with the wind howling mournfully around the house. A few days later he was still making preliminary notes for it when Wordsworth and Dorothy arrived.

"I've brought the first four verses of my new poem," Wordsworth told him excitedly. "I only started it yesterday. I'm calling it *Immortality*. I've based it on the themes of despondency and hope, like in your poem *The Mad Monk*."

Samuel decided not to tell them about his new poem. They might not approve of it. But, whether he ever published it or not, he was determined to write it. The ideas were crowding into his mind and they had to be written down, even if he was the only one who ever read them.

Sara welcomed the Wordsworths more cordially than usual. Samuel suspected it was because they had so few visitors that it made a change for her to have someone to talk to. Or maybe she was just making an effort for him. Whatever the reason it was good to see her and Dorothy getting on, even if only on a superficial level.

Dorothy made a fuss of both children, exclaiming at how much they had grown. Hartley was so excited to see her and it warmed his heart to see her taking Derwent onto her lap so that he wouldn't feel left out. What a shame she would never have children of her own, he thought, watching her with them. But maybe Wordsworth and Mary would have a family in due course and she could live her life through them.

Sara continued to be in a good mood for the rest of their visit. He could tell it was an effort for her but he was just pleased there was some reprieve. They hadn't talked about their problems. They both shied away from any confrontation. Nothing would mend their broken marriage but if they could exist together civilly it would be bearable.

He had kept to his promise and not told her about Annette so he had to wait until he was out for a walk with Wordsworth and Dorothy to find out what was happening.

"We have written to Mary," Dorothy said. Samuel smiled at the thought of poor Mary receiving joint love letters from Wordsworth and Dorothy. Surely she must want a letter exclusively from her lover. But she was probably used to it by now; Wordsworth and Dorothy did everything together.

"I've arranged to go and see her," Wordsworth said. "I'd like to explain everything to her myself."

Samuel sighed. "I still think you're going about it the wrong way," he said. "Honesty isn't always the best policy when it comes to wives."

"That might be *your* experience," Wordsworth said. "But I don't agree."

"Women are tricky creatures..."

"Even me?" Dorothy asked.

"Especially you," Samuel laughed. "They're more prone to worries and nervous disorders."

"Well, that's true enough," Dorothy said. "But you men worry too." She glanced at Wordsworth. "One thing's for certain though," she went on. "I've told Mary we won't be moving in with them at Gallow Hill."

Samuel stopped and looked at her. "Were you seriously considering it?"

"Mary wanted it," Wordsworth said. "She can't bear the idea of leaving her family, especially her sisters. We could all have stayed together."

Samuel let his breath out shakily in relief. The thought of them all living so far from him was unbearable.

The next day, while Wordsworth and Dorothy went over to see the Calverts at Windy Brow, Samuel picked up his pen and began writing his new poem. It was the right time. He was ready. He knew it as the words flowed from his fingers onto the page. He wrote it as a letter to Sarah Hutchinson, telling her all the things he wanted so much to say, if only she would listen.

That night Wordsworth knocked on the door to his room. "Can I talk with you?" he asked. Samuel was in bed. He and Wordsworth had climbed Skiddaw two days ago and he was still recovering: his knees were swollen and painful and he felt completely exhausted. But Wordsworth always listened to him; it was only fair he should reciprocate.

"Yes, of course," he said, pushing back the bedclothes to get out of bed.

"No, no…" Wordsworth said quickly. "Stay where you are." He pulled a chair up to Samuel's bedside and put his candle down on the floor next to the bed.

"I still don't know what to do," he said.

"About Annette?" Samuel was beginning to lose his patience on the subject. "It's obvious what you should do. Write to her. Tell her there's no chance. Marry Mary as soon as you can, before she decides she shouldn't have you."

"She would never do that," Wordsworth said decisively.

"If she thought some other poor woman was suffering because of her she well might," Samuel said. "Women are strange creatures, the way they think."

"And Annette *is* suffering," Wordsworth said sadly. "She has no money."

"You'll still support her, I presume? Her and Caroline?"

"Of course, when I can. She knows that. But that's another reason to go and see her. We can regularise the arrangement, legally, so she knows I won't abandon them both when I'm married and have other obligations."

"As long as she doesn't get her hopes up," Samuel said. "She might think when you see her and Caroline you will change your mind and marry her. That's why you shouldn't go. It's not right, really it isn't."

Wordsworth shook his head. "You won't dissuade me," he said. "I have to see her in person. I have to tell her myself that I am marrying someone else. Make a proper arrangement for them both. It is only fair."

"But you risk losing Mary," Samuel said. "You're crazy. You must seize happiness while you can."

Wordsworth shook his head. "Mary will understand. I know her. She will see that it is the honourable thing to do."

"You don't know women like I do," Samuel said. "She might refuse to marry you."

"It's a risk I have to take," Wordsworth said. "Dorothy agrees with me. And there's Caroline. This is my only chance to see her, now, before I'm married. And while the peace lasts. Who knows how long that will be?"

They talked all night but by morning Samuel had been unable to persuade him to change his mind. The next morning Wordsworth and Dorothy set off for Pooley Bridge, where Dorothy would stay with their friends the Clarksons while Wordsworth went on alone to see Mary and tell her about his visit to France to see Annette and Caroline.

“I still think you shouldn’t do it,” Samuel said to Wordsworth when they parted.

“I must,” Wordsworth said, finally.

As Samuel walked home he was already looking forward to getting back to his new poem. Thoughts and phrases floated into his mind but he tried not to hold on to them too firmly. Sometimes it was better to let them whirl around for a while before committing them to paper.

He worked on it furiously all the time the Wordsworths were away, writing, re-writing, creating, honing. At this rate, he thought, he might even be able to finish the first draft by the time they came home. He was desperate to know how Wordsworth’s confession to Mary had gone so, as soon as he heard they were back in Grasmere, he walked over with the poem in his bag. He could tell straight away things hadn’t gone well. Dorothy looked pale and strained. “I’m not at all well,” she said.

Wordsworth too, looked poorly. “Mary is so ill,” he said. “I’m so worried about her. She can’t eat. She’s very thin. It’s all my fault.”

“I will write to her,” Dorothy said quickly. “She will listen to me.”

“But the wedding’s still going ahead?” Samuel asked. “Mary was all right about everything?”

“Yes, yes, of course. She understood. I knew she would. So now we need to sort out our trip to France. Dorothy and I will meet Annette in Calais — ”

"Calais?" Samuel said. "I thought you said she lived in Blois?"

"Yes, but it's such a long journey for us. If we meet in Calais it's about the same distance for them to travel, to Calais via Paris, as for us to come from Grasmere via Dover. We're thinking of leaving it 'til the summer just to make sure the peace treaty lasts. Then Dorothy and I can make a bit of a holiday of it by the seaside while I sort out the legal stuff."

"So have you fixed a date for the wedding?"

"Late summer I hope. As soon as we return from France. Maybe I'll get a special licence to save having the banns read in church."

"There's no rush is there?" Dorothy said quickly. "That will be in the middle of harvest. Tom won't want to spare Mary at that time."

"No, of course. And we'll have to visit our brother Christopher in London to sort out the financial situation."

"I can manage on very little," Dorothy said, blushing. "Now you'll have a wife to support." Her blush deepened and Samuel wondered again how this strange three-sided relationship would work. Wordsworth and Dorothy were so intimate: they touched, kissed, cuddled and caressed almost like lovers. When they had lived abroad people had often mistaken them for a married couple. If Wordsworth said she was his sister they assumed he meant mistress. But the intimacy of marriage was something different. How would Dorothy feel, knowing what was going on behind the bedroom door so close to her in that tiny cottage?

"Christopher and I will sort out some sort of allowance for you, Dorothy." Wordsworth was saying. Samuel saw him squeeze her arm reassuringly. "There's no need to worry." He turned to Samuel. "I've written some new poems," he said, brightening a little. "Dorothy has been transcribing them for me. They're short poems, based on nature. I've finished the one on the butterfly; I'll read it to you later."

"I've written a new poem too," Samuel said proudly. He'd been bursting to tell them since he arrived but he could see they were both preoccupied. "I'll read it to you tomorrow," he said, "when you're both feeling a bit better."

He couldn't have chosen a better morning. It was late April, the beginning of spring up in the north. The air was crisp and cool, the light sharp, the sun shone from a clear blue sky. Dorothy had opened the window and the sound of birdsong drifted in.

He began in a clear, confident tone. As he read he could feel their reaction. Dorothy's hand had flown to her mouth and when he risked a glance he saw tears in her eyes. She reached for her handkerchief and sniffed. Wordsworth's head dropped to his chest. Samuel could tell he was listening intently, nodding his head every so often.

Dorothy stood up the moment he had finished.

"I'm sorry Samuel." She was crying in earnest now. "It's just too painful." She rushed out of the room and Samuel heard the front door to the cottage open and close.

"I hope she's taken a shawl," Wordsworth said quickly. "It's still quite cold."

"What do you think?" Samuel asked impatiently.

"It's excellent. Very, very good. But Dorothy's right, it's too personal. I know it's how you feel but, Samuel, you can't possibly let anyone else read it."

"I know," Samuel said sadly. "This is the problem of a writer. The conflict between the private and public life. Maybe if I change it…"

Wordsworth shook his head. "Everyone will wonder who it refers to."

"A writer can use his imagination can't he? I'll say that's what I've done. You know it's good, you've said so. If I leave out Sarah's name…"

Dorothy was gone all morning. Wordsworth kept going to the window to look for her. "She's so wound up at the moment," he said, "with all this worry about Mary and Annette. She's been getting dreadful headaches and bowel trouble."

She returned eventually but her walk didn't seem have helped at all.

"Everywhere looks so dreary," she said sadly. "Even the sunshine didn't lift my spirits. And the baby lambs gambolling, you know how they usually make me smile, William. Today they just made me sadder still. The primroses are coming out and there are still a few daffodils. Do you remember the ones we saw at

Ullswater, William? How many there were, how they tossed their heads and danced in the wind?"

"We can go out later," Wordsworth said. "You'll feel happier if we go with you."

Much as it had upset her, Samuel didn't regret writing the poem. It had been cathartic and it had crystallised his true feelings in his mind. Out on the hills with Wordsworth and Dorothy he knew this was where he belonged. Wherever they went, he would go too.

As for his poem to Sarah Hutchinson, or Asra as he called her in his notebook, he would start to work on it when he got back to Keswick. He could rewrite it, omitting all references to her. Only the people he knew him well would know it was meant for her.

In early May spring finally arrived; the leaves came out on the trees and the days became longer, days of unusually warm sunshine and sudden sharp showers. Samuel walked out as often as he could, taking paths he had walked with Wordsworth and Dorothy. One morning he stopped to take a drink of fresh spring water from the rock that they called 'Sarah's Rock' after she had carved her initials on it. Two weeks ago he had carved his own initials, and Dorothy's, above hers but it had been growing dark when he did it and he saw now they needed deepening. The rock seemed to symbolise the group, the charmed circle he belonged to. Wordsworth's initials should also be there, and Mary's, their names carved forever as an emblem of their friendship.

There was one set of initials that would never be there: his wife's. She didn't belong. She would never belong. Writing his poem to Sarah Hutchinson had made one thing abundantly clear to him: his marriage was over. His future didn't lie with Sara. They must separate.

Chapter Fourteen

"Say something, Sara," Samuel said.

"I don't know what to say," she said quietly. "Leave me alone will you? I need to think."

She could scarcely believe she'd heard it yet the moment the words were out of his mouth she knew he meant it. This wasn't one of those hurtful remarks flung at each other when they were angry, something to regret and apologise for later when tempers had cooled. This was cold, rehearsed; he meant it. "We must separate." She never would have believed she'd hear it from his lips. She knew how important religion was to Samuel. Marriage was sacred, not something to be taken lightly. People divorced, of course they did, but not often and not *them*. In their very worst moments, their most violent arguments, she had never thought he would leave her.

Questions crowded into her mind. Where did he expect her to live? She couldn't stay here alone. They could scarcely afford the rent as it was. Samuel would never be able to run two households. Single women, spinsters like Dorothy, widows like her sister Mary, usually lived with their nearest male relative. They needed a man to run the household; despite Mary Wollstonecraft's best attempts, businessmen, traders, landlords and the like wouldn't deal with a woman. But Sara's brother George was only sixteen, he could scarcely support himself, let alone anyone else. And she couldn't move back in with her mother; Samuel was already paying her an allowance and it wouldn't stretch to Sara and the two boys. That left Samuel's relatives in Devon. Was this to be her fate? Thrust into the role of the poor relative reliant on family to support her?

She had wanted so much for the boys: school, university, travel, careers. But these things cost money. Maybe Samuel would take the boys away from her. The thought cut like a knife. By law he was their guardian if they separated. She didn't think Samuel would do it but the threat would always be hanging over her.

And behind all this lay the stigma of being *separated*. They might as well be divorced for all society would make of it. Whatever the truth, and she was blameless enough, everyone would always believe it was *her* fault her marriage had failed.

"We make each other unhappy," Samuel had said. Well, that was true enough. They were constantly at each other's throats and lately it seemed to be getting worse. Samuel spent more and more time shut up in his study, writing. She knew she should be pleased he was working but he was always distant from her when he was writing, deep in thought, muttering phrases out loud, hurrying off to write something down, and whatever it was he was working on at the moment was making him more distant than usual.

She couldn't deny that their marriage had always been stormy. She knew deep down it was partly her fault: she had a quick temper. Her mother had warned her to curb it when she first became involved with Samuel. "Men don't like a woman who constantly contradicts them," she had said. "They like a quiet life." But Sara had never seen why she should keep quiet if something annoyed her. What was the point in bottling it all up? Far better to say how you feel and get it out in the open. When they were first married Samuel had admired her outspokenness and honesty. He had listened to her opinions. Now everything she said annoyed him.

But whatever was wrong with their marriage, whoever was at fault, one thing was crystal clear to her: she would do anything to avoid a separation. She spent a sleepless night rehearsing what she would say to Samuel. She would stay calm. She would remind him of his marriage vows, his responsibility to her and the children. Had he thought what it would be like to be parted from them? He missed them so much when he was away from them. And they missed him. She would ask Samuel what she could do to make things better between them. She would agree to anything.

But the next day Samuel was still adamant. "I can see no future for us," he said. "Not as we are now."

"At least tell me what I've done wrong," she pleaded.

"Everything," he said heavily. "You run me down, you hate my friends, you're cold, you have no sympathy when I'm ill, you don't support me."

All Sara's good intentions vanished as hurt gripped her chest like a vice. "While *you're* fault free I suppose," she snarled. "That's all I ever get from you: criticisms. Whatever I do, whatever I say, it's wrong and not as good or clever or witty as the Wordsworths or the Hutchinsons or Godwin or any other of your learned friends!"

"You see, Sara? It's hopeless. How can we go on when we agree on nothing?" He turned to leave the room. Suddenly he clutched his arm, then his chest. She watched in horror as he crumpled at the waist. If she hadn't caught him he would have fallen.

"Samuel!" she cried. "Are you all right?"

"A pain," he gasped. "Here, in my side. My chest, oh, I don't know where…"

"Come and sit down. Lean on me."

He was ill, he was dying. The thought made her realise how she truly felt. She couldn't lose him. They may not always be the best of friends but she loved him, she needed him. She didn't care what he did, where he went, who else he loved. The thought of losing him forever was unbearable.

She helped him up to bed, made him comfortable, put a cool, damp cloth on his forehead and tiptoed out as he fell asleep. Later on, when she heard him moving around, she went in.

"Samuel," she said quietly. "Can I talk to you?"

"Please, Sara, can't it wait until I'm better?" he sighed.

"I won't lose my temper. I promise," she said quietly. "I just want to say I'll do anything. I'll change, I promise. Just don't leave me. I couldn't manage without you. I'll be better. More understanding. I won't criticise you."

She saw him hesitate.

"Give me another chance," she said. "If not for my own sake then for the boys."

She saw him struggling with the idea. Then he said. "We'll try then. Both of us. We'll be kinder to each other."

"Thank you, Samuel," she said. "Oh, thank you." She took his hand and kissed it. He patted her head gently.

They were a long way from being right again, of course, but it was a start. And when Samuel came to her room a few days later she didn't turn him away. She hadn't forgotten he had called her 'cold'. She returned his kisses with as much feeling as she could, did her best to respond to his touch. But some of the trust had gone. It would take more than a night of lovemaking to restore it.

She tried hard. She knew Samuel was trying too but it wasn't easy. The habit of bickering at each other was hard to break and the slightest thing would set them off again. It was like treading on eggshells. Sara had a very good reason for persevering, though. She had suspected it for a while but by early June she knew for definite: she was pregnant again.

She hoped Samuel would be pleased but she saw his face fall before he quickly recovered. "Why, that's splendid," he said. She could see he didn't mean it but he would come round to the idea. He never enjoyed her pregnancies — she was usually poorly throughout and it interfered with his writing — but once the baby was born, once he set eyes on his new son, it would be different. It always brought them closer, that special time just after the birth, the knowledge that they had created a new life.

At least she didn't have to worry when she wrote to Edith this time to tell her; after nearly seven years of marriage Edith was pregnant. The baby was due in September, four months before Sara's. The news couldn't have come at a better time for poor Edith, who had been having so many problems. Southey's position as secretary to the Irish chancellor had meant a move from Dublin, which she had loved, back to London, which she had always hated. She soon became depressed again. Then Southey's mother became ill and Edith couldn't cope with looking after her while she herself felt so ill. Not knowing what else to do, Southey sent for their sister Mary to help out. Edith was refusing to eat again; she wouldn't take any of the medicines the doctors recommended or follow any of their diets. When they eventually realised she was pregnant Southey left his job in London and moved the whole household, including his mother and Mary Lovell and her son, down to Bristol.

Edith was so pleased to be pregnant at last that she didn't mind what she had but Sara longed for a girl this time. A little girl to dress in pretty clothes and play with, instead of the rough and tumble little boys she had always had. And daughters were so much more loyal than sons. As boys grew up they became independent, they stopped confiding in their mothers. A daughter would always be there for her, would always be on her side. But Sara had had three boys already. It was bound to be a boy.

It was hard to think that fat little Derwent, not yet two and just beginning to talk, would no longer be the baby of the family. Hartley, at six years old, was fast becoming an image of his father; not to look at, he was like neither of them really with his skinny little body and elfin face, but in his ways. He told her the other day that he had been thinking, "What would it be if there was nothing; if all the men and women and trees and grass and birds and beasts and the sky and the ground were all gone? If there were darkness and coldness and nothing to be dark and cold."

"What did you say to him?" Samuel asked when she told him.

"I told him to go outside and play," she laughed. "He's just like you, Samuel, with his strange ideas."

"I'm glad of it," Samuel said. "He feels things so deeply."

"He certainly loves it here," Sara said. "It's always *his* kitchen, *his* garden, *his* field. He doesn't need friends. And he hates going away from home, even into town."

The children were her strongest weapon in the fight against separation. She was sure Samuel wouldn't leave her now she was pregnant again but she never missed an opportunity to remind him how unhappy it would make them if the children's world was turned upside down, their safe home disrupted. She would do whatever it took to save her marriage and she made an effort to take more interest in the Wordsworths.

"Dorothy will find it strange when Mary is living in her house won't she?" she asked Samuel. "No longer mistress in her household. I would hate it."

"She's known Mary a long time," Samuel said. "I suppose they'll settle down together easily enough. But it will be a big change for all of us."

"The marriage seems to be taking a long time to organise," she went on.

"I suppose there's no rush," Samuel said quickly. "I think Mary's brother needs her on the farm. And Wordsworth and Dorothy are going to have a holiday first."

Sara struggled to stop herself from laughing. It was ridiculous. Wordsworth and Dorothy had had years together on their own. Why did they suddenly need a few more weeks alone?

"They're going to France," he went on.

"To *France*?" she repeated. "What on earth for?"

"I told you. A holiday," Samuel said tersely.

There must be more to it than that, Sara thought, but Samuel obviously wasn't going to tell her and she didn't want to risk another argument.

She had always had the impression that Dorothy didn't think she looked after Samuel properly so the next time he went over there she sent over some clean clothes for him. She enclosed a little love note with them, hoping it would make him smile to think of her.

He came home soaked to the skin. "It was raining by the time I got to Dunmail Raise," he grumbled, shaking out his wet hat. "It was too late to turn back so I had to keep going. I had a dreadful walk over there as well."

"It didn't rain here on Thursday," Sara said. It had been a beautiful day. All her sheets had dried on the line.

"Then I was attacked by a cow," he went on.

"A cow?" Sara laughed, though she could see Samuel didn't find it funny. "Not a bull then?"

"I *do* know the difference, Sara. A big cow. Luckily it didn't have horns. It's not funny," he went on as she snorted with laughter again. "You weren't there; it was very frightening!"

"How's Dorothy?" she asked, struggling to control herself.

"Not well. Neither of them are. They're not sleeping well."

"Wordsworth too? I thought he'd be excited about the wedding."

"They'll be coming to stay in a few weeks, by the way. On their way to France. A night here, then on to Gallow Hill to say goodbye to Mary, then down to London to see their brother Christopher who deals with their finances."

"Yes, that's fine," Sara said, her mind on beds to make up, food to buy. "There must be things to sort out prior to the wedding," she went on, remembering she was trying to take an interest in Samuel's friends.

Summer was late coming, as it always was up here in the north, but finally the leaves came out on the trees and the temperature began to rise. Sara usually looked forward to the end of the long winter, a chance to go outside again without the risk of falling on icy roads or getting soaked in the constantly pouring rain, but her pregnancy had brought on the usual nausea. Every morning she woke retching. Getting breakfast for the children and Samuel was an ordeal; even the smell of food cooking turned her stomach.

Luckily Samuel spent most of his time either scribbling away in his study or walking on the mountains. "I'm just off to post these letters," he would say cheerfully, patting his bulging bag. He wrote to Wordsworth and Dorothy almost daily, then there were letters to Southey, Godwin, Poole and Davy. "I've sent them versions of my new poem to read," he told her one day.

"When am I going to see it?" she asked.

"Oh, it's not ready yet. When I've revised it a bit," he said vaguely. "I'm translating a German poem too, by Gessner. It's an exercise to see if I can do it."

It was so tempting to complain, "None of this is making us any money," but this was the sort of thing she had promised not to say. "That sounds interesting," she said carefully, instead.

There was no point in trying to understand the workings of Samuel's mind. They both had to accept that they thought very differently. Even if he read some of his work to her the chances were she wouldn't like it; she didn't understand half of it. Some of Wordsworth's poetry was equally incomprehensible, although she had liked the shorter ones he had read to them recently.

She was feeling a little less nauseous by the time the Wordsworths were due to arrive.

"I'll meet them part-way," Samuel said.

Sara looked out at the threatening clouds. "It looks like rain," she said. "And they're coming by cart with all their luggage. You don't need to meet them, do you?"

"Oh, a bit of rain never hurt me, Sara," he said cheerfully.

"It might bring on your rheumatism."

"Well, my Sally-Pally won't mind nursing me if it does," he said.

"No, of course," she said meekly. "Well, enjoy your walk."

She watched him go, eager to leave her as always. And when he came back she would have to swallow her pride and be nice to them. Pride was one of the things Samuel had accused her of. It was hard trying to be this person that she wasn't. She thought of Dorothy, reliant on her brothers for her income; Mary Hutchinson, who was moving away from her family when she married; Edith who traipsed around Europe with Southey. She was no worse off than any other woman. They all had to do whatever their men wanted.

Chapter Fifteen

Sara had been right, it started raining almost as soon as he left. He had arranged to meet Wordsworth and Dorothy at Sarah's Rock and as he walked he caught up with another walker, a pleasant, good-looking man who told him he was from Wythburn.

"I'm stopping here," Samuel told him when they got to the rock. "I'm waiting for my friends, a man and a woman. If you see them on the road you might say I'm here."

"Yes, of course," the young man said. "I've enjoyed our talk. I hope we meet again one day."

Samuel sat down on the side of the road and looked at the rock that would always make him think of Sarah Hutchinson, though maybe they should find a different name for it now it held so many initials. They had added Mary's and John's initials, so now William's initials were at the top, then MH for Mary Hutchinson, then Dorothy's initials, Samuel's, John's and SH for Sarah Hutchinson right at the bottom where they had first been carved: a permanent memorial to a group of friends who belonged together forever.

He hadn't stopped writing to Sarah. His promise to be a better husband didn't include banishing her from his heart or his life. But he'd made a promise to Sarah too, not to write any more love letters. So instead he kept to safe subjects like Hartley and Derwent. She didn't seem to mind hearing about them. If it was a long way from the relationship he wanted, at least he still had the pleasure of reading her replies, seeing her writing on the page, her name at the bottom of each letter.

She knew all about the Wordsworths' trip to France, of course, and the reason for it; she and Mary were so close that nothing was secret between them. But he was careful not to say too much about it in his letters: you never knew who might read them. He liked this secret, known only to them, binding him closer to the Wordsworths and Hutchinsons.

It rained again while he was waiting for Wordsworth and Dorothy to arrive and he leant against the rock to get some shelter. At last he heard the steady thud of horses' hooves and the squeak of the hefty cartwheels. The cart lumbered to a halt and Dorothy leant out.

"We were told you'd be waiting here," she said as Samuel clambered aboard. "We had a very good description of you from such a handsome young man. He was very taken with you."

"You have a long journey ahead of you," Samuel said, glancing round at the boxes and bags behind them.

"It won't be too bad," Wordsworth said. "We'll break it up to make it easier for Dorothy: a few days with you, then on to the Clarksons before we go up to Gallow Hill to see Mary."

"That's a long detour," Samuel said. "An extra hundred miles or so."

"But I must see her first," Wordsworth said, his face reddening. "It's only right."

"We'll spend some time with her," Dorothy said, "then take the coach down to London to see our brother and on to Dover."

"Everything's sorted out with the finances now is it?" Samuel asked. The Wordsworth family had been waiting nearly twenty years for their father's inheritance. It was a complicated business entailing a debt owed by their father's employer Lord Lowther. A few weeks ago they had had the good news that the debts would finally be paid and they would come into their inheritance.

"Yes and no," Wordsworth said. "Our brother Richard wants us to claim interest on the debt."

"That will delay things," Samuel said. He knew Wordsworth must need the money, with the trip to France and the marriage coming up.

"Yes, but it's not just that," Wordsworth said. "I think we should settle for what we can get. If we ask for too much it may go to court, then we risk losing it all in legal fees. But Richard's been fighting nearly all his life for this money. He's a lawyer and he says he knows best, so we have no choice."

They reached Greta Hall at tea-time. Sara was waiting at the door and Samuel noticed the quick look of surprise cross Dorothy's face when she saw her; Sara was only a few months pregnant but her body had already ballooned. Samuel hated it when she was pregnant. She was always ill. He heard her rushing for the pot in the morning to vomit in, then at breakfast she would groan at the sight of food and hold her stomach, her face pasty and bloated. The thought of another child was more than he could bear. Hartley could pretty well look after himself and Derwent was beginning to walk and talk. They had their established routines but a new baby would throw the household into disarray with his constant crying, nappy changing and feeding. He was sure it would be a boy. One more boy to provide food for while he was young, educate and prepare for a profession when he grew up. One more boy to tie him forever to Sara and domesticity. Every fibre of his being railed against it.

Wordsworth had all this to look forward to but it would be different for him. He and Mary were suited; they would have the perfect marriage, the perfect family, while he was stuck with Sara. It wasn't fair. He could hear her now, prattling away to Dorothy, the sort of light, frothy, social chit-chat she reserved for visitors. To Samuel's ears it sounded false but at least it was an improvement on the cool reception she usually gave them.

Dorothy seemed to be happy to join in with the domestic talk. "We've been busy getting the house ready for Mary," she was saying. "I washed all the curtains and we've whitewashed the ceilings and painted the walls. Oh, and we've changed bedrooms: William and Mary will have my old one downstairs and I'll have a room upstairs."

Samuel saw the colour rising in her cheeks as she said it. It was a small cottage. Noise travelled easily from room to room. They had obviously realised that the newlyweds would need as much privacy as possible.

"So, your last holiday alone?" Sara was asking.

"Yes."

"You must be looking forward to it."

He saw Dorothy trying to raise a smile. "Of course but…" She hesitated. "It will all be so different. I'm just trying to make the most of each present day."

He saw the exasperation on Sara's face. "Anyone would think she was going to a funeral," she said later to Samuel. "Not looking forward to her brother's wedding. I don't know what all the fuss is about…" She stopped, remembering her promise not to criticise his friends. These were the flash-points that set off their arguments. Their marriage was like a smouldering fire: one wrong word, one spark, and the flames leapt into a full-blown conflagration with raging arguments that could last for days, subsiding maybe for a few hours, only to ignite again.

Wordsworth's marriage would be calm, as calm as the lakes he loved so much. Oh, there might be the odd ripple now and again, clouds might come over and darken the surface of the water. But mostly it would be serene, safe, a haven for him and Dorothy.

Wordsworth had told them over dinner how he had written a poem about the preparations they had made for Mary. "You should see the work we've done on the house and in the garden," he said.

He saw Sara trying to look interested. Samuel had already read the poem, which Wordsworth was calling *Going for Mary*.

"I've made a few changes," Wordsworth said.

"Which it didn't need," Dorothy laughed.

"And Sarah has copied it out for me," Wordsworth went on unabated. "I'm still not entirely happy with it."

"It's perfect," Dorothy said firmly.

"And I've changed the title to *Our Departure*. Though I'm not sure it really needs a title at all. It's a private poem, for the family. I don't think I'll ever publish it."

"I look forward to hearing it," Sara said politely.

But if she ever did read it, Samuel knew instinctively that she wouldn't appreciate it. It was deeply nostalgic, a wistful, fond farewell to a way of life that would never be repeated. Mary would be brought like a flower to the cottage garden in Grasmere and transplanted into Wordsworth's and Dorothy's lives. It was the sort of imagery Samuel understood and Sara never would.

Since she had no idea of the real reason Wordsworth and Dorothy were going 'on holiday' she continued to think of their trip as ridiculous. She might be outwardly interested and solicitous but he knew what she was thinking.

They were due to leave the next morning but Dorothy woke up with a bad headache and it was pouring with rain so they decided to stay one more day. It was cool and dreary for mid-July, the sort of day when the clouds hung low over the mountains and the rain fell in a constant miserable drizzle. After breakfast, Sara stoked up the fire in the parlour and they pulled their chairs up around it, Dorothy with her eyes closed, leaning her head against the back of the chair, Wordsworth and Samuel reading, Sara stitching some sort of tiny clothes for the new baby.

The rain pattered gently against the windowpane, there was the odd gentle crackle of wood from the fire and the swish of a page as Wordsworth or Samuel turned it over in their book. The children were playing upstairs in their room and occasionally there was a burst of thundering feet, a raised voice from one of the boys or the maid. It reminded Samuel of the time he and Sara had stayed at Alfoxton Park in the spring of 1798. Sara had been pregnant then too, with poor little Berkeley. Then, as now, she sighed every so often, shifting her place on her chair, leaning backwards and forwards, rubbing her back or her swollen stomach.

"Shall I bring you a footstool?" Wordsworth asked her. Sara looked up at him with the sort of smile she used to give Samuel. "That's so kind of you but I really can't stay long. I have the children's lunch to prepare."

Oh, if only Samuel could be going to France with Wordsworth and Dorothy. He longed for wings to escape this dreary domestic existence. His friends were the only thing that made life bearable and they were going away.

"Do you remember how seasick you were when we made our Channel crossing?" Samuel asked Dorothy.

"I was just thinking the same thing," she said. "I'm hoping it won't happen again."

Did she know how much he longed to be going with them?

"It's only for a few weeks," she said, giving him a wan smile. Ah, so she *did* know. He smiled back, careful not to let Sara see. But she hadn't noticed. She was unpicking a stitch, frowning in concentration.

A few weeks, then the wedding, the honeymoon and summer would be over. Mary would come to live with them, be transplanted into their lives, the three of them in the little cottage at Grasmere. Where would that leave Samuel? He didn't want to be left out in the cold.

"I wish you'd think about coming to live here," he said. "There's plenty of room. We wouldn't be in each other's way."

His words fell into an awkward little silence. They all knew why Dorothy wouldn't want to live at Greta Hall. Sara's face had turned red, Dorothy's was stony. Wordsworth gave him a sympathetic little shrug. Like Samuel, he wouldn't care where he lived as long as he had somewhere quiet to write.

Samuel half hoped it would be raining the next morning or that Dorothy's headache would be worse or she would wake up with the bowel trouble she was so prone to, so they would have to stay a bit longer. But the rain had stopped. It was still a cool, grey morning, the air and the ground damp from yesterday's rain, but there was no reason not to go.

"Are you sure you shouldn't stay longer?" he asked Dorothy. "You're still very pale."

He ignored the look he saw flit across Sara's face. They all knew she would be glad to see the back of them, however hard she tried to hide it.

"The fresh air will do me good," Dorothy said. "And we really must go now. We want to spend some time with Mary before we go down to London."

"I'll walk with you," Samuel said. "Just a little way," he added, seeing Sara's face.

They parted after about six or seven miles. Samuel sat by the roadside and watched them until they disappeared from sight. Whatever happened in France, nothing would be the same now. Everything would change. Maybe not for the worse, but it would definitely change.

Chapter Sixteen

Sara felt a huge weight lift from her mind when the Wordsworths had left. Samuel was always nicer to her when they weren't around. She knew what they thought of her; they wanted her out of the way. If she and Samuel separated they would take the children from her and Dorothy would look after them. Sara would fight that with every fibre of her being. The Wordsworth-Hutchinson ménage could live where they liked, here even, bring Miss Sarah as well if they wanted, John Wordsworth too; she didn't care as long as she could keep her children. They were the only ones who loved her and needed her.

Now that the Wordsworths had gone she and Samuel would have the summer to themselves. Her condition was beginning to show so she couldn't socialise but they could go for short walks on their own, now that Samuel wouldn't be going over to Grasmere every other day and staying away for weeks at a time. Hartley especially would love to have Papa home. He enjoyed the games they played together and the lessons Samuel was supposed to be teaching him.

But she should have known that Samuel would never be happy on his own with her. It wasn't long after the Wordsworths had left that a visitor arrived. Samuel seemed as surprised as she was when they saw him labouring up the steep drive with his baggage.

"Who is it?" she asked.

"I have no idea," he said. "I haven't invited anyone."

"You're *always* inviting people," she said.

"William Sotheby," the man introduced himself.

"Ah, Sotheby!" Samuel wrung the man's hand enthusiastically. "So wonderful to meet you at last. My wife…"

Sara bobbed a curtsy, noticing with a sweep of her eye the number of bags the man had brought.

"I hope you don't mind, Mrs Coleridge," he said quickly. "Mr Coleridge said to come any time."

"No, of course," Sara said. "You're very welcome. Stay as long as you like."

Her heart sank at the thought of the bed to make, the meals to prepare, while she was feeling sick all the time. And she didn't like to expose her figure to strangers. But there was no choice.

"Sotheby is a poet and a playwright," Samuel said. "His sonnets are wonderful."

The man shook his head deprecatingly. "Nothing as to your work, dear sir," he said. "I am honoured to meet you at last."

She saw Samuel basking in the adulation. Maybe this new man was just what he needed; he was always excited when he had new people to impress with his brilliance. And at least it was someone outside the Wordsworth circle. He was older than them, maybe mid-forties, confident but with a touch of shyness, his manners impeccable but in a relaxed way; he was obviously used to London society.

Samuel took him out for long walks every day; he was always keen to show new visitors why he loved it so much here. She never understood what they found to talk about but there was a constant flow of conversation, their heads bent towards each other as they set out walking, the low rumble of their voices behind the study door, where they retreated every evening.

In the end he didn't stay long. He was, "moving on," he said vaguely. "Come again," Samuel urged him. "Any time. For as long as you like. A week, a month, a year…"

The weather turned the day Sotheby left, grey skies and lashing rain replacing the warm sunshine. Caged up in the house, Samuel's mood turned like the weather. Day after day he sat hunched over his desk. Sara could sense his restlessness. "Can't you keep those children quiet?" he yelled one morning. "I'm trying to work."

Hartley, who had been racing up and down the hallway stopped in his tracks, his face crumpling.

"Come on Hartley," Sara said, taking his arm. "Papa's trying to work."

Derwent's piercing wail still rose from the bedroom. "I'll take them next door," Sara said. "Mr Jackson likes to see them," she added pointedly.

A few days later Samuel suddenly announced, "There's a library I need to go to at St Bees on the west coast. They have some excellent rare books. I shall make it into a walking tour."

Objections rose to Sara's lips; the rain might have stopped but dampness still hung in the air and it was cold for early August. He would walk for miles then come back with his aches and pains ten times worse and she would be expected to look after him when she was still feeling so bad herself. Really, he was nothing more than a selfish child. Why couldn't he stay at home like any other ordinary man? It was exasperating. She burned with the injustice of it all. At one time she would have poured it out in a long diatribe of vitriol but she had promised not to criticise. And if he couldn't face up to the responsibilities of his family then she would have to be the strong one, the adult. If she didn't indulge him in his whims and fancies, if she stood against him in any way, he only became ill and fractious and took it out on her and the children. So, instead of grumbling at him, she made sure he had a clean shirt and stockings to put in his knapsack along with his cravat and night cap, tea and sugar in paper twists, and the notebook, quills and portable ink-well that he always took with him.

"I've drawn a map of my route," he said, waving it in front of her. "I reckon I should be back in ten days or so."

The whole house seemed to breathe a sigh of relief when he had gone. Hartley, who had kept away from Papa as much as possible for fear of being snapped at, now began hurtling around the house like a maniac again, asking his endless questions and making her laugh with his funny games. Derwent was too young, really, to notice the friction but even he was sleeping better at night and grizzling less during the day. It was true that the children of warring parents suffered. But if the parents separated wouldn't they suffer more? The boys needed a father. She didn't want to deprive them of one through her own selfishness.

When she and Samuel were first together, when they were planning to emigrate to America and the principles of Pantisocracy were being hotly debated, they had agreed as a group that the marriage contract could be dissolved if it was agreeable to one or both parties. It was one of Mary Wollstonecraft's firmest principles that nothing should make a man and woman live together once mutual love and respect had gone. But what good had that done the poor woman? Sara had been as shocked as anyone when she read, in William Godwin's memoir of his wife, how Mary's lover had abandoned her with an illegitimate baby, justified by the very principles that she herself believed in. They were a long way from female equality. A woman on her own, for whatever reason, struggled financially and socially. Sara didn't want it happening to her.

Samuel arrived home nine days later with his clothes wet and muddy and great rips in his breeches.

"Whatever's happened to you?" Sara asked.

"I had a fall," Samuel said, laughing. "Coming down Scafell Pike. I got wedged…"

"Yes, yes, you can tell me later." She knew what Samuel was like when he started on one of his stories. "Don't move. Take off your hat and coat. And your boots; you're traipsing mud everywhere."

"You look like a tramp, Papa!" Hartley laughed. "Papa, the vagrant."

"Come here, you scamp!" Samuel made to grab him and Hartley darted out of his reach, screaming, "No, no! You're dirty! Ugh!" as Samuel pretended to wipe his dirty hands all over him.

"Come on, Sara," Samuel said, seeing the look on her face. "It's only a bit of dirt. It'll wash off."

"You'll need new breeches, Samuel. They're expensive."

"But the whole trip only cost just over thirteen shillings. Except I gave four shillings away to some poor children I saw by the roadside and some poor travellers."

"You should have kept it to pay for the clothes repairs," Sara said acidly.

"I was hoping they might have started the work on the house while I was gone," Samuel said to her later.

Sara shook her head. "Mr Jackson said there's a delay. You'd think they would want to get on with it during the summer wouldn't you? But then it's been so wet."

They had had such problems with the front of the house being draughty and poorly built that, as Samuel pointed out, even if Mr Jackson hadn't said he would have it rebuilt it would probably have fallen down on its own. Sara was dreading the upheaval but looking forward to having a house that wasn't letting in every breath of wind that blew down from the mountains.

She had just started preparing dinner the next day when Hartley rushed in. "Mama, Mama, there's a man and a woman coming up the drive." Sara's heart sank. She had told Samuel specifically not to invite any more visitors this summer.

"I didn't Sara, I honestly didn't!" he said when she rushed in to accuse him. He looked out of the window. "Why, it's Charles and Mary Lamb, Sara!" he said excitedly, rapping his knuckles loudly on the window. The man below looked up, took off his hat and swept a low theatrical bow that made Samuel burst out laughing. "Come on, Sara," he said. "You know how much you like them, especially Mary."

"But, Samuel," Sara said, determined not to be sidetracked, "the beds to make, the meals to cook, with me like this." She gestured to her stomach. "And the builders due in any day."

But they couldn't turn them away. "You said come any time!" Lamb laughed, clutching Samuel's hand. "So we came. I knew you wouldn't mind. Mary's been a little delicate lately." He dropped his voice. Mary was upstairs, washing her hands and face in Sara's room. "I thought the change of scenery would do her good. And your company, Mrs Coleridge." He turned a beaming smile on Sara. "You've always been so kind to her."

Mary Lamb suffered dreadfully from a mental condition. She had been in and out of asylums for the last six years since she had stabbed her mother to death in a frenzy. Without her brother's support she would never be allowed out at all. He had dedicated his life to her.

While Sara rushed around finding aired sheets for the beds and trying to think of what to add to this evening's meal to make it stretch to four instead of two, Samuel took Lamb into his study. "But this is splendid!" she heard Lamb exclaim. "What a place to work in! So big and comfortable. A comfy sofa!" She heard him sigh as he sank down on it. "And a fire, even in August. You have it all, dear friend; you are so lucky."

"But he doesn't realise it," Sara thought, shuffling along the corridor with the heavy pile of sheets.

"Let me help you," Mary said, reaching out to take them from her.

"Oh no, please," Sara said. "You're our guests. It's my pleasure."

She couldn't deny it was nice to have company and of all people Charles and Mary Lamb were the easiest. Samuel had known Lamb since they were boys at school in Christ's Hospital. He wasn't blind to his faults like the Wordsworths were. There had been rifts over the years, always of Samuel's making, but the friendship persisted. And Sara couldn't help admiring Lamb's support for his sister. She noticed how his eyes fell on her regularly, making sure she was included in the conversation, that she wasn't too tired, too warm, too cold. If only Sara had someone like that instead of Samuel, who was regaling them with his story about his fall on Scafell Pike.

"There was a stepped series of ledges I had to slide down one at a time." He held up his hands to demonstrate them. "The rock burned my skin and the effort made my muscles tremble. I threw my faithful broomstick down before me and had dropped to the next ledge with only two left to go when I realised the next drop was too far down. I looked up: too far to climb back up too. I was like the sheep that get stuck in such places, utterly alone. My limbs were trembling. I lay on my back to collect myself. *'I will die here,'* I thought. For some reason the idea made me laugh like a madman."

"Only you would laugh," Lamb said, shaking his head.

"Then I looked up," Samuel said, raising his eyes to the ceiling. "I saw the crags towering above me, the huge grey clouds above them. God had created these. And God had created me. I felt a kind of divine revelation. I bless you, God, for the powers of reason and will you have given me, I thought. I don't know how to go down or up but I am calm and fearless and confident. If this were a dream how frightened I would be. I would scream aloud in fear, unable to think of a way out. Yet it is real and you, O God, have given me the power of reason and logic to get myself out of this situation."

"So how did you get down?" Lamb asked.

"Oh, that," Samuel said blithely, as if it had nothing at all to do with the story. "I found a sort of gulley in the rock face behind me, like a chimney, and I slid down inside it. God showed me, you see. He gave me the power of logic and reason."

"If only God would show you how to look after your wife and children," Sara thought, *"and provide the money to buy new clothes to replace the ones you destroyed during your divine revelation."*

But Samuel hadn't finished. "The sky had turned dark," he went on, lowering his voice dramatically. "The clouds rolled down. There was a rumble of thunder."

Oh, he was good at this. Even Sara could feel the electricity.

Suddenly he jumped up from his seat. "A flash of lightning!" he boomed, waving his arm. "Rain fell from above." He looked up to the ceiling. "I ran for shelter in a sheepfold. When the storm had passed I stood and shouted the names of the people I love loud across the valley. Echo after echo came back to me: Sara, Hartley, Derwent, Wordsworth, Dorothy… I wished I could stay there forever like some mad, gentle shepherd." He sat down, took a drink of water, wiped his forehead.

"Tomorrow I will take you both out," he said expansively, "and show you my mountains and my lakes."

"I'm half afraid of your mountains," Lamb said, laughing shakily. "Like great floundering bears and monsters. Maybe we're safer just walking around here."

Sara had seen him glancing nervously at Mary during Samuel's performance. Mary had been with him every step of the way, leaning forward in her chair, her hands gripped tightly together, her eyes never leaving his face. She flinched when he waved his arms in the air, jumped when he leapt up from the chair. Her eyes shone in the candlelight and her face was flushed pink.

"Oh, I shan't take you anywhere dangerous, don't worry," Samuel said. "Just the foothills and the lakeside. I promise to look after you both."

"I can stay here with you, Sara," Mary said. "I'm a bit tired anyway. I can help you in the house, look after the children while you have a rest."

"No, no," Sara said quickly. She was touched, but the last thing she wanted was this mentally fragile creature looking after highly strung Hartley, with his strange thoughts and ideas, and boisterous Derwent with his tantrums.

The weather, which had been miserable for weeks, turned overnight to warmth and sunshine. Sara watched enviously as the three of them set off day after day in their holiday mood, the two men shouldering the knapsacks of food she had prepared for them, Mary holding her brother's arm. She didn't want to go with them. Even if she hadn't been pregnant with two small children to look after she had never wanted to go on those long energetic walks Samuel was so keen on but, as each morning dawned bright and sunny, she began to long for dreary, wet days so they would stay at home with her.

As it was, she was on her own all day with the children. She was happy enough with her household routine — running the house was the only thing she had control over — but sometimes she longed for adult conversation. The servants were the only grown-ups she spoke to and she couldn't have any proper conversation with them.

After three weeks of traipsing around the countryside with Samuel it was becoming obvious that Charles Lamb was dying to get back to London. "It's beautiful, of course it is," she heard him tell Samuel, "the mountains and lakes. It's that thing that tourists call 'romantic'. But I don't know how you can bear the isolation. I think I would mope and pine away without Fleet Street and The Strand."

"That's just because you're a city boy!" Samuel laughed. "I was brought up in the country…" Sara closed her eyes and waited for Samuel to start on his usual long story of what a hard childhood he had had. As if it had been any worse than hers or the Wordsworths, or Charles and Mary Lamb's for that matter; all had suffered poverty and the loss of one or both parents. But Samuel added neglect to his list of hardships, sent up to school in London at nine years old when his father died. He had never got over it. But

Lamb knew it all of course, so Samuel simply said, "Anyway, I can come down to your beloved city whenever I want. I shall come for the winter. Unless I can find someone to go abroad with. I can't stay here. The climate is too bad for my health."

It was the first Sara had heard of him going away and indignation seethed through her. The baby was due in January; surely Samuel wasn't thinking of going away when she needed him most? But she couldn't say anything in front of the Lambs. She waited until they had gone.

"You're not really thinking of going away, are you?" she asked as lightly as possible.

"I haven't decided anything for definite yet," he said.

"But the baby…" she began.

"Oh, you don't want me around while you're having it," he said quickly. "It's not like it's our first. And my Sally-Pally has managed perfectly well on her own before."

Samuel had been up in Birmingham, looking for work, when Hartley had arrived several weeks sooner than expected. Sara had gone through the whole thing, her first baby, on her own, the midwife only arriving in time to deal with the afterbirth. Berkeley had arrived equally easily, born in the cottage in Nether Stowey while Samuel was preaching in Taunton. But he had been home for Derwent's birth and it had brought them closer. She had hoped it would be the same for the new baby.

"You know how my rheumatism plays up in the bad weather," Samuel was saying.

"That's all you ever think about, yourself!" she burst out.

"*You're* the one being unreasonable, not me. The last thing you want is me ill in bed while you're having the baby."

"I want you to be like other husbands! Do you think Southey would leave Edith at a time like this? Or Wordsworth would leave Mary?"

Oh, it was satisfying the way he recoiled at the thought of Wordsworth and Mary having a baby. "You know I'm right, Samuel," she went on, pressing her point home. "You owe it to me to stay. I'm your wife. This is your home."

"I told you, I haven't decided anything for definite yet. I'm waiting to hear from Sotheby. He said he might come up here for the winter."

Sara thought of the urbane city gent. He was like Lamb. He didn't mind the odd few weeks up here in the summer but he would never come all the way up here in the depths of winter, cut off from city life and the civilised company he enjoyed.

But that wasn't the point. "So you'd stay if Sotheby came up but not if it's just me," she said spitefully.

"I've told you before, I need the company of like-minded people, Sara."

"And I'm not like-minded?"

"You're not a writer," he said. "I thought I'd ask Southey and Edith too."

She was almost deflected again by the idea of having Edith up here, Edith and the new baby. The children could meet their cousin. She and Edith would look after them all together. And Southey was such an old friend, like a real brother to her. He wasn't blind to Samuel's faults like everyone else seemed to be. But it was impossible.

"Oh, Samuel, how do you think I'd cope with the new baby coming?"

"Edith would help you."

"Her baby's due in September! Even if she waits a few months it would be chaos, you know it would, with two small babies in the house. You're just not thinking. Why can't you be content with me and the boys? Why do we have to constantly have other people around?"

"I need…" he began.

"*You* need, *you* need. That's all I ever hear. What about *me?* What about the children?"

"I wish you'd try to understand, Sara. I'm not like other people. I have to have a certain way of life so I can work: peace and quiet, no distractions, friends to inspire and support me. I can't just sit on my own here day after day. I get so…" His voice trailed off. "Lonely," he said finally. "Unhappy."

"So I don't make you happy," Sara snapped.

"Not like this you don't."

"Well, you don't make *me* happy either."

She slammed the door behind her. That was it, she thought. She'd had enough of pandering to him. What was the point of her trying to keep to their agreement when he didn't? The fragile truce was over, the few months of accord gone like the summer weather. They were back to where they had started.

Chapter Seventeen

Samuel was lonely when the Lambs left. Lonely and miserable. Sitting at his desk in his study he would suddenly find tears of self-pity running down his face. It was the weather, he told himself. Autumn and winter were the worst times because he couldn't get out of the house. And there were no more visitors, Wordsworth and Dorothy were still away and Sara hated him. Ah, here was the real problem. If he had someone who loved him, looked after him, made his home into a haven of peace and comfort instead of a prison… But there was only one person he wanted: Sarah Hutchinson. Asra. Writing to her was his only consolation but it was a delicate business. How he wished he could pour out his feelings to this woman he loved! But he had promised not to so, instead, he filled the pages with ordinary matters like the walks he had been on, the people he had seen, what the children had been doing (especially Hartley who was always doing or saying something unusual or amusing). Nonetheless, the letters were a far cry from anything he would have written to any other female friend and nothing like the letters he ever wrote to his wife. Asra was a kindred spirit; she understood him like no one else. The people he wrote about, the walks he went on, even the stories of the children were designed to appeal to her particular humour and interests.

At the end of August he had sent her a study of the Lake District waterfalls he had visited with Charles and Mary Lamb. He was fascinated by the way the water flowed. It was like life: sometimes calm and peaceful, sometimes frenetic. It made him think of the fallen angels from heaven. "Flight and confusion and destruction," he wrote to Asra, "but all harmonised into one majestic thing. The mad water rushes through its sinuous bed or, rather, prison of rock," he went on, "with such rapid curves, as if it turned the corners not from the mechanic force, but with foreknowledge, like a fierce and skilled driver. Great masses of water, one after the other, that in twilight one might have feelingly compared them to a vast crowd of huge white bears, rushing one after the other against the wind, their long white hair shattering abroad in the wind."

The water, with its constant rushing impulse, made him think about the underlying energy of nature, so far beyond the control of man. The waterfalls were like a perpetual prayer-wheel, worshipping their maker. "What a sight it is to look down on such a cataract!" he wrote. "The wheels that circumvolve in it, the eating up and plunging forward of that infinity of pearls and glass bulbs, the continual change of the matter, the perpetual sameness of the form, it is an awful image and shadow of God and the world."

But that had been back in the summer. September had brought rain but there was no one to go out with even when it wasn't raining. Standing at his study window, he watched the children playing in the garden, their long hair blowing in the wind, Hartley, whippet-thin, a spirit of nature, his arms outstretched like a bird's wings, revelling in the way the wind blew him this way and that; Derwent, solid and sturdy, a true Coleridge, his feet firmly planted, his body only swaying slightly.

With the sudden end to summer, the autumn wind howling around the house and down the chimneys, Samuel's nightmares began again: he dreamt he was back at school, he was in trouble, hiding from one of the masters, running through the corridors, up onto the rooftops, anywhere to escape the flogging. He was followed by ghostly figures, his limbs heavy as lead as he tried to escape. His fingers scrambled madly to close bolts on doors that failed to hold them.

Hartley had started sleeping badly too. He had always been an imaginative child and Samuel could sympathise with the little boy when he begged for a candle to be left alight so that he could make sure monsters and ghosts weren't lurking in the darkness.

With all the visitors gone and the weather so bad, there were no more excuses for Samuel not to work. He knew his *Letter to Sarah Hutchinson* was good, one of his best pieces of work, and that it ought to be published. But he couldn't possibly do that in its current form; people who knew him would know who it was about and those who didn't would try to guess her identity. And the references to his marriage were too intimate. He spent hours working on it, chopping bits out, moving bits around, until finally it became *Dejection: An Ode,* now much shorter, the words and meaning skilfully altered so that all references to Sarah were erased. In its new form the poem took on a different meaning, expressing Samuel's depression and his inability to write poetry or to enjoy nature when he was feeling so low. He wrote it in the style of Wordsworth's *Immortality Ode* and he knew Wordsworth would recognise it as a reply to his poem *Resolution and Independence.*

He had a store of other poems that he had written in the summer about Sarah, along with twenty brief epigrams. He set to work on those, too, so he could submit them to the *Morning Post* for publication. He wanted to include a poem about his walks on the mountains, his divine revelation, the waterfalls he had described to Sarah Hutchinson, but however hard he tried he just couldn't transform the imagery from prose into poetry. In the end he turned to a German poem he knew, by Frederica Brun, about the mountains and glaciers of Chamonix, which had just the effect he wanted to achieve. Once he had translated it, he had the structure he was looking for and simply added in his own observations. The finished poem was now more his than Brun's so he didn't see the point of saying it was a translation. It was, however, still redolent of an alpine landscape rather than the north of England so, when he sent it for publication, he wrote an introduction saying he had written it in Chamonix, though he had never been there in his life.

Back in the writing routine, he dashed off the first in a planned series of four articles for the newspaper, comparing the French Republic under Bonaparte with the Roman Republic under the Caesars. He then went on to start another series, in the form of open letters addressed to the leader of the Whig party, Charles James Fox, challenging his view of Bonaparte as a peacemaker, and followed it up with an article on Jacobinism in England. He was proud of this article, which asked why the government was so relentless in persecuting former radicals. He himself had been one of the many who had been excited by the French Revolution but had since changed their minds. He ended the article by saying he was contemptuous of those, "Who would turn an error in speculative politics into a sort of sin against the Holy Ghost, which in some miraculous and inexplicable manner shuts out not only mercy but even repentance."

Journalism wasn't just about politics, of course, and when Samuel heard about the scandal of the 'Beauty of Buttermere' he knew it would stimulate public interest. He had stopped at Buttermere on his walking tour in August and drunk tea outside the inn that was renowned in the area for the beauty of the innkeeper's daughter, Mary Robinson. Mary had unfortunately been taken in by a handsome charming confidence trickster, John Hatfield, who told everyone he was the Honourable Colonel Alex Augustus Hope, MP. Promising her a title and wealth he persuaded her to elope with him but he was already married and was exposed as a conman, forger and bigamist.

Samuel hurriedly gathered together all the material he could on the case and began a series of articles, which he planned to bring out in dramatic instalments, filled with all the gothic touches he knew the public would enjoy: romantic trysts, love letters, dashes at dusk over the Glaramara Pass. Mary was the beautiful but tragic heroine, an innocent country girl, Hatfield the cold-hearted city-dwelling seducer. Tragic though the story was, it fascinated Samuel, just as it fascinated his readers. It had all the makings of a gothic novel. He kept all his notes; it was the sort of thing he could write a poem about.

He had arranged for *Dejection: An Ode* to be published on 4th October, Wordsworth's wedding day and the seventh anniversary of his own marriage to Sara. He dedicated it *To Edmund,* knowing Wordsworth would recognise that as a literary reference to himself.

The night before Wordsworth's wedding Samuel had one of his bad dreams. Wordsworth and Mary were in it and a woman who looked, from the distance, like Dorothy. When she came closer, though, she wasn't like Dorothy at all: her body was fat and bloated, she had wild red hair, the face of the roughest sort of harlot. He woke up in a sweat then fell asleep again, only to find himself pursued by a dreadful pale woman who he knew carried some shameful disease which she could pass on to him by kissing him.

The Wordsworths came back on 6th October and Samuel hurried over to see them. They hadn't had a proper honeymoon but had taken a circuitous route home visiting some of their favourite places, including the ruins of Helmsley Castle and Rievaulx Abbey and the waterfalls in Wensleydale.

"I was ill a lot of the time," Dorothy told Samuel, "with headaches and sickness. It wasn't easy, you know." She dropped her voice, though Mary was in the kitchen and Wordsworth had gone out. "Revisiting the places I had visited on my own with William. But Mary looked after me so well. Really, I couldn't wish for a better sister."

"You're looking better now," Samuel said.

"It's so good to be home. It was dark when we got back but we explored the garden by candlelight to see how things had grown. And on Friday Mary and I walked on the hillside, then to John's Grove and then up to Rydal. Our first walk as sisters."

Mary had been seamlessly amalgamated into life in Grasmere. They were all so blissfully happy and Samuel couldn't help feeling jealous. Of course, this was the honeymoon period. He and Sara had been happy in their tiny cottage in Clevedon with the aeolian harp in the window, the roses and jasmine scenting the air. He had written poems to Sara like Wordsworth wrote them to Mary. But he had hardly known Sara when he married her. Wordsworth had known Mary for a long time. She had been a friend before she was his lover. Maybe this was the answer to a happy marriage. Samuel had rushed into love with his eyes closed, woken up to find himself married to a stranger.

"I have to get away," he told Wordsworth. "My life is intolerable. Never a kind word. You can't imagine what it's like."

Wordsworth and Dorothy exchanged glances. They had told him before how they hated visiting when Sara was there. She made them feel so uncomfortable.

"But the baby's due so soon," Wordsworth said. "You'll wait until she has it, surely?"

"She doesn't need me," Samuel said. "When I'm there she spends all her time carping at me. She's happier when it's just her and the children. Anyway, I've asked Southey and Edith to come up."

He was still hoping that they would. It would solve all his problems at a stroke. Edith would help Sara with the house and the children and Southey would be company for Samuel when he came home. They would be a buffer between him and Sara. She couldn't scream at him with another couple living there.

"So where will you go?" Wordsworth asked.

Samuel had been thinking about this for some time. "Tom Wedgwood is looking for a travelling companion," he said.

"But you said you didn't want to do that last time," Dorothy said. "Two invalids travelling together, you said."

"And I hear he's dosing himself with laudanum all the time," Wordsworth added. "Apparently he's given to dreadful moods of depression and temper."

But Tom was the only one Samuel knew who had the money to pay for a trip overseas. Surely he could put up with his illness and bad moods if it meant getting away.

Samuel was dying to know how things had gone with Annette and Caroline but he had to wait until the two women had gone to bed to ask Wordsworth.

"It was… difficult," Wordsworth said slowly. "But not as bad as I expected. We've both changed. She didn't seem to want much from me. Just to know I wouldn't take Caroline away. But it's all legal now."

"And Caroline? What was she like?"

"A little French girl," Wordsworth said. "A stranger. I can't think of her as my daughter."

So that was that. Wordsworth and Dorothy and Mary could put it behind them and start their new life together. It seemed a good time for him to go away.

He delayed telling Sara as long as possible but Tom Wedgwood kept asking when he was coming. Alone in his room he practised several ways to break it to her, leading up to it gradually, but in the end he just said bluntly, "I'm going away."

Sara looked up from the breakfast table, glanced at Hartley, shook her head at Samuel crossly. But he had chosen this moment deliberately. She wouldn't make a scene in front of the children.

"With Tom Wedgwood," he said, even though she hadn't asked. "For his health."

"And yours," she said acidly.

"Yes, of course. We talked about this."

"As you like, Samuel," she said. Even Hartley, young as he was, couldn't have mistaken the hatred in her voice. "You have no idea how long you'll be gone?" Her hand had moved involuntarily to the bulge in her stomach.

"Oh, we're going abroad," he said quickly. May as well get it all out in the open now he had started. "Italy probably. I won't be back 'til spring at the soonest."

Now she did react. Her fist came down on the table with a thump that made all the china rattle and Hartley jumped nervously, tears rushing to his eyes.

"Are you all right Mama?" he asked.

"Just a pain, Hartley," Sara said quickly. "Here, in my heart."

"Your heart? Will you die?"

"No, no!" She rushed over to him quickly, pulled his head into her stomach. "It's gone now. You've made it all better…"

Samuel left them at the table. They would be fine without him. The worst was over. He hummed quietly to himself as he began to pack.

He left Keswick on 4th November, a cold and dreary day. Hartley stood at the doorway a long time, watching him go with great sad eyes, waving goodbye whenever Samuel turned round. Oh, how the children pulled at his heart strings. He felt them stretching between him and Hartley, Derwent and the coming baby, a bond too deep to break.

He had arranged to go down to Cote House, Tom Wedgwood's house at Westbury, near Bristol. Tom seemed to have decided now on France for their travels. "You are aware," Samuel had written to him, "that my whole knowledge of French does not extend beyond the power of limping slowly, not without a Dictionary Crutch, through an easy French book and that, as to pronunciation, all my organs of speech from the bottom of my larynx to the edge of my lips are utterly and naturally anti-Gallican."

At Penrith, Samuel's thoughts, as ever, turned to Sarah Hutchinson. He knew she was staying there with her aunt on her way to spend Christmas with the Wordsworths at Grasmere. She was so close he could almost feel her. His mind was full of her as he queued for a seat on the London mail coach.

Then he heard the words, "Sorry, we're full."

A groan came from the man in front of Samuel, "But I have to get to London. My daughter's expecting me."

But Samuel's heart had soared. He'd have to spend the night in Penrith. He could call on Sarah. It would be rude not to.

She was surprised to see him of course. She came hurrying to the front hallway when she heard his voice.

"Samuel, what are you doing here? Has something happened? To Mary, Dorothy?"

"No, no. I find myself marooned here, that's all," he said, taking hold of her hands and squeezing them reassuringly. "Until I can get the London coach tomorrow morning."

"Well, you must stay, of course," Sarah's aunt said politely.

Their old intimacy was long gone but at least he could see her, look at that face he loved so much, hear that voice. With her aunt hovering around, conversation was of the usual social type: how Tom and Jack and George were, the work on the farms, Mary's wedding of course. "Dorothy didn't go," Sarah told him. "She stayed home with me to help with the wedding breakfast. She was very overwrought. I'm so looking forward to seeing Mary again. I do miss her."

Samuel sat down to write to Sara that night. Should he tell her where he was? But why shouldn't he? He had nothing to hide. But he was nervous as he wrote the letter. He always seemed to care for his wife far more when he was away from her. He knew she would be jealous. But they had discussed this many times. She must love his friends like he loved them.

"My dear love, write as cheerfully as possible," he wrote. "I am tenderer and more fluttery and bowel-weak than most. I cannot bear anything gloomy, unless when it is quite necessary. Be assured I will bring back (come home when I will) a pure, affectionate and husbandly heart."

But it wasn't enough. Her reply, which was waiting for him at Cote House, was worse than he expected. In a long tirade, Sara accused him of disloyalty, of going behind her back, of abandoning him when she needed him most. His throat tightened and his heart began to hammer. Was he having a heart attack? He sat down shakily, gathered his thoughts. She was overreacting, he decided, as his heart began to settle down and his bowels stopped churning. Then he read the letter again. There were phrases in there, harsh words, words he could never forget. He composed a reply, explaining away every accusation. He had never been less than honest with her, he said. But he must have been *too* honest. The letter that came back said she had fainted when she read his reply. Suddenly he was scared. He had never known Sara to faint. She would lose the baby. She would die. They would both die. It was all his fault.

Again his heart constricted, beating so hard he could hardly breathe. An excruciating spasm shot through his bowels. He had to rush to the pot. When he got up he measured twenty drops of laudanum into a glass and drank it down. His bowels stopped churning. He felt calmer. He woke in the early hours of the morning, justifications swarming in his mind. Finally he gave up sleep and got up to write to her.

"You must see by this the importance of tranquillity to me," he wrote. "The desire of writing you lay so heavy on my mind that I woke at four o'clock. I beg you *instantly* to get a nurse. Try to get Mrs Railton. To be sure there is a mawkish 'so-vary-good'ness about her character, and her face and dress have far too much of the smug-doleful in them for my taste, but she is certainly an excellent nurse. At all events get somebody immediately. Have a fire in your bedroom. If you are seriously ill or unhappy at my absence I will return at all hazards for I know you will not *will* it, though you might *wish* it, except for a serious cause."

He paused. He had to make Sara understand that everything he did was for the best. He wasn't like other husbands. He needed different things: space, peace and quiet, nature, the love and support of the people he loved.

"I owe duties, and solemn ones, to you as my wife," he wrote. "But I owe equally solemn ones to myself, to my children, to my friends and to society. I can neither retain my happiness nor my faculties unless I move, live and love in perfect freedom. Permit me, my dear Sara, without offence to you, as heaven knows it is without any feeling of pride in myself to say that in sex, acquirements and in the quantity and quality of natural endowments, whether of feeling or of intellect, you are the inferior. Therefore it would be preposterous to expect that I should see with your eyes and dismiss my friends from my heart only because you have chosen not to give them any share of your heart; but is it not preposterous, in me, on the contrary I have a right to expect and demand that you should to a certain degree love and act kindly to those whom I deem worthy of my love."

Samuel's first sight of Tom Wedgwood caught him unawares. He had lost a huge amount of weight but his stomach was distended. "I can't eat," he said. "I'm in so much pain. And everything goes straight through me."

Samuel wondered if he would be well enough to travel but he was still very keen. "I thought we'd go up to Wales first," he said. "To visit my cousins in Pembrokeshire. You'll like them."

Tom was paying for everything. Samuel had no choice but to follow him, wherever he suggested. They stayed the first night at St Clears in Carmarthenshire. When they arrived Tom collapsed onto the bed.

"I don't know what I'd do without this." He gestured to the little brown bottle of laudanum.

"I know, I know," Samuel said. "People like you and me, who suffer from our stomach and bowels, need a stimulant and opium is far better than alcohol and less harmful than tea."

He left Tom sleeping peacefully and strolled down the road to Laugharne, which he had been told had a castle well worth seeing. The tide was out when he got there, exposing long stretches of sand and mudflats. The castle was right on the estuary, crumbling ivy-covered walls standing out against the grey sky. He could hear the murmuring of the sea in the distance, the cries of seagulls. Here, the gorse was still bravely flowering, yellow blossoms clinging to the scrubby bushes, and petals of white tansy blew in the wind.

He walked on into the town, past a collection of elegant, well-kept houses. One had two bird cages suspended outside, with a screaming parrot in each. Chickens perched on top of the cages, and a fine cockerel, "with a bold, brave old English face," Samuel told Tom when he got back. "I waited for him to crow but he wouldn't. So I went on down to the church, a white building with a grey steeple. I stopped to look at the gravestones; you know how much I like epitaphs."

He had knelt down on the damp ground, trying to make out the words on the tombstones encrusted with lichen and smattered with the bright red droppings from the birds who had feasted on the yew berries above.

"Some of them were so touching," he told Tom, "I copied them down in my notebook. There was one gravestone to the wives and daughters of Evan Jones. He lived forty-one years after they had all died and the poor man's name and dates had to be squeezed in at the bottom with no room for an epitaph at all."

Tom didn't seem to be listening. His eyes were closed, his face grey with pain. He wouldn't join Samuel for dinner but had a dish of thin soup sent up to his room.

He was up early the next morning though, looking forward to the next stage of their journey. "You'll like my cousins," he said again. "And it's a beautiful area. There are some lovely walks."

Cresselly House was a fine Palladian villa, built of the local mellow yellow stone in the modern symmetrical style. Tom's cousins welcomed them at the door and, while Tom went to his room to rest after the journey, Samuel sat down to read the letter from Sara that had been handed to him when he arrived. His hand shook when he opened it, he was so terrified of what she would say, but in fact it was a lovely letter, so tender, so keen to make sure their marriage would work, that his heart melted. He wrote back immediately, "God love you and have you in his keeping my blessed Sara and speedily restore me to you. I have a faith, a heavenly faith, that our future days will be days of peace and affectionate happiness. Oh, that I were now with you! I feel it very, very hard to be from you at this trying time. I dare not think a moment concerning you in this relation or I shall be immediately ill. But I shall soon return and bring you back a confident and affectionate husband. Again and again my dearest, dearest Sara, my wife and my love and indeed my very hope, may God preserve you."

Cresselly House was obviously a good omen, he decided. If the baby was a boy, they would call it Cresselly. If it was a girl, which seemed highly unlikely, he liked Rotha, after the River Rothay, or Algretha, or Lovenna. But he was sure it would be a boy.

Once Tom had recovered from the journey, he turned out to be good company and Samuel regretted ever having thought they couldn't be travelling companions. "He possesses the finest, the subtlest mind and taste I have met with," he wrote to Sara.

Tom had always been interested in science and scientific experiments and he had an enquiring mind. Travel interested him too, different cultures, new experiences. It was a shame he was so obviously dying; the swelling in his abdomen must be some sort of tumour. The constant pain and nausea made him bad-tempered and the opium he took to relieve the pain dulled his mind. His travel plans became more and more vague.

"Tom Wedgwood's hopes and schemes are again all afloat," Samuel wrote to Sara. "Cornwall perhaps, Ireland perhaps, Cumberland, possibly. Naples, or Madeira, or Tenerife. I don't see any likelihood of our going to the moon or to either of the planets or fixed stars but that's all I can say. Write immediately my dear love and direct to me… Where? That's the puzzle."

Tom had given him a £50 advance on his annuity and he slipped it in with the letter, imagining Sara's surprise and pleasure when she saw it. With luck it would cover the Greta Hall rent and all the outstanding bills.

In the meantime he was in no hurry to move from Cresselly House. During the day he went for long walks in the beautiful countryside then came back to his comfortable room and worked undisturbed on his newspaper articles, the bright fire constantly replenished by one of the many servants.

The family prided itself on its local farms and the produce they provided for the table: there was plenty of meat swimming in creamy sauces; huge game pies; sweet, candied fruit from the exotic glasshouses; ices made from the ice hacked out of the icehouse down by the river; puddings served with thick, fresh cream. Samuel had never eaten so well.

After they had dined, they retired to the music room in comfortable armchairs, drawn up around another crackling fire, and talked, read books or listened while Tom played the pianoforte. The ladies of the house, Jessica, Emma and Frances, flirted gently with Samuel in a way that reminded him nostalgically of the evenings at Gallow Hill with the Hutchinson sisters.

He and Sara were getting on well now that they had some distance between them. This was the perfect time to make her understand how important his relationship with Sarah Hutchinson was to him. He knew she wanted a female friend to be with her when she had the baby. Sarah Hutchinson was spending Christmas with the Wordsworths. It couldn't be better. He wrote to Sara saying it would be a great comfort to him if one of the women would be with her. "Sarah rather than the other two," he went on confidently, "as you will hardly have another opportunity of having her by yourself and to yourself and of learning to know her, such as she is, really is. Much of our common love depends on your loving those whom I love."

Their stay at Cresselly House finally came to an end. It was December and Christmas was approaching. Tom still had no definite plans for going abroad and Samuel wasn't even sure he was up to it, so they made their way back down through South Wales, stopping off at various places until the only thing left to do really was to head back to Greta Hall, where Samuel thought Tom could recover for a while and they could make arrangements to go abroad sometime in the new year. He wrote to Sara to say they would arrive on Christmas Day. He knew the baby was due on or around that date. She must thoroughly air and warm Tom's room, he told her, likewise the bed and bedding. She could hire an extra servant to help her: Tom would pay. There must be extra food. Although Tom ate little he was used to the very best so she must get a couple of chickens and a pound or so of the best salt potted butter that Tom liked so much. Tom had said he would only stay a night or two, he didn't want to be in the way, but if the weather was bad or he was ill, he might have to stay longer.

The last thing Samuel wanted was to arrive home with a male guest, especially a bachelor, to find Sara in the throes of labour, so he asked her to arrange for Mr Jackson to send a message to the post office in Kendal letting him know what was happening. When they arrived in Kendal, however, in the early hours of Christmas Eve morning, there was no message waiting for them.

"What shall we do?" Tom asked.

"Sara won't want us turning up unannounced," Samuel said firmly. "Let's go on to Grasmere. Wordsworth and Dorothy will be happy to see us."

"And Sarah will be there." His heart leapt at the thought.

It was Dorothy who hurried out of the cottage when the cart drew up outside. "Oh, Samuel, you don't know then?" she burst out.

For an awful moment he thought something had happened to Sara. Then he saw she was smiling. "The baby?" he asked quickly.

"A girl!" she laughed. "Yesterday morning at half past six."

"A *girl?"* Samuel said incredulously. "I'm the father of a *girl?* I thought I could only have boys."

"You'll come in?" Dorothy said. "You can't go without refreshments."

"Yes, of course. But then I must go."

"Sarah has toothache," Dorothy was saying as she led them into the cottage. "And Mary is feeling sick." She said it in such a meaningful way that Samuel knew instantly that Mary was pregnant. So soon. So much would change. The cottage was too small for a baby, surely. But he couldn't think of that now. Wordsworth hurried over to greet him, slapped him on the back heartily. "A girl!" he laughed. "Who would have thought it?" Samuel laughed with him but his eyes were drawn like a magnet to the figure hunched over by the fireside, a cloth wrapped around her jaw. Toothache was something he could sympathise with; he suffered dreadfully from it himself. He hurried over to take Sarah's hands between his but she shrank back, glancing up at Tom Wedgwood.

"Oh, never mind Tom," Samuel said cheerfully, although she hadn't actually said anything. "He's my friend. He knows me."

She made to rise from her chair to bob a curtsy but Tom waved it away. "Please, Miss Hutchinson. We won't stay. We're intruding." He looked meaningfully at Samuel. Of course he must go to Sara and the baby but his heart belonged here with this other Sarah, the pale creature by the fire. She knew it too. It was written in every fibre of her being, however hard she tried to hide it.

"I'll come again soon," he said. "When Sara is more settled. We'll bring the new baby, the little Coleridgiella! "

"Oh, we'd love to see them," Mary said. The way she blushed as she said it, her hand hovering above her own belly, confirmed Samuel's suspicions though it was obviously too soon for any official announcement.

Sara had taken on Mrs Railton, the woman with the saintly do-goodness about her. He liked to think it was because Sarah had toothache but maybe she just preferred someone more experienced. The woman greeted Samuel at the bedroom door with folded arms like a gaoler.

"Mrs Coleridge is feeding the baby," she said sternly.

"Please," Sara called. "Let my husband come in. I don't mind."

One look at the fat little baby in Sara's arms made Samuel realise that none of the unusual names he had chosen would be suitable. He sat down on the edge of the bed next to Sara and put his hand gently on the baby's head. "We'll call her Sara," he said.

Chapter Eighteen

Sara entered baby Sara's name and date of birth, 23rd December 1802, in the family Bible herself. No point waiting for Samuel to do it as he had scarcely spent any time at home recently.

Tom Wedgwood had left after a couple of days. The house was too cold, he said, for an invalid. His friend Luff had a warm house at Glenridding and he would stay there until he and Samuel went away. It was easier without him there. He was a pleasant enough man but so demanding with his constant need for special food, a warm bed and a fire in his room. True, he paid for all his extras, but it really wasn't appropriate for a bachelor to be staying in a house where she was nursing a new baby.

When he had gone, Samuel spent most of his time tramping over the hills between Derwent Water and Ullswater to Glenridding to see Tom and his friend Luff. He had brought back special walking boots from Wales. "These will keep my feet dry Sara," he enthused. "Look at the fineness of this leather. And this cuff, see, it's oilskin and comes six inches up my leg to stop the water coming in."

Sara was tempted to ask how much they had cost but at least he had sent enough money to settle the bills.

When he wasn't over with Tom Wedgwood he was with the Wordsworths at Grasmere, of course. Anywhere but home here with her and the children. How foolish she had been to hope that the new baby might bring them together. They were further apart than ever.

"You are a good woman with a pleasing person and a healthy understanding," he wrote to her. "Superior certainly to nine women in ten of our own rank or the rank above us and I will be not only contented but grateful if you will let me be quite tranquil and — above all my dear, dear Sara! — have confidence in my honour and virtue and suffer me to love and to be beloved without jealousy or pain. Depend on it, my dear wife, that the more you sympathise with me, in my kind manners and kind feelings to those of Grasmere, the more I shall be likely to sympathise with you in your opinions respecting their faults and imperfections. I am no idolator at present and I solemnly assure you that if I prefer many parts of their characters, opinions, feelings and habits to the same part of yours, I do likewise prefer much, very much of your character to theirs. Of course, I speak chiefly of Dorothy and William because Mrs Wordsworth and her sister are far less remote from you than they."

Cruel, cruel words. What had she done? What had she *ever* done to deserve a husband like this? Her first reaction was to tear the letter up and throw the pieces into the fire. No one should read words like this. But she must keep it. If it came to a separation or, worse still, divorce, here was the proof that she wasn't to blame. Despite all the provocation her letters back to him had been warm and loving. No one could accuse her of being unkind. She knew she was pitied. Her mother, Edith, Southey, her other sisters: they all felt sorry for her. She hated it. She would keep the outward show of a happy marriage even if it wasn't true.

The letter went on to say that he was bringing Sarah Hutchinson over the next day to spend some time with her. Did the poor girl realise what was going on? Or did she sit next to him at the table at Grasmere helping him write the letter? Did they laugh together as he wrote it? Did Wordsworth and Dorothy and Mary all join in? But she was just being paranoid. The idea was ridiculous. She knew Sarah Hutchinson. She was no scheming minx, no tempting siren. It was a social visit, nothing more.

It was hard to believe Miss Hutchinson didn't know the depth of Samuel's feelings towards her. Maybe she was flattered, but she wasn't trying to break up their marriage. And even if she did, even if she really *was* in love with Samuel, would she have the courage to live with him? People did it. Mary Wollstonecraft had lived openly with Gilbert Imlay. But it took a very brave woman to flout convention. The Wordsworths and Hutchinsons might be an unusual lot but she couldn't see them going that far; Sarah's brothers would never allow it.

Samuel obviously thought it was more than just a social visit. The letter went on to say that he had some 'few reasons' for wanting Sarah to be with her immediately. "I will tell you when I am alone with you," he wrote. She couldn't imagine what the reasons might be. Did he want Sarah to see the new baby? He had wanted her to be at the birth. Was he thinking of taking the children to live with him and the Wordsworths and Hutchinsons? If Mary had a baby they could bring all the children up together, with Dorothy and Sarah to help look after them. They would all live together in the sort of Pantisocratic community Samuel had always wanted and she would be left alone. She would rather die.

"In one thing, my dear love!" he ended the letter, "I do prefer you to any woman I ever knew. I have the most unbounded confidence in your discretion and know it to be well-grounded."

How could he call her his dear love and say he liked her better than anyone else, then say such hurtful things to her? The man was impossible. He didn't know himself what he really wanted. And what was all this about discretion? She wouldn't dream of telling everyone their marriage problems. It was embarrassing enough as it was without anyone else knowing.

Samuel didn't say what time they were arriving. All day she looked out for the sight of them coming up the drive. She didn't tell the children Papa might be coming because they would be disappointed if he didn't turn up. By nightfall they still hadn't arrived so Sara put the children to bed early. If Hartley had known his papa was coming over he would never have settled but, as it was, she allowed him the last stub of his candle so he would get to sleep. She sat down with her sewing, expecting at any moment to hear the sound of a carriage, Sarah's and Samuel's voices outside. She jumped at every sound, strained her ears to listen, but it was only the fire crackling, the house creaking, the night-time sounds of owls hooting and foxes barking.

No letter of explanation came. Clearly the whole idea had been in Samuel's mind. Miss Hutchinson had never had any intention of coming over. If Sara didn't know him differently she would have thought he'd been drinking when he'd written it and forgotten all about it. But Samuel never did things like that; everything was deliberate, thought out, even if it made no sense to anyone else.

Dorothy wrote several times inviting her over, saying how much they were looking forward to seeing the new baby. It seemed rude to refuse so she accepted each time. But when it came to it she couldn't face it. She had this crazy idea she would get there and they would make her leave the children with them.

She should send an apology, of course she should, some explanation, anything would do. And if it were anyone else she would, it was how she'd been brought up, but she was past caring with them. Let them think what they liked.

Anyway, she had her new baby to think of, the most beautiful girl in the world. Edith had had a girl too. They had named her Margaret after Southey's mother who had died just before she was born. She would love to see Edith again. The two girls were only tiny babies but they were so close in age, they were sure to be close friends, like her and Edith. Maybe Samuel could persuade them to live up here.

But whatever happened Sara at last had the little girl she had longed for. She was pleased Samuel hadn't gone for any of those outlandish names. Sara, without the 'h', after her. The alternative, that he had called her after Sarah Hutchinson, was unthinkable.

She had been more nervous this time than usual. Childbirth was dangerous; she might die. Or she might live and the baby might die. She had lost Berkeley, and Derwent had been desperately ill just after he was born. She hadn't told Samuel how scared she had been. He just couldn't cope with other people's problems. Anything that upset him affected his health and then he was in a dreadful state with pains in his stomach, chest and bowels. It just wasn't worth it.

The birth might have been as easy as all her others but she seemed to take longer to recover. Tired and sore, she dragged herself from the bed to the chair to feed baby Sara, then crawled back to bed.

"It's quite natural to be like this," the indomitable Mrs Railton assured her. "It's your third. Your body's getting tired."

"Fourth," Sara corrected her for the umpteenth time. "I've had four babies. I told you…" Tears came to her eyes.

"Yes of course, I know," Mrs Railton said briskly. "We need to concentrate on the living ones now, don't we?"

The weather was cold, wet and stormy with high winds that howled round the house. Hartley went down with scarlet fever and croup and baby Sara developed thrush. Sara, still feeling dreadful, had to haul herself out of bed; there was too much for Mrs Railton to do on her own.

Then Samuel came home one day more bedraggled than she had ever seen him. "It was dreadful, Sara," he said, stumbling through the door. "I was coming over the Kirkstone Pass when there was a storm such as I have never known before. The wind was so strong, the cold so intense, the rain pelted across my face like pieces of flint. My hands were shrivelled. I had to carry my stick under my arm."

The next day he woke unable to move: his knees were swollen and his hands couldn't grip anything. She had to help him in and out of bed, lift a cup to his lips for him to drink, a spoon for him to eat.

From his sick bed, he planned his trip abroad.

"Tom says we'll go to Paris first," he informed Sara. "Then on through Switzerland to Rome, Naples and perhaps Sicily."

"And Tom's well enough for all this now, is he?" Sara asked.

"Oh, he'll be fine once we get somewhere warm. And he knows it's what I need too: warmth and sunshine. My joints will improve along with my stomach and my bowels. I'll come home a new man."

Back in the kitchen, going through the same mundane chores of peeling and chopping and cooking, Sara allowed herself to imagine what it must be like to be Samuel, to come and go as he wished without any responsibilities. It was a fairy tale life he led; a life devoted solely to himself. Nothing and no one must upset him otherwise he couldn't work. She knew he was clever, of course, a genius maybe. Certainly *he* thought he was. But did that give him the right to have everything always *his* way? As she looked out of the rain lashed window to the dreary grey sky and mountains she thought wistfully of the blue skies and sunshine he spoke of, dry, dusty roads, orange and lemon groves, whitewashed houses, freedom. She had often dreamt of travel, back when she had first known Samuel. She was good at languages; if they had gone abroad she would have easily picked up the language of whatever country they ended up in. Samuel still talked of setting up a commune overseas with the Wordsworths, the Hutchinson sisters, Edith and Southey. But Dorothy had been travelling with Samuel and Wordsworth. She had told Sara about the dirty streets and houses, the insects crawling over the food in the markets, the ragged, filthy children in the streets, the danger of disease everywhere. Sara would never take Hartley, Derwent and baby Sara anywhere like that. Edith would never take Margaret. And Wordsworth and

Mary would have a baby before long, she was sure of it. The time for them to travel had gone now. She never regretted having the children but it changed things. Except for Samuel. As he kept reminding her, he was free to do what he liked, go where he liked. So she wasn't surprised when, as soon as he was well again, he announced he was leaving.

"We're going down to Blandford Forum first," he said. "To stay with Josiah Wedgwood for a month or so. Then we're leaving for Paris and on to Italy and Sicily."

She didn't ask when he would be back but a trip like that, it couldn't be less than nine months, a year maybe. He would miss baby Sara's first tooth, her first steps maybe, first words, Derwent's breeching ceremony, the boys' birthdays… How could he do it?

Chapter Nineteen

Sara was in the kitchen when he went to say goodbye. He could hear her banging pots and pans and issuing sharp instructions to one of the maids. He stood in the doorway waiting but she hadn't heard him come in and in the end he crossed the hot, steamy room, dodging the maid who chose that moment to dart across with a pan of something in her hand. "Oh, sorry sir." She bobbed a half curtsy. Sara turned, took in at a glance his travelling clothes, walking stick and knapsack and wiped her hands on her apron.

"So you're off?"

"Yes." There didn't seem to be much else to say and for a moment they stood awkwardly opposite each other.

"I'll get the children," she said.

"Do you need to? I hate these goodbye scenes."

"*You're* the one who makes them all, Samuel," she spat out. "You could try staying home like any other husband."

"Sara don't, please. You know I have to go. With my health…"

"Your *health,* your *health*! If it wasn't that it would be some other reason. Why don't you just come out and say you can't stand living with me?"

"If you made my home a place of comfort instead of a place of torment maybe I would."

"*Me?* How can it be me? *You're* the one with the bad moods, the constant grumbling, shouting at me and the children. I do everything for you. I cook and clean and wash. What do *you* do?"

"I work. All the time. You've read my articles haven't you? My poetry? Oh no, I forgot you prefer Southey's to mine!"

He suddenly became aware of the maid standing staring at them. "Sara let's not start arguing again just when I'm leaving," he said.

"Huh! We argue all the time anyway. I don't see what difference it makes."

"Well, it's just as well I'm going then." What was the point of being nice to the woman? Whatever he did, whatever he said, it was wrong.

"Off with another drug addict," she said sarcastically.

"What?"

"Tom Wedgwood. He's as bad as you. Always at that little glass bottle."

"Have some pity, Sara. He's in pain. He may be dying. It's the only thing that keeps him going."

"*You're* not dying though. And you can't let it alone either."

"For my joints."

"And to 'relax' you. That's where all the money goes, Samuel. I've told you before. How d'you expect me to manage while you're away?"

"I'll send you money. I always do."

"Not always. I had to ask Tom Poole when you were away in Germany."

"Why do you always have to drag up things that happened years ago? I've just said I'll make sure you and the children are provided for. Why can't you trust me?"

"*Trust* you? *Trust* you? What makes you think I'd *ever* do that?"

"If only you would, Sara. It's all I ask. Your life would be much easier if you'd just let me do what I know to be best and *trust* that it's the right thing. Now, let's just go and find the children so I can get this over and done with."

Hartley looked up distractedly from the game he had been playing on the floor of the parlour. "Say goodbye to Papa," Sara prompted him. "He'll be gone a long time."

Samuel saw the reluctance in Hartley's face as he dragged himself to his feet, the distant look in his eyes. What would a few more months mean to him? Samuel didn't see much of him anyway.

Derwent wouldn't even come to him and squirmed away to cuddle closer to Sara when Samuel tried to kiss him. As for the baby, well, she was only a few weeks old. There was no point in doing anything other than touching the tiny, curled hand above her cot blanket.

And yet, despite the fact that his children didn't seem to care whether he was going or not and his wife did her best to make him feel guilty, Samuel felt his heart lift the moment the door closed behind him. The feelings of guilt that Sara had planted in his chest, and the pain at leaving the children, faded away as he got into a steady stride. There was nothing like it, the freedom of the open road, the excitement of travel. It didn't matter where, as long as he could get away.

Tom Wedgwood and his brother Josiah both had houses in a village called Tarrant Gunville near Blandford Forum in Dorset.

Tom's house, Eastbury Park, had once been a palatial mansion. Designed by the famous architect Vanburgh, it was built for George Dodington, who had made a fortune when he was paymaster of the navy. It took twenty-one years to build and was finished in about 1738. The show front was 570 feet across, with the main house in the middle and stables and service rooms on either side. At the time it was one of the grandest and most superb in the land, set in beautifully landscaped parkland and gardens and fitted out sumptuously inside with gilded and moulded ceilings and luxurious fabrics and furniture.

When Dodington died it was inherited by his nephew, Bubb Dodington, and after that it passed on to Earl Temple. A big house like that was expensive to run and Earl Temple didn't want it so he put it up for sale. But no one else wanted it either and in desperation he offered an annuity of £200 a year to anyone who would live there. No one accepted. In 1763 the elegant furniture was sold and the only thing that could be done was to demolish it. The building was so immense that it took several years and large amounts of dynamite to destroy but by 1782 it had gone except for the stables. Three years before Samuel's visit these had been made into a house, with a new wing built to connect the front block and the coach house.

Josiah's house, nearby Gunville House, had only been built four years ago and, like the other Wedgwood houses that Samuel had stayed in, was modern, warm and comfortable with an army of staff to see to all their needs. It was so comfortable that he began to doubt if anything would ever come of Tom's plans to go abroad. He seemed worse than ever.

"They say it's a thickening of the gut," he told Samuel.

"What we need," Samuel said, "is something to pick us both up, take us away from this world and into another. I've heard of a new drug called bang, or Indian hemp, that gives you the most amazing high. I've written to John Wordsworth and to Sir Joseph Banks to see if they can get us any."

Tom was the only one Samuel could talk to like this, him and Humphry Davy. Both were interested in the effects of drugs, though Davy's interest was more scientific. He and Samuel had tried out laughing gas at the Pneumatic Institute in Bristol. Tom, like Samuel, took laudanum for pain, but they both knew it had another effect too. Sara had been right about that though he would never admit it to her. He didn't just take it for pain. It lifted him. It made him feel better about everything: Sara's nagging, the constant struggle to find inspiration, the worries about work and money, the impossible situation with Sarah Hutchinson, all became more tolerable after a few drops from that little brown bottle. True, it played havoc with his bowels and stomach but it was a small price to pay. He traced his dependence on the drug back to when he began using it for his painful knees but in fact he had been aware of the effect as far back as his university days when he took it for toothache. But he couldn't afford to buy it in those days. Instead he had relied on the cheap alcohol in the ale houses to give him the high he needed.

Tom still seemed reluctant to move from the comfort of Gunville but Samuel was restless so he decided to go down to Nether Stowey to stay with Poole. It was the middle of February when the drug arrived at Poole's house from Kew Gardens with a note from Sir Joseph Banks, "It seems beyond a doubt that the nepenthe was a preparation of the bang known to the ancients."

There were no instructions as to the size of the dose. "We will have a fair trial of bang," Samuel wrote to Tom Wedgwood. "Do bring down some of the hyoseyamine pills and I will give a fair trial of opium, hensbane and nepenthe."

He didn't tell Poole what the mysterious package was. He would be shocked and disappointed if he knew Samuel was wasting time and money on drugs.

He met Tom at Cote House in Westbury but they waited until they were back in Gunville to experiment with the drugs. They tried them out on consecutive evenings: the hyoscyamine made them both feel woozy, the hensbane made them think they could fly, the long-awaited nepenthe was the most disappointing, simply making them so relaxed that they fell asleep. They decided overall that the opium they both already took in their liquid laudanum, or mixed with mysterious spices as Kendal Black Drop, had the best effect.

Maybe it was the effect of the drug-taking session but Tom's mood suddenly changed from lethargy to action. "We must go away immediately," he announced one morning. "I'm fed up with hanging around here. I'll get someone to book the passage." He looked Samuel up and down as though he were seeing him for the first time. "You can't go to France like that," he said. "You must have some new clothes."

"But — " Samuel began, reddening.

"I'll pay," Tom said quickly. "I can't have you going dressed like that. What would people think in Paris? In Rome? Milan?" He started laughing and Samuel joined in. The sooner they got going the better. No more delays. It was what he wanted.

A tailor turned up at the house and Samuel was measured for a whole wardrobe of new clothes that arrived the following week. But by then Tom's mood had changed again. Now he seemed worried about Samuel. "Are you sure you're well enough to come with me? I feel so bad again. How will we manage if we're both ill? Maybe it's all a mistake."

Samuel's chance of escape seemed to be slipping away from him. He had been relying on Tom to pay for the trip.

At the beginning of March, Tom went back to Cote House. "I just don't feel up to going away," he said mournfully.

Not knowing where else to go, Samuel went up to London. If Tom didn't want to go abroad with him he would have to find a way of going on his own. He couldn't go back to Sara; he made her unhappy. And there was no future in his relationship with Sarah Hutchinson. He made her unhappy, too. The Wordsworths would never come abroad with him now; he had been right about Mary, he heard she was expecting a baby in July, just nine months after they had married. If children came as easily as this, they might move from the cottage in Grasmere to somewhere bigger but they would never go overseas.

It was an evil day when he married Sara, he thought, but whatever he felt for her, he couldn't leave her unprovided for. He wrote to Southey, asking him yet again if he and Edith would come and live at Greta Hall. Southey was an old and trusted friend. Samuel had already confided to him that he and Sara weren't getting on.

"If our mutual unstableness continues," he wrote now, "and (as it assuredly will do if it continues) increases and strengthens, why then, it is better for her and my children that I should live apart." He went on to point out the advantages of living at Greta Hall. "If it suited you, you might have one kitchen, or (if Edith and Sara thought it would answer) we might have the two kitchens in common. You might have, I say, the whole ground floor, consisting of two sweet wing-rooms, commanding the loveliest view of Borrowdale. The highest room in the house is a very large one intended for two but suffered to remain one for my desire. It would be a capital healthy nursery."

The only fly in the ointment was Edith's sister, Mary, who had been living with them since Edith's bad illness in London. Mary was a widow with no financial support of any kind. Her late husband's family had never approved of their marriage and now refused to help her and her eight-year-old son. She had been a great support to Edith when she was ill and Samuel knew Southey would not abandon her now. The problem was that Sara had never got on with Mary like she did with Edith. Even Southey agreed that she was difficult, bad-tempered and moody and often caused arguments between him and Edith. Sara knew it too. She would refuse to have her there. Maybe Southey could pay Mary an allowance. He wasn't particularly bothered how Southey did it, he just wanted Sara looked after so he could go away indefinitely. He and

Southey didn't always get on; he always seemed so perfect and Samuel preferred his bachelor friends Lamb, Poole and Tom Wedgwood. And Edith was nothing but a bore, even in her most positive times. But Sara liked them. He could be satisfied he'd done his best for her. That was all that mattered.

When he had finished writing the letter to Southey he went to a broker and took out a life assurance policy in Sara's name which would give her £1,000 if he died. Hanging, drowning and suicide were not covered. The premium was high, at £27 a year, but it was worth it. He made his will at the same time, leaving the interest on the assurance policy to Sara and, after her death, to their daughter Sara. The boys could always earn their own living.

He stayed in London a fortnight, visiting Sotheby, Davy and Lamb. The moment he saw Mary Lamb he realised something was very wrong: her face was drawn and anxious, she couldn't sit still for a moment, she twisted her hands together all the time, nibbled the ends of her fingers, wrung her hands and pulled at the strands of hair around her face. This was nothing like the woman he had seen last summer, walking with him by the lakes, talking to him cheerfully and intelligently. One evening it all came to a head: for no reason that he could make out she suddenly started shrieking and yelling, throwing herself around the room, sobbing hysterically. It was terrifying. Samuel had seen Sara in a hysterical state before but it was nothing like this. Charles followed her as she flung herself around, trying to calm her, talking to her in a steady monotone voice, but she was beyond any reason. "I'll have to take her to the asylum again," he said. "I don't know what else to do. It breaks my heart."

"I'll take her for you," Samuel said, "if it's easier."

"Would you?" Charles' face lit up. "I so hate doing it. She begs me not to. I feel dreadful."

It was the least he could do for the friend who had always stood by him. But it was an awful journey. Mary sobbed and cried, clutched at his arm. "Take me home. I'll be good, I promise."

The asylum looked like a prison, the strapping women who dragged Mary inside like prison warders. No wonder Charles hated doing it. Samuel's hands shook all the way back and he felt sick to the stomach. Charles was sitting with his head in his hands when he went in. "She'll be fine," Samuel said as cheerfully as he could.

"It breaks my heart to see her like that," Charles said again. "She can be so sweet, so kind, so *clever*."

"Maybe it's that," Samuel said. "The cleverness. Women can't cope with it like we can. Too much learning, too much thinking, it brings on hysteria. It makes you realise, doesn't it, how fragile we all are, mentally and physically; one thing wrong, even a small thing, and it upsets our balance."

When he wasn't out with his bachelor friends, Samuel found himself invited to some of the big social gatherings. These were good places to meet influential people like Sir George Beaumont, people it was worth impressing and fostering for the financial backing they could provide. Sometimes Samuel caught sight of Humphry Davy across the crowded room. Davy was already well established as a celebrity but Samuel knew he should be taking advantage of the opportunities these society events afforded him. But when a group of Sotheby's rich friends offered to produce a private edition of *Christabel*, on the best quality paper with decorative illustrations, Samuel turned it down. They were doing it for all the wrong reasons: they didn't *know* the work, Sotheby had only described it to them; they certainly didn't appreciate it for its worth. He would rather it were published on its own merit, on cheap paper if necessary, when he was good and ready.

His London publisher, Longman, said he would print a third edition of his collection of poems from 1797 and offered to include his more recent ones. He knew it made good sense, both commercially and professionally, but it seemed such an effort to submit the new work with all the transcribing and correcting necessary, so he told him just to proceed with the old ones.

He was relieved when Lamb offered to do the proofreading for him as it was another tedious job that he hated.

"I classed them as nearly as I could according to dates," Lamb wrote to him. "Can you send me any wishes about the book?"

Lamb never seemed to mind helping him. "Bless you, old sophist," he went on, "who next to human nature taught me all the corruption I was capable of knowing… When shall we two smoke again?"

Samuel felt a twinge of jealousy when he heard that Tom Wedgwood had gone to France with someone else. The news surprised him in more than one way; not only could he scarcely believe Tom had galvanised himself after all his prevarications and his illness but it seemed increasingly likely there would be another war with France. Maybe Tom hadn't realised this or maybe he was just so desperate to get away that he was prepared to risk it. Samuel wasn't; he had missed his opportunity to flee the country and there was only one thing left to do. He packed up his bags and books and arranged to go back home.

It was early April and spring had started arriving in London with warmer days, fresh green leaves on the trees, spring flowers appearing in the parks and gardens. As the coach travelled northwards the skies became grey again, the branches still leafless, the roadsides muddy and bare. The coach was dirty and draughty, the rooms in the inns they stopped at cold and unwelcoming. An old man sitting opposite Samuel began sneezing when they left the city, pulling out a series of disgusting looking handkerchiefs from his pockets to wipe his nose and blow it noisily. By the next day he had started coughing and wheezing, gasping for air and spitting out of the window.

Samuel, wrapped in his greatcoat, did his best to stay as far away as possible from him but it was no good. Soon he was sneezing and coughing as well, turning hot and cold and feeling rotten, along with many of the other passengers.

Nothing, though, could prevent his heart from lifting at the first sight of the familiar grey mountains on the horizon, the craggy outcrops and shaggy sheep, the tumbling brooks, the forbidding dark stone of the buildings.

It was good to be back in the land he loved so much. If only home didn't also mean Sara.

Chapter Twenty

Sara could see Samuel was ill the moment she saw him staggering up the path. Her heart sank. The last three months had been drama free. Once she had got used to the idea that Samuel would be gone for a long time, life had gone on smoothly in the same old routine. She hadn't been totally surprised when Samuel said he wasn't going away after all. She had long since given up believing anything he said. Neither was she surprised when she heard that Tom Wedgwood had gone with someone else. Samuel was always falling out with his friends. She didn't know how they put up with him. But *she* had no choice; it was her duty. The man struggling up to the house would bring nothing but chaos into her life but she was his wife. She pulled a cloak on over her day dress and pinafore and hurried out to meet him.

"Papa! It's Papa!" She heard Hartley's voice behind her. "Papa! Papa!" Derwent chimed in.

"Stay inside boys!" she said sharply. "It's cold out here and Papa's not well."

But she couldn't keep them away from Samuel forever. They crowded around him as he took his coat and boots off, struggled to get onto his lap, into his arms. Of course, it was the novelty, but Sara felt a stab of jealousy. *She* was the one who looked after them all the time. She never had a welcome like that when she came back from town. They took her for granted.

"I feel so bad," Samuel said. "I shall have to go to bed."

"Of course, of course. Come on. Leave Papa alone, boys. He's not well. He will see you later when he's better."

The doctor was called. "It's influenza," he said, shaking his head. "There's a lot around at the moment. He must stay in bed. Keep the room warm. No draughts. Light food only."

Sara knew the drill. Back to nursing Samuel. She had done it so many times before. Predictably, the illness inflamed his joints as well. His hands and knees were stiff and swollen and she had to help him in and out of bed to use the pot. By then Derwent was beginning to sneeze and cough, then one of the servants and finally Sara herself succumbed. Mrs Railton was already working for a young mother who had just had a baby and there was so much illness about that many of the other nurses in the area were busy too, so Sara struggled on with Mrs Wilson from next door to help out. It was a dreadful month; Hartley was the only one who didn't go down with it, running around as boisterously as usual, wondering why everyone was in their rooms.

"I've been back for weeks and Wordsworth hasn't been to see me once," Samuel moaned. "I'd go and see him if he were ill."

"Mary's baby is due in three months," Sara said. "He's obviously worried he'd give her your flu. Most people *think* of their wives and loved ones."

She hadn't been to see the Wordsworths and they didn't visit her. Samuel was their only link and with him away there was no point in pretending a friendship that didn't exist. But Samuel talked about them all the time. She had been surprised when he told her that their baby was due in July.

"That was quick work!" she laughed. "Edith would have given anything to conceive that quickly."

"They're going to move house in June," Samuel said.

"Just before the baby comes?"

"Dorothy says they'll have a big wash when they get there, ready for the baby. 'Our baby', she calls it." He laughed. "As though all three of them were having it!"

Sara laughed with him. She always liked it when he found something denigrating to say about the Wordsworths. "I thought they might move house with the baby coming," she said. "That cottage is far too small for children. Where are they going? Somewhere in the village?"

"She doesn't say. They were talking of somewhere nearer Keswick. I wish they'd come here. There's plenty of room."

"It would never work, Samuel, you know it wouldn't," she said quickly. "Anyway, I thought you were going away. Then we'd all be stuck with each other."

"It's a big house."

"With one kitchen and one wash house. One household to run with two mistresses, three with Dorothy. It would be impossible."

Samuel sighed. "We could make another kitchen. A whole separate suite of rooms. But they're coming into their inheritance soon. I suppose they'll be able to afford a bigger place of their own. Dorothy says she's already bought new clothes."

"Dorothy? New clothes?" Sara could hardly believe it. "Lucky her, " she went on. She couldn't remember the last time she had bought new clothes. Her old ones were turned and altered and mended as much as she could.

Wordsworth's next letter wasn't so much to Samuel's liking. "He wants me to give him my thoughts on *The Recluse*," he grumbled, tossing the letter to one side disparagingly.

"I thought that's what you do," Sara said. "Criticise each other's work, suggest improvements." She picked the letter up, smoothed it and put it back on the desk. He'd be turning everything upside down to look for it later.

"It's the way he says it," he said tetchily. "I'm not his servant. He should come over here and ask me himself. We could discuss it properly."

He had started having nightmares again, waking up in the night screaming. Sara's sympathy for him had worn thin but she was worried he would wake the children so night after night she went in, as she had so many times before, and put her arms around his shaking shoulders, shushing him as though he were Hartley or Derwent, while he clung to her.

"It was dreadful, Sara," he sobbed one night. "You and I were dead but we wanted to find the children. We didn't know where they were; we looked everywhere. Then I was back at school and my hand was hurting…" He looked at his hand as if to see if it was damaged. "I'd touched something corrosive. Other boys were peeking at me. And girls, the nurses' daughters I think, they said to me, 'You're not at school.' I said, 'Yes, I am, I'm only twenty.' Then I remembered I was thirty, and not at school, and I was confused."

"Dreams, Samuel, only dreams," Sara said, as she had said so many times before. "Go back to sleep."

"Stay with me Sara, until I go to sleep."

Sara was tired. Baby Sara would wake for a feed at five, then she might catch a few more precious minutes before Derwent woke and then Hartley. But if she left Samuel now he would be calling out for her again. "Yes, of course," she said. "Now settle down. I'll be right here next to you."

Sara's day revolved around the children. Now, with the warmer weather coming, she could send the boys outside to play and put baby Sara's crib outside the back door while she pegged out the washing.

Sara was a lovely baby, plump and pretty. If the boys were jealous they seldom showed it. Hartley was seven now; the baby was little more than a nuisance when she cried. Derwent, not yet three so still little more than a baby himself, had more reason to resent the attention lavished on his little sister, but he was a placid little boy and accepted easily whatever happened around him.

News that Mary's baby had been born took them all by surprise. It was 18th June. The Wordsworths had been married on 4th October. Sara counted it up on her fingers: barely eight months. Of course, Mary might have her dates wrong. Sara often got muddled with hers. Or the baby could be premature. The alternative was unthinkable; the Hutchinsons might be a free and easy lot but Sara couldn't imagine Mary's brothers allowing her to be alone, unchaperoned, with Wordsworth. And even if they had, it was hard for Sara to imagine the dour man she knew getting carried away by sexual passion.

The baby was a boy. "John," Samuel told her. "After their brother. Dorothy says he's stout and healthy."

"So not premature, obviously," Sara thought.

"And sleeps through the night."

"Already?" Sara asked, sceptically.

"A paragon apparently." Samuel laughed. "They've got rid of the nurse already. Dorothy is doing all the looking after."

"Mary's lucky, having family to help her," Sara said.

"I'm still hoping Southey and Edith will come up."

"I don't think they will, Samuel. Not now they have Margaret. They won't want to risk the journey. "

Another visitor turned up, however, arriving, like all Samuel's friends did, with no prior warning. Sara recognised the young man from a distance. "William Hazlitt is here!" she called to Samuel. "Were you expecting him?"

"No… Well, yes… Well, you know…"

She had last seen Hazlitt when he had visited them in Nether Stowey just after she had had Berkeley. He had been barely twenty then, shy, unassuming and in awe of Samuel and Wordsworth. A different young man stood before her now. Where before he could scarcely look her in the face now his eyes swept over her whole body appreciatively. "Mrs Coleridge, it's a pleasure."

Unused to compliments, Sara found herself blushing but when the maid came in with a tray of tea she saw the same admiring look fall on her instead. She was a pretty dark-eyed girl of about fifteen and she too reddened under his gaze, the china rattling on the tray as she put it down on the table.

Hazlitt's opinions had changed too and he wasn't afraid to express them. Sara heard his raised voice from the study. "You, sir, a committed republican like myself, now to flaunt these lily-livered liberal views in the *Morning Post*!"

It didn't sound like a serious argument though. She knew Samuel enjoyed nothing better than what he called 'debate' and she heard him laugh before he replied, "I am older than you are, my young friend. I see things differently."

Samuel and Hazlitt had met when Samuel was preaching in the Unitarian chapel in Shrewsbury. At this time, before the Wedgwood brothers had offered an annuity of £150 for Samuel to be free to write, he was intending becoming a minister. The same career had been mapped out for Hazlitt by his father, who was minister of the chapel in nearby Wem. He sent Hazlitt to the Unitarian college in Hackney in London to prepare for the ministry. The college taught the classics, maths, history, government and science in addition to religion and by the end of two years Hazlitt found he had lost his faith and changed his mind about his career. He didn't want to upset his father by telling him outright but left before doing any of the preparation for ministry.

His education left him with a burning interest in liberty and the rights of man and the importance of the individual in effecting change in the world by sticking to their principles. He hated tyranny of any sort and felt it important to speak out against it, at whatever cost.

Back at home, Hazlitt told them, he began to take an interest in contemporary politics as well and to delve further into the philosophy he had begun to study at Hackney. "I read all the philosophers," he said. "John Locke, David Hartley, George Berkeley, David Hume. Oh, and the French ones: Claude Adrien Helvétius, Étienne Bonnot de Condillac, the Marquis de Condorcet and Baron d'Holbach."

The only two Sara recognised were David Hartley and George Berkeley and that was only because Samuel had named two of their children after them, but she saw Samuel nod in recognition. "And I decided to become a philosopher," Hazlitt was saying, grandly. "It's the idea of man as a social and political animal that really interests me. And the philosophy of the mind."

Samuel leant across the table. "And what about Rousseau?"

Sara's interest began to wane as they argued on and on, bringing up other ideas and names of other great thinkers like Edmund Burke and William Godwin. "I'm not entirely sure that I agree with Godwin's philosophy," Hazlitt said.

Sara saw Samuel give a little start of surprise to hear the great Godwin questioned, though she had spent enough time with Samuel and Godwin to know that Samuel himself often disagreed with his views. "But he gives me a lot to think about," Hazlitt went on.

It amazed Sara how much talk could go on incessantly about things that really didn't seem to matter much. Talk wouldn't pay the bills.

"I'm working on a treatise," Hazlitt was saying. "On the natural disinterestedness of the human mind. I intend to disprove the idea that man is naturally selfish. Have you heard of Joseph Fawcett? He's a retired Unitarian minister and a keen reformer like Godwin. He's helped me with my reading. He says I must read and dissect works like *Paradise Lost* and *Tristram Shandy*."

"You were lucky," Sara said, "being able to devote all your time to studying."

"Yes, but I knew it couldn't go on," Hazlitt said. "My father would expect me to earn my own living. I spent some time with my older brother John in London. He's an artist, he studied under Joshua Reynolds, you know, the great portrait painter."

Samuel nodded.

"Well, my brother is very talented and earning a very good living from painting miniatures. So I asked him to give me lessons. I went to picture galleries and I began to realise I did actually have a talent myself. It comes from my mother's side of the family. I do portraits in the style of Rembrandt and people pay well. The one I did of my father was exhibited by the Royal Academy and last year I had a commission to copy several works of the Old Masters in the Louvre in Paris. It was hard work. I caught a glimpse of Napoleon while I was there." His eyes shone with passion. "The man who rescued the common man from the oppression of the monarchy."

It was a portrait commission that had brought him up to the north and he had taken advantage of it to come and see Samuel.

"I'll do one of you and Wordsworth if you like."

"Oh, I don't know..." Samuel said.

"Or one of your children? Hartley maybe? He has such an interesting face; I'd love to capture his expression. There's a lot of vulnerability, thoughtfulness…"

"Oh yes, Samuel," Sara said. "I'd love one of Hartley." She had noticed how kind Hazlitt was to the children. It was unusual for a young man in his twenties. He got down on the floor and played with Hartley's toy soldiers with him, shielding them from Derwent's clumsy interference and making lots of realistic fighting noises. Even Hartley could be easily persuaded to sit still for him.

"I don't try to flatter my subjects," he warned. "I like to show them as they truly are."

"That's fine," Sara said. "You should do it, Samuel. If not one of you then one of Hartley."

If only Samuel would realise, like Hazlitt and Southey did, that money had to be earned somehow. The Wedgwood annuity should have been enough to live on but it never stretched to cover all Samuel's habits: the books, the travel and the opium. Especially the opium. She had no idea if any of Samuel's friends knew the extent of Samuel's addiction. It was something she never dared ask him. And she was too loyal to tell anyone, even Edith.

He said it helped him sleep but she was sure it was the opium that gave him nightmares; it certainly played havoc with his bowels and his stomach and made him lethargic. Or maybe he had always been lazy and she hadn't noticed. To hear him speak you'd think he did nothing but work. There was always some project on hand, some new and brilliant idea he'd had.

"I'm working on a vast metaphysical work at present," she heard him tell Hazlitt. "*An Instrument of Practical Reasoning.* I shall preface it with a twelve-part introduction to the history of logic, from Plato and Aristotle to Descartes, Condillac and Hartley. I shall then write my own *Organum*, a detailed analysis of all possible modes of true, probable and false reasoning, arranged philosophically. It should run to 500 pages. I could have the first 250 pages ready at a fortnight's notice."

Sara saw the look of scepticism on Hazlitt's face. Did Samuel really think anyone would believe he could do it?

Then there was his idea for a six- or eight-volume history of British literature, a *Bibliotheca Britannica,* which would include extracts from the British poets and prose writers together with their biographies, as well as a history of metaphysics, theology, medicine, alchemy, surgery and chemistry. "I'll get experts to contribute," he said. "Walter Scott could write on the Scottish poets for example. I've written to Southey about it. He thinks it's an excellent idea. And Longman says he will publish it."

But these were long-term schemes. None would bring in the immediate money they needed to live on. The next time Sara had some cash she took £10 out, put it in an envelope and locked it away in her desk, an emergency fund to be used only as a last resort.

Hazlitt stayed on in the area through the summer, a regular visitor to Greta Hall.

Their landlord and neighbour, Mr Jackson, went away in July and August and Sara was impressed when she heard that his side of the house was to be rented by Sir George and Lady Beaumont.

"Oh, I met them in the winter," Samuel said blithely when she passed the news on to him excitedly.

"You *met* them. A baronet and his wife?"

"They attended one of the literary evenings I went to in London."

"They're interested in literature? You should keep in with people like that Samuel. Maybe they would give you their patronage."

"They're more interested in Wordsworth," Samuel said.

"Well, you need to work on them, Samuel. It's important for our future."

She invited them round as soon as she could. Lady Beaumont was gushing but underneath the society sheen she had a keen interest in literature and music. Sir George was cool and aloof but by the end of their visit Sara saw him begin to warm to Samuel's particular brand of charm. He nodded with interest as Samuel churned out the same plans he had expostulated to Hazlitt.

"I enjoyed your article in the *Morning Post* on the situation with France," Sir George said.

"Just the first in a series I intend to write," Samuel said, "*The Men and the Times.* England shouldn't be afraid of standing alone against the continent. We must think for ourselves. Let France bribe or puzzle all Europe into a confederacy against us, I will not fear for my country. The words of Isaiah will be truly prophetic: 'they trod the wine-press alone and of the nations there was none with them.'"

Sir George and Lady Beaumont seemed very taken with the Wordsworths.

"It's a long way for you to travel each time you want to see each other," Sir George said. "Is there any land for sale around here? I was thinking, maybe, I could have a house built for them nearer you. Somewhere more spacious. I don't know how they manage in that poky little cottage."

"I can find out," Samuel was saying just as Sara said, "They love that little cottage." She was quite sure Wordsworth would never accept charity, even if it was presented as some sort of loan, and Samuel was the only one who wanted them to live closer to each other.

With Hazlitt and then the Beaumonts needing entertaining at home, Samuel had spent less time than usual out walking on his beloved mountains. Sara sensed his restlessness and she wasn't surprised when he began to talk of going away again.

"Malta or Madeira," he told her. "Somewhere with a naval base. I could get an administrative post."

"Are you sure?" Sara asked doubtfully.

"I've written all those articles on foreign affairs," he said confidently. "I'm sure they would take me on as a civil servant. And I have contacts. There's John

Stoddart in Malta. I know him well. He's just been made Judge Advocate over there. It makes sense, doesn't it? To live and work somewhere warm. It would cure me of illness."

It wasn't just his joints that troubled him now; he was breathless and wheezing a lot of the time and the doctor had diagnosed atonic gout. Maybe a long spell abroad would be the answer to all their problems. If he wasn't in pain, he wouldn't have to take opium and there would be more money available. And a break from the Wordsworths and Sarah Hutchinson might cure him of his infatuation with all of them. Away from their influence he could work and write. He would come back a changed man. She could only hope.

Nothing more was said about the idea for a while and she wondered if he'd dropped it, like he had done so many others.

So she was surprised when he returned from a visit to Grasmere with quite a different scheme. "Wordsworth and Dorothy are planning a tour of Scotland," he said.

"So soon after the baby?" Sara asked incredulously.

"Oh, Mary doesn't need Wordsworth around. And he needs a break from domestication."

"But she needs Dorothy, surely? I thought Dorothy couldn't bear to be parted from the precious child?"

"Well, she's a bit worried about it," he admitted. "But Sarah is coming to stay with Mary while they go."

She saw his face light up with pleasure, as it always did, at the mention of that hated woman's name. But at least he wasn't suggesting he stayed behind so he could go and see her. "And Dorothy's always wanted to go to Scotland," he went on. "It will be time on her own with me and Wordsworth, just like old times."

So it was Samuel's idea really. The chances of it all going ahead were remote. Dorothy would decide not to go, she would miss the baby too much and they changed so quickly at that age. And Wordsworth wouldn't go without her. But the next time Wordsworth came over she heard him talking enthusiastically about it. "We'll go up to Carlisle first, then on to Longtown and then Glasgow," she heard him tell Samuel. "That's the route I took two years ago when I went with Montagu and the Rush family. I'm dying to show you and Dorothy all the places. You'll love it."

Sara remembered Basil Montagu. Wordsworth and Dorothy had been looking after his four-year-old son when they came to live at Alfoxton Park near Nether Stowey. Wordsworth had met Montagu eight years before in London. Montagu was a widower. His family hadn't approved of his marriage and then his wife had died in childbirth, leaving him with a son to look after and support on his own. When Wordsworth and Dorothy set up house together at Racedown Lodge in Dorset, Montagu paid them to look after and tutor little Basil. Wordsworth and Dorothy weren't the best of surrogate parents but in the end Montagu couldn't afford to pay them anyway and little Basil had to go back to his father. Montagu stayed in touch with

Wordsworth, however, and when he became a successful barrister he paid Wordsworth back part of the money he owed him and invited him to his wedding to Miss Laura Rush, the daughter of a wealthy Suffolk landowner. The marriage was to be in Glasgow and the wedding party, travelling up in two carriages, picked up Wordsworth on the way through.

"It was the sort of journey I hate," Wordsworth was saying. "Cooped up in carriages with Montagu, the Rushes and their six children. But they were making a tour of the area while they were there and I didn't know if I'd ever get another chance to see Scotland. This time we'll do it properly. And maybe I'll get some inspiration. I haven't written anything new for ages."

Wordsworth wanted it to be a walking tour but he was worried Samuel wouldn't be up to it. "He's bought a jaunting car," Samuel told Sara, "and he'll drive."

Wordsworth brought it over to show them. It was an odd-looking vehicle, a low open cart, with a dicky box for the driver, hanging seats for three people either side and space in the middle for children and luggage. Samuel looked doubtfully at the stout, ancient-looking horse Wordsworth had bought to pull it.

"It was a good price," Wordsworth laughed. "I'm told it has spirit."

Dorothy and Mary had come over too, sitting on the hanging seats either side with Mary holding baby Johnny in her arms. Of course Hartley and Derwent were desperate to have a ride so Sara let the maid take them, the two boys wedged safely in the pit in the middle.

Wordsworth brought it over again a few days later and asked Sara if she would like to ride part of the way back with them. "Oh, Mama, Mama, can we come too? *Please, please,*" Hartley begged. They set off, the horse going at such a slow pace and Sara's feet so close to the ground that she could have jumped off easily and walked alongside.

Soon it was time for Samuel to leave his family once more. "I'll stay the night at Grasmere before we go," he said. "So we can make an early start." It was a fine evening and Sara stood at the doorway in the warm sunshine, watching him go. Six weeks. It was the middle of August already. Summer would be well and truly over by the time he came back. How long before he would say he had to get away for the winter? Would he ever settle down and stay at home? Did she even want him to?

Chapter Twenty-One

Samuel was hoping to find Sarah Hutchinson at the cottage when he arrived. "She couldn't come," Mary explained. "She was needed to help with the harvest. Joanna's here instead," she added jauntily, although he could see she was disappointed. Joanna was a good-hearted, generous girl but she was much younger and had never been as close to Mary as Sarah was. The suspicion that Sarah was avoiding him darted through Samuel's mind but he dismissed it. She would surely have been able to tolerate his company for one evening in order to see her new nephew and spend six weeks with the sister she loved so much.

They were sitting in the garden having tea when they heard the sound of voices coming down the lane towards them.

"It sounds like Rogers," Wordsworth said. Samuel's heart sank. He had met Samuel Rogers two years ago when he had arrived on Wordsworth's doorstep with a letter of introduction from Josiah Wedgwood. Rogers was a well-known published poet who came from a wealthy banking family but Samuel found him a bit of a bore. It turned out that he and his sister were also on their way up to Scotland on a tour. Samuel could see that Wordsworth enjoyed Rogers' company and for one awful moment he thought he might suggest they travel together but nothing was said.

"I don't know what you see in him," he said after they had left. "He's so jealous of everyone and everything."

"He does have a petty-minded attitude," Wordsworth admitted. "But I don't see why it bothers you so much."

But their visit had put Samuel in a thoroughly bad mood and he went to bed feeling grumpy and unsettled.

The following morning, the day they were due to set off, Dorothy woke up with one of her bilious attacks. "She can't possibly travel like this," Wordsworth said as Joanna hurried from her room with a foul-smelling bowl covered with a cloth. Samuel had slept badly: he was used to disturbed nights with baby Sara but Greta Hall was a big house, he only heard her distantly and usually managed to get back to sleep. The cottage was tiny, baby Johnny's ear-splitting cries from Wordsworth's bedroom on the ground floor resounded through the whole house, and it seemed to Samuel that he woke nearly every hour.

The next morning they finally set off, Wordsworth perched up on the dicky box, Dorothy hunched over, holding her stomach, on the seat next to Samuel. By the time they reached Keswick, Samuel was feeling very bad. Maybe it was sitting still in one position for so long, but his knees were locked solid and swollen up. Soon his feet became painful too.

"It's my gout," he told Wordsworth. "It's so bad. I think I might have a paralytic stroke."

"Maybe you shouldn't come," Wordsworth said.

But the alternative, going home to Sara, was so much worse.

"I'll be all right," Samuel said determinedly, reaching for his opium bottle.

He and Dorothy had both decided to keep a journal. After all, they didn't know when they might get another chance to do a tour like this. Samuel wasn't sure what he would do with his; maybe he could write it up for publication when they returned. Dorothy said she would write hers up properly too. "I think my friend Mrs Clarkson would be interested to read it," she said.

They stayed the first night in Hesket Newmarket at the Queens Head, a basic sort of inn, clean enough but with a spitting pot full of sawdust in the main parlour. Portraits of the owner's children hung either side of the fireplace, both dressed in their best clothes, the young lad with a parrot in his hand, the young girl holding a rose. Their round goggle eyes seemed to follow Samuel round the room.

Samuel was pleased when they arrived in Carlisle the next day in time for the trial of the infamous forger and bigamist John Hatfield, seducer of Mary Robinson, the Beauty of Buttermere. Having followed proceedings so closely and written the newspaper articles, Samuel had been hoping he could get to the trial. Wordsworth and Dorothy came with him to the court where they heard Hatfield given the death sentence.

"You should see if you can get an interview with him," Dorothy said.

Permission was granted and Dorothy waited outside while Samuel and Wordsworth went in to see him. Samuel couldn't get over how vain the man was, so proud of what he had done. "I shall never understand how anyone could behave like him," he said to Wordsworth.

While they had been in with him, Dorothy had started talking to a man who had been imprisoned for debt. "You'll never believe this!" she said excitedly when they came out. "This man was a sailor with our brother John when he was serving under our cousin Captain Wordsworth!"

Wordsworth and Samuel introduced themselves and also expressed their surprise at such an amazing coincidence. As they turned to leave Samuel saw Dorothy nudge Wordsworth and whisper something into his ear. Wordsworth reached into his pocket and unobtrusively passed the man a shilling.

From Carlisle they travelled on to Longtown and from there to Dumfries where, to their surprise, they ran into Rogers and his sister, who were staying in the same inn as them.

"Come and see us later on," Rogers said expansively. "When we're settled into our rooms."

"You two go," Samuel said to Wordsworth once they were on their own. "I don't think I can stand spending any more time with that man."

They didn't stay long. Wordsworth was keen to go and look for Robert Burns' grave. He had loved Burns' poetry since he was very young and had introduced Dorothy to it.

"We asked a local bookseller," Wordsworth said excitedly when they returned. "And he told us where to look in the churchyard. The grave has no marker."

"And we went to call on Mrs Burns afterwards," Dorothy said. "I couldn't believe she'd be living in such a dilapidated house. The maid said the family were at the seaside but she let us in. It wasn't much better inside. But scrupulously clean," she added approvingly.

They were still talking about it the next day. "You'd think they had family to help them out," Dorothy said worriedly.

"Or friends," Wordsworth agreed. "He was a great poet. His family shouldn't be left in penury."

Samuel wasn't particularly interested. "Doesn't this countryside remind you of the area around Gallow Hill?" he asked, hoping they would change the subject. With any luck Dorothy would start talking about Mary, then Sarah. He could say her name aloud, instead of having to whisper it in the darkness of his room or write it over and over again in his notebook.

"I suppose there's a vague similarity," Wordsworth said, looking around him.

"There's nothing we can do to help is there?" Dorothy said, picking up her conversation with Wordsworth as if Samuel hadn't spoken at all, and he realised they were back to worrying about the Burns family.

That evening he decided not to join them on their evening walk. "My knees are painful," he told them. The truth was, they didn't seem to need him; they were happier just with each other. He sat in his room, on his own, writing up his journal but he couldn't stop thinking of Sarah Hutchinson. He picked up his private notebook. "Oh, Asra," he wrote, "wherever I am, my heart aches for you."

It was so unfair. Wordsworth always had someone to be with, if it wasn't Mary it was Dorothy, while he had no one.

Samuel didn't think much of the Scots people. They were a dour race, he thought, who muttered in an accent he found hard to make out. The innkeepers were a surly bunch who looked at them suspiciously and it wasn't always easy to find accommodation for three people. In one inn there was only one room left. Samuel couldn't deprive Dorothy of a bed and Wordsworth was the only one who could share a room with her so he ended up sleeping on three chairs put together in the parlour.

The poverty in the countryside was appalling, worse than any they had seen in the Lakes. Many people went round barefoot and clothed in little more than rags. The houses were dirty and dilapidated, falling-down hovels, with scrawny starving children sitting listlessly outside.

After the initial novelty of the jaunting car had worn off, it became a nightmare: there was no shelter from the wind or rain and the wheels made a creaking, grating sound that set his teeth on edge. By the end of the day he was stiff and painful from the damp and the cramped position.

"I don't know how much longer I can go on with this," he grumbled. "I'm in so much pain."

"You've taken some laudanum, have you?" Dorothy asked.

"Yes, but it's not enough," he said. "Dr Beddoes has brought out a new gout medicine. I shall have to try it."

"You should stop the laudanum altogether," Wordsworth said severely. "It's the cause of all your troubles. The more you take, the more you need. It *changes* you Samuel, makes you moody, upsets your stomach and bowels, gives you nightmares."

"But you're not in pain like I am," Samuel protested. "I *can't* give it up. If it weren't for this accursed weather… It has the same effect on me as the little old lady and gentleman in one of those weather vanes."

Wordsworth was keen for them to go to the Falls of Clyde at Corra Linn, which he had visited two years ago with Montagu and the Rush family. They were shown the way by a girl of about twelve, who didn't bother to hide her yawns of boredom as Wordsworth and Dorothy stood in raptures in front of the waterfall. Their next stop was Hamilton Palace.

"The Duke of Hamilton has a fine picture gallery," Wordsworth told them. They walked up to the front door but the porter looked them up and down disdainfully. "I can't let you in," he said.

"But I came two years ago," Wordsworth protested. "With my friends, the Montagus and Rushes."

The man raised his eyes sceptically and Samuel suddenly realised how they must look. When Wordsworth visited last time he had been with a wedding party, well dressed, in a smart carriage. Now they looked like peasants. No wonder the man wouldn't let them in.

"Well, could we walk in the grounds?" Wordsworth asked. "I remember they were beautiful. I would like to show my sister and my friend."

"Absolutely not," the porter said. "The Duke's family would be most unhappy to see you walking about."

They travelled on to Glasgow, a dirty, noisy, busy city, where they didn't bother to stop, heading on instead up the west bank of Loch Lomond, which reminded them of Ullswater. Wordsworth's plan was to cross Lake Lomond on the ferry but first he wanted to take them up to see the Trossachs. Here, the scenery was stunning, the hillsides covered in heather ranging from white to pale purple, dark purple, crimson and rose. "Like fabric," Samuel murmured, trying to capture the sight in words in his notebook. "Shot silk and ribbons."

Huge mountain peaks towered on the distant horizon, waterfalls tumbled down the hills amongst the rocks and stunted trees. They drove on until it began to get dark.

"We should find somewhere to stay soon," Wordsworth said. But there was no inn on the roadside.

"We've come too far," he said anxiously. "We can't go on much further in the dark but we'll never get back either."

"We'll have to ask at one of the cottages," Dorothy said. "It's the only thing we can do."

They knocked on the door of the next house they came to. It took a while to convince the couple that they were simple travellers who just needed something to eat and somewhere to rest but eventually they let them in. The woman in particular spoke with such a strong accent that it was hard to make out a word she said but she made them tea and brought out barley bread, cheese and butter. By that time the couple seemed to have changed their minds about them and allowed them to stay the night.

The next morning they went back to the ferry station. It was a misty morning, grey and chill. The thought of a trip on a cold, damp boat was more than Samuel could bear. Wordsworth and Dorothy got on board and Wordsworth looked up at Samuel. "Come on then," he said.

"No," said Samuel. Maybe it was childish but suddenly he was fed up with being ordered around by Wordsworth, doing everything he said, according to his Grand Plan.

"Don't be silly," Wordsworth said, sternly. "Come on, the boat is leaving."

"No, I'm not coming."

He strode off triumphantly, not even turning to watch the boat leave, a great feeling of freedom surging through him. He would go back up to the Trossachs; it was beautiful up there and on his own he would be as free as air. He could go where he liked, stop when he wanted, not have to listen all day to Dorothy reciting Wordsworth's poetry or reading bits of her journal aloud. Neither of them had asked to hear *his* journal. He took it out now. The small square notebook had become squashed and misshapen from having been squeezed into his pocket in the damp weather. Trying to write on the bumpy road had made the writing almost illegible. Much of it was written in pencil, smudged with finger marks and smeared with rain and mud, but he would keep on with it.

It was evening when he returned to the ferry station and waited for the ferry to come in. Wordsworth and Dorothy had met an artist from Edinburgh on board and the ferryman offered all four of them accommodation at the ferry house for the night.

It was a primitive one-roomed croft, the walls black and glistening from the thick peat smoke that filled the room. They had a good meal though, cooked on the leaping flames of the fire. Samuel's shoes were wet through. If he had known he would be doing serious walking he would have brought his walking boots. Now he thrust his feet right up to the warm fire to dry them. Suddenly there was a strong smell of smouldering leather and looking down he saw that his shoes were on fire. He struggled to get them off. One came off fairly easily but by the time he had got out of the other one his foot and the front of his calf were burnt and his shoes, the only pair he had brought with him, had split along the seams.

The artist was good company and after a day apart Samuel felt more inclined to be friendly with Wordsworth and Dorothy. They sat and talked about what they had each done until it was time to go to bed. Dorothy was shown up to the hayloft above the one room and Wordsworth, Samuel and the artist were given blankets and shown out to the barn to sleep on the hay.

The next morning, having made his protest, Samuel felt obliged to go with Wordsworth and Dorothy by boat to the end of the lake. But he kept thinking of his day of freedom, the steady rhythm of walking at his own pace, the fresh air, the exhilaration he had felt. Sitting on a cold, damp boat while the scenery slid by just didn't appeal to him but he could see how much Wordsworth and Dorothy were enjoying it. He was glad when they reached their destination and he could get out and stretch his legs.

But as they walked it began raining again and Samuel's feet were soon wet through from his leaking shoes. They sheltered when they could under the dripping trees but by the time they reached the next ferry point they were thoroughly soaked. A tiny tumbledown shack stood by the jetty. There was no one else around. Wordsworth pushed at the rickety door hopefully. Samuel thought of a warm fireside, someone there who could give them hot tea maybe, even though he could see there was no smoke rising from the chimney. The air inside struck damp and chill. Cold raindrops dripped dismally from the leaky roof, falling in great puddles on the floor. They waited and waited while the rain fell incessantly and they grew colder and colder. Finally the ferry arrived.

"We've been waiting for hours," Wordsworth complained.

"We had to take the folk to the preaching," The ferryman said as Highlanders and their children flooded off the boat, talking in their unintelligible tongue.

They were so grateful to be on their way that they didn't bother to ask what preaching or where it was or why the ferry had to be taken up with it rather than running its scheduled service.

The next day Samuel woke up knowing he didn't want to go on. Wordsworth and Dorothy were enjoying themselves. He wasn't. He was a nuisance to them.

"It's all too much for me," he said to Wordsworth. "The damp is making my rheumatism so much worse. If I go any further it will be the death of me. You two go on; I'll walk back to Stirling and get a coach back home from Edinburgh."

They divided their money. "I don't need much," Samuel said. "Six guineas will be enough. You'll need more, with the two of you and the rest of the tour."

"Thank you," Wordsworth said. "We plan to go on westwards then come back via Melrose to visit Walter Scott."

The moment they had parted Samuel felt relief flooding through him. He didn't know how he would have stood another day of cold and rain. In a boat or in the open carriage, it made no difference. The long walk to Stirling would be worth it to get into the shelter of a covered carriage.

He took the ferry back to East Tarbet. It was still raining, the drops of rain falling on the pale surface of the lake like dancing nymphs or fairies. In the town he arranged to have most of his luggage sent on to Edinburgh before setting off. The moment he started walking he felt his spirits lift and his body respond.

The wind and the rain eased and the mist lifted from the mountains. The countryside that had seemed damp and drear suddenly became more appealing. Maybe he wouldn't go straight back to Edinburgh. He could take his own tour at his own pace, free from the confines of that dratted jaunting car, could rest when he wanted, stay as long as he liked, it would be easier to find a room at an inn now it was just one person and he didn't have to slavishly go along with everything Wordsworth had planned.

He headed north again, along the line of Scottish forts to Inverness. It was the end of August, it should have been warm, but although the rain and wind had stopped it was still cool and he wished he had brought his warm coat. His burnt shoes flapped at every step and let in water but he pressed on regardless, ignoring the pain in his feet and legs, the tiredness that overwhelmed him. He had very few clothes with him and he soon he began to look and smell like a tramp: dirty, dishevelled, covered in mud, the splits in his shoes getting worse and worse. The six guineas he had taken for his share had never been meant for a tour like this and after he had paid for accommodation he was left with very little for food so he managed on tea, porridge, beer and oatcakes.

He tried to buy new shoes in every town he came to but there were none ready-made and he had no time to wait for handmade ones. He wrote to Sara asking her to borrow £10 from someone, anyone, and send it to Perth, the nearest big town he would reach, so he would be able to buy some decent food.

Strangers were rare in the Highlands, tourists on foot like him even more so. At Fort Augustus he was arrested and charged with spying. Even up here there were rumours of a French invasion and he had been seen scribbling notes in his notebook.

"I'm just a traveller," he protested. "A poet and a philosopher. This is my journal, look: descriptions that's all, phrases and words… " And the distances between towns… He could see that might look suspicious. He kept his own private notebook well hidden. Much of it was written in Latin but even so no one was allowed to read it. Eventually, after a lot of huffing and puffing by officials and a lot of muttering in Gaelic that Samuel couldn't understand, he was allowed to go free.

By the time he reached Fort William he was totally exhausted. He collapsed in the street and had to ask a passer-by to give him his arm and help him to the nearest inn. When he was told it was full he had to find his way, alone this time, to the next one. Tears were running down his face by the time he saw the inn sign swinging slowly in the wind and he burst into the parlour, sobbing uncontrollably. At the same time he felt a churning in his bowels and had to rush from the room clutching his stomach. He had never had such a bad bout of diarrhoea. Maybe he had drunk some bad water. Or maybe it was just because he had been eating so badly. Usually he would take opium to relieve it but after what Wordsworth had said he was making a supreme effort to cut down on it.

The effects of withdrawal were horrendous: he broke down in hysterical sobbing attacks, shaking all over as if he were having a fit. His nightmares returned, only worse than ever. He dreaded going to sleep, knowing the terrors that would follow, and woke up every night screaming. Here, there was no Sara to comfort him, only his landlord and fellow guests to yell curses at him or hammer on the bedroom door.

He jotted down the distances he had travelled from the signposts between places and added them up at the end of each day. By the time he reached Perth on 11th September, eight days after he had set off, he had walked 263 miles.

He had been writing to Sara and his friends regularly and letters from them followed him round from place to place. The letters he opened at Perth changed all his plans: Southey's baby daughter Margaret, just eleven months old, had died after a short but dreadfully painful illness. Not knowing what else to do, Southey had brought Edith up to Greta Hall to be with Sara. Samuel threw his bag onto the floor of his room, asked for pen and paper to be sent up and sat down to write a letter straight away. "Oh dear friend!" he wrote. "It is idle to talk of what I feel. I am stunned at present. And this beginning to write makes a beginning of living feeling within me. Whatever comfort I can be to you, I will… My children shall be yours 'til it pleases God to send you another."

He abandoned all plans to travel further north. Southey needed him. He must go back home.

Chapter Twenty-Two

Sara knew only too well what Edith was going through. And at least she had a loving husband to comfort her; when Berkeley died Sara had been all alone. It was the biggest resentment in her marriage, the one she could never, would never, get over.

Poor Edith. Poor Southey. They had waited six years for a baby and she had been taken away from them.

"It was terrible Sara, terrible," Edith sobbed. "We thought she was just teething. But the fever increased. She had fits. She died in such dreadful pain."

"I know, I know," Sara said. Useless to tell Edith that Berkeley had gone through the same. It wouldn't help.

She had longed to see Edith again, but not like this. She and Southey were shadows of their former selves. But Southey would pull through; she wasn't so sure of Edith, always prone to depression, now worse than Sara had ever seen her.

"I had to get her away," Southey said. "The house in Bristol just kept reminding her of the baby.

And my mother had died there, too. It was awful. You two have always been so close. And your baby is much the same age as Margaret. I thought that I could graft her into the wound while it is still fresh."

It was a crazy idea, the sort of thing only a man would think. Edith had been distraught when she saw baby Sara, so nearly the same age as the baby she had lost, so closely related to her.

"You look so well," Southey had said to Sara when he first saw her. But compared with Edith, anyone would look well. She was so thin, so wan, so worn out, like a wraith.

"I don't want another baby," she sobbed to Sara. "Not when there's a chance I might lose it again."

"I felt like that too," Sara said. "After I'd lost Berkeley. But I went on to have Derwent and Sara. Nothing replaces the one you've lost. But it helps."

"But you already had Hartley," Edith said. "I've got no one. We waited so long. It probably won't happen again."

"Whatever happens it's God's will," Sara said, "and we have to accept it."

Despite the circumstances, even though it was hard to wake each morning and go to sleep every night with the sound of Edith sobbing, despite all this, she was still pleased to have Edith with her again. She remembered only too well how she herself had suffered when Berkeley died, she simply wouldn't have coped without Edith and Southey. Edith had sat with her day after day while she cried non-stop, she had taken care of Hartley, only three years old at the time and bewildered by what was happening. Southey had made all the funeral arrangements for Berkeley and paid for them. This was her chance to give back something of what she owed them.

They had been there just over a week when Samuel came home, bursting through the door noisily, looking and smelling disgusting.

"Southey, my friend, my poor, poor friend." He flung his arms around him and Sara saw Southey, such a neat, dapper man, recoil slightly.

"I had such a journey," he exclaimed, flinging himself down on the nearest chair before Sara could find a cloth to cover it.

"Pooh, Papa, you smell!" Hartley yelled, holding his nose, but he and Derwent clambered up onto his lap anyway.

"Ah, *that's* why no one wanted to sit next to me on the coach!" Samuel laughed.

It was hard to resist Samuel when he was in one of his boisterous moods, even though it didn't seem quite fitting with the funereal atmosphere in the house. But maybe that's what they all needed, a bit of light relief.

Samuel held court at the dinner table with his stories of the Scottish, with their unintelligible dialects, and the places he had stayed.

"Sometimes I had to spend the night in a barn on the hay," he laughed.

"Like Jesus in the manger," Hartley said knowingly.

"We've been reading the Bible," Sara explained. She was keen to show Samuel she hadn't neglected Hartley's education.

"In Edinburgh I climbed up to Arthur's Seat at sunset," Samuel said. He loved nothing more than a rapt audience. "I watched the ships way below me in the harbour. They looked like your little wooden ones, Hartley, as though I could pluck them up out of the water and play with them. I counted fifty-four peaks on the mountains around me and, oh, there were hundreds of little houses below me in the valley, each one with a curl of smoke rising from them. One smoking chimney, one family sitting by the fireside."

He made it sound lovely. Sara could almost see herself there.

"I'm getting to like your mountains here," Southey said into the silence. Samuel's face lit up. "Really? You must stay. You know it's what I want."

"The view from your library window is just wonderful," Southey said. "The way the light shifts and shades, the sunshine slanting in great shafts, lighting up the books on the shelves. Oh, if only I were a painter rather than a poet. I would love to capture it."

Sara noticed he had avoided the subject of moving in. She couldn't allow herself to think it would ever happen. She and Edith had managed perfectly well sharing a kitchen and the wash house. They could live together easily. She didn't fool herself that Samuel would stay for long. With Edith and Southey here her life would be so much better. Southey could have one of the spare bedrooms for a study. He could write just as easily here as he could in Bristol. It would be a fresh start for both of them, like the fresh start *she* had always been hoping for. It never happened for her. But she could make it happen for them. Her gift to them. Here, away from all the old associations with Margaret, Edith would grow strong again. Southey liked to eat well. He had the money to buy good food. She would feed Edith up. She would soon be pregnant again.

"Tomorrow I will take you for a really long walk," Samuel was telling Southey. "Over the fells, through Borrowdale…"

She hoped it would give Southey a chance to talk about Margaret. Any mention of the baby sent Edith off into a fit of weeping so he couldn't talk about her when she was around. One afternoon when she had gone to bed he looked over at Sara with baby Sara asleep on her lap.

"Maybe it was a mistake bringing Edith up here," he said sadly. "I didn't realise how hard it would be for her to see you so…" He searched for the word. "Fulfilled," he said. "Yes, fulfilled and glowing with maternal happiness." He smiled over at her half-shyly but she accepted the compliment as it was meant. She had known Southey since he was a small boy; they could say anything to each other.

"The sight and smell and sounds of a baby," he went on wistfully. "*I* feel it too. It brings back such strong memories. She was lovely, you know, our

Margaret. Oh, I know every parent thinks that of their child, but she really was beautiful. I wish you could have seen her."

Sara's heart contracted as she remembered Berkeley. He was a beautiful baby too, quite her best-looking child, everyone commented on how perfect he was. Even the smallpox scarring didn't diminish his looks. She still missed him. She would always miss him. She remembered each birthday, each anniversary of his death.

"She had lovely grey eyes," Southey said, half to himself, "and a little flat nose. She was a big, strong girl. Strong-willed too." He gave a half-choked laugh. "The Passionate Pearl, we called her."

"Yes," said Sara. Edith had told her in her letters about the little girl's temper. Not even a year old and the whole household revolved around her and her tantrums. She was obviously indulged. A little brother or sister would have done her good.

Now that Samuel had come home visitors began to arrive again. The Wordsworths came with baby Johnny, grown into a great fat slug of a boy with tiny, beady eyes half-hidden in the rolls of fat in his face. Sara loved babies but even she tired of Dorothy's constant crowing about him.

"Just look at him. Only three months old but nearly as big as baby Sara. Does she sleep through the night? Johnny's such a good boy. He hardly ever cries."

"Oh, he has his moments," Mary laughed. "When Sarah was here he cried non-stop. It was the first time she'd seen him, too."

Sara saw Samuel redden. He hadn't told her Sarah Hutchinson had been to stay.

But she wasn't going to show that it bothered her at all. "How is your sister?" she asked.

"Not at all well," Mary said, shaking her head. "Her nerves, you know."

Samuel was looking awkward now. He got up and stared out of the window.

"Our brother has been given notice at the farm at Gallow Hill," Mary said, as if that explained everything, though everyone knew it was Samuel's fault poor Miss Hutchinson was in such a state.

It was a relief when the Wordsworths left but soon another visitor arrived. Hazlitt had come to paint Samuel's portrait. He might be easier to entertain than the Wordsworths but she had to keep a close eye on the maids, who seemed to find him irresistible. When he wasn't hanging around with them, he spent hours closeted with Samuel in his study, where she heard so much talking going on she wasn't sure how Hazlitt was able to do any painting.

Sara was relieved that her sister Mary hadn't come up with Southey and Edith. She had never got on with her like she did with Edith. Mary was a difficult lady, always causing trouble between people just for the sake of it, and since her husband died and his family refused to have anything to do with her or her son Robert, she had grown bitter towards everyone.

"She's looking for a position as a governess," Southey told her.

"She'd be good at that," Sara said encouragingly. She didn't see why Southey should be supporting Mary when a woman in her position was usually supported by her husband's family. But at least they hadn't taken her son away from her, which often happened in the circumstances. "She was always the brightest of the lot of us," Sara went on.

"I don't know about that," Southey said. "I always thought *you* were the cleverest."

"Much good it's done me," Sara muttered.

"You can educate the children," he said.

"Yes. Samuel should be doing it of course. But with his health…"

"Huh," Southey grunted.

"No, it's true," she protested. No one was going to say she had ever been disloyal to her husband. "If only he could get better, then everything else would just fall into place."

"The eternal optimist!" Southey laughed.

Sara was so sure that Mary would find a position in Bristol that her heart sank when a letter arrived from her.

"She'll have to come up here," Southey said after he had read it. "There are no positions available at all.

And she has nowhere to live, no one to turn to. We can't refuse her, Sara."

"No, of course," Sara said quickly. She couldn't turn her own sister from the door. Maybe she wouldn't stay long. But whatever happened, however long any of them stayed, Southey already contributed unquestioningly to the household costs and she knew he would add in a bit more for Mary and Robert.

Hartley was already looking forward to his cousin, only a year older than him, coming to stay. It was a big house, Sara thought, maybe Mary would keep herself to herself.

There had been a small but perceptible improvement in Edith since she had been with them. She could still be heard crying sometimes but she came downstairs more, spent time with Sara and the children and began to eat the meals that Sara put in front of her.

"It's because of you," Southey told Sara. "I don't know how I'd have coped without you."

When Hazlitt left at the end of September, Samuel said he was going to take Southey on a walking tour.

"I hope he'll be all right," Sara said to Edith. "Samuel's tours are very strenuous."

"I don't know how he does it," Edith said. "One moment he's crippled in bed and the next moment he's walking halfway across Scotland."

"I know. It's hard to understand," Sara agreed. "But he's trying this new medicine from Dr Beddoes, invented by a Mr Welles. It seems to be working wonders."

Samuel had worked out an ambitious route: Caldbeck, Cockermouth, Lorton, Ennerdale.

"We can explore the fells," he said excitedly. "Saddleback, Bowscale, Uldale, Loweswater…"

Sara assumed they would be gone for weeks but by the time they reached Caldbeck it seemed Southey had had enough and a few days later they were back home.

Shortly afterwards Mary and Robert arrived. Sara had tried to warn Hartley that just because Robert was much the same age, and his cousin, it didn't necessarily mean they would be friends. But Hartley had only ever had Derwent, who was four years younger, to play with and Robert had clearly been equally starved of friends of his own age so the boys hit it off immediately. Mary was her same prickly self, moaning about the long journey, the cold weather, the dreadful food at the inns. Sara watched her as she spoke. She was still a pretty woman, she was young and Robert was a pleasant, friendly little boy. If only she could meet a man, she could marry again. The fact that she had once been an actress stood in her way; it had probably hindered her prospects as a governess too. But it was more than that; she was just so miserable and pessimistic all the time. But she was family. She had nowhere else to go. Sara had to make her feel welcome, however hard it might be.

When Sara woke to hear Edith retching one morning she didn't take much notice. Edith had always suffered from a bad stomach. But when it was still happening a week later, Sara began to wonder. By lunchtime Edith had always recovered from the sickness. She ate well. She was definitely putting on weight. There was a glow to her face in the evening candlelight. She treated Southey more tenderly than she had for a long time. With a mother's instinct and a woman's intuition Sara knew: Edith was expecting another baby.

Chapter Twenty-Three

"It's just the best news ever," Samuel said, grasping Southey's arm.

"It's early days yet," Southey said. "Anything could happen. I probably shouldn't be telling you but I just couldn't keep it to myself."

"Does Sara know?"

"You know what women are like," Southey laughed. "Of course she knows. Oh Samuel, coming up here is the best thing we could have done. The change of scene, being with Sara, it's made all the difference in the world to Edith. I can't tell you how grateful I am."

This was the moment Samuel had been waiting for. "Stay," he said. "Stay here, Southey. You know what it's like now. You like it here, you said you do, the walks, the mountains, the lakes. We'll make it a proper arrangement. Divide the house up so you can have your own space. A separate kitchen if that's what the women need. Your own study. Edith is happy here, you said it yourself."

Southey was already smiling. "I agree," he said. "I'll talk to Edith about it. If she agrees I'll cancel the tenancy on the house in Bristol and pay you half the rent on this place. Of course it means Mary will have to stay."

Samuel sighed, "I know." Mary had already been causing arguments with Edith and Sara. "But the women will have to sort it out between them, won't they? They're sisters. They've probably always argued. I was thinking," he went on. "I need to get away, somewhere warm, for my health."

"Yes…" Southey said cautiously.

"Would you promise not to leave until I come back? It would make all the difference to me to know that Sara was well looked after."

"Of course," Southey said. "I owe her that for what she's done for Edith."

It was Samuel's thirty-first birthday in October. "Oh me!" he wrote in his diary. "My very heart dies! This year has been one painful dream! I have done nothing! Oh for God's sake, let me whip and spur, so that Christmas may not pass without something having been done."

It was a day of strong winds and driving rain, too stormy to venture out. He stood at his study window, looking out at the trees lashed by the wind and rain, the grey sky and the grey lake. He felt like the weather: miserable, cold, tormented. "Oh Asra, Asra, why am I not happy?" he wrote in his journal. "Why have I not an unencumbered heart? These beloved books still before me, this noble room, the very centre to which a whole world of beauty converges, the deep reservoir into which all these streams and currents of lovely forms flow, my own mind so populace, so active, so full of noble schemes, so capable of realising them, this heart so loving, so filled with noble affections. Oh Asra, wherefore am I not happy? Why, for years have I not enjoyed one pure and sincere pleasure? One full joy? One genuine delight that rings sharp to the beat of the finger?"

If only he could say this to Asra herself. She was the only one who would understand. Sometimes he fantasised that Sara was dead, that he was free to marry Asra. She would become mother to his children, they would have children of their own. He saw himself in bed with her, slipping her nightdress off her shoulders, exposing her beautiful bounteous breasts, his hand sliding down, lower, lower…

Afterwards he felt dreadful. To look forward to someone's death, it was the last taboo, the ultimate sin. Only God had the power to give and take life.

But if he couldn't have Asra, at least he could write to her. She wrote back asking him not to write so passionately but he couldn't help himself. He knew she loved him as he loved her. If he hadn't already been married, she would have married him, he was sure of it. What woman would want to be a spinster, at the beck and call of any family who needed her, reliant on family for support? Especially a woman like Sarah. He tortured himself with the thought of her marrying someone else. John Wordsworth maybe. John had liked Mary at one time. Why not marry her sister Sarah? They could all live together. The idea was unbearable.

Asra had refused to see him when she came to Grasmere at the end of September. "She is too ill,"

Dorothy had told him. "William has ridden over to Keswick to see Dr Edmondson for advice."

He knew they blamed him.

But Sarah had feelings too. Asra, his Asra, she had admitted those feelings to him, he had written them down in his notebook. And not just the things she said but every incident that showed she cared for him: the way her face lit up when she saw him, she and Mary cuddling up to him on the sofa at Gallow Hill, her small hand on his arm when they walked, the afternoons by the fire looking at books together. When he doubted it, he read and re-read them. She loved him, he loved her. It was a hopeless situation.

He didn't see so much of the Wordsworths nowadays. They didn't come over to visit him and he didn't see why he should be the one always visiting them. Wordsworth was becoming lazy. It was having all those adoring women fawning over him all the time: Mary, Dorothy and the Hutchinson sisters. Samuel had women living with him too but they did nothing but criticise him whereas Wordsworth's women worshipped him. They would do anything for him. If he had the slightest ache or pain they rushed around him to help. He had become such a hypochondriac. And he didn't seem to be doing any real work, just wasting time on short nature poems, spending hours writing and re-writing them and ending up ill and exhausted while he should really be working on his great philosophic poem, *The Prelude*. Samuel had the chance to talk to him about it when he came over to Greta Hall at the end of October.

"You really should get on with it," he said. "I know it will be a great work. You will be seen by posterity as the first and greatest philosophical poet. Picture it as a journey on which you will sail on an open ocean with a steady wind, no short tacks to hold you up, no reefing and hauling and untangling of ropes. This is your destiny, an epic work, not the short compositions you've been turning out."

"You're right of course," Wordsworth said. "But it's been so hard to galvanise myself since we came back from Scotland. I went to Ambleside to volunteer for the defence regiments in case there's an invasion, you know, along with most of the other men in Grasmere."

"You did?" Samuel asked. Since war with France had been resumed the threat of invasion was again very real. The last time it happened he and Wordsworth had supported the French. Now Wordsworth had leapt to the defence of his country.

"I've written to Sir George Beaumont," Samuel said, feeling he should show he was supporting his country as well. "I've told him I now see how wrong my radical opinions were. I was young, hot-headed, full of anger against injustice. The drivel of a babe."

While they were talking Hazlitt arrived. He had come back to do more work on Samuel's portrait. Sara showed him in with icy politeness. She never seemed to have taken to him. "I have to keep an eye on the maids when he's here," she complained to Samuel.

Hazlitt and Wordsworth, both atheists, got on quite well and began discussing religion. Hazlitt's argument was that there couldn't possibly be a god who would allow such vice and misery in the world. When Wordsworth agreed with him Samuel couldn't keep quiet any longer.

"How can you speak so irreverently of the divine being who created you?" he burst out. "How can you not believe that every wonder you see around you," he gestured towards the view of the mountains outside the window, "that *this* is not made by God?"

"A god who gives you pain," Hazlitt replied scornfully, "who makes you suffer, who makes innocent children suffer, who lets them die. I can't believe your divine being would allow that…"

On and on he went in the same vein, his anger like a furnace, until finally he stormed out of the room.

"I don't mind what he thinks," Samuel said to Wordsworth. "But I care about *you*. Don't be swayed by his petty arguments. God gave us suffering for a reason. Everyone has their cross to bear and we have to choose between good and evil."

He picked up the subject again with Hazlitt when he returned three days later. While he sat for his portrait he tried to convince him of the existence of the Almighty. But although Hazlitt listened this time, rather than losing his temper, Samuel still summed him up with bleak satisfaction in his notebook later on as, "Worthless, soul-less and God-less."

Still feeling unsettled by it, he went to bed early but woke two hours later screaming with terror. Thinking there was a fire or an intruder, everyone rushed from their rooms to help him — Southey, Edith, Mary, the maids and of course Sara, who he heard telling them all to go back, that she would see to it. Even while she sat with him he couldn't stop screaming. "It was dreadful Sara, the fires, the torment, a world without God…"

After she had gone he lit his candle and stirred up the fire in the grate. Then he sat at his desk and wrote a counter-argument to Hazlitt and Wordsworth.

Despite their disagreements, he continued his sittings with Hazlitt so that the portrait could be finished.

"It's a very good likeness of you," Wordsworth said when Samuel showed it to him.

"I think I look too lugubrious," Samuel said.

"What were you talking about while it was being painted?" Wordsworth laughed. "Religion again?"

"Well, yes, some of the time, but not always, not when it was started."

"No, seriously, it's very like you. The expression you have when you're thinking deeply. And the features are exactly correct. It's the best I've seen of you."

As autumn wore on, the household settled into a routine. The three women argued and grumbled, but basically they got on pretty well. The children played together in much the same way, with the occasional shriek of discord but mostly quite happily. Southey worked in his study and walked out with Samuel in the afternoon if the weather was dry.

With the onset of colder weather, Samuel's joints began to get bad again. He was still sleeping badly and feeling depressed. Now that Southey had provided him with his means of escape he didn't know where to go or how. He only knew that he must. It was his only hope. Wordsworth was right, Sara was right: he was addicted to opium. If he could go somewhere warm, cure his aches and pains, then he could give it up altogether. Once he had broken the habit he would never take it up again.

But, although he was so often unhappy here, he had grown to love Greta Hall, his study with its books from floor to ceiling, its tall windows looking out on the mountains and the lake, the driving rain lashing against them or the wind rattling the windowpanes. His warm bright fire, his armchair pulled up close to it, the desk where he wrote, his own bed. And the lakes and mountains, the walks he loved so much, with Wordsworth and Dorothy nearby, Mary and Sarah. He would be cut off from all this for a very long time.

But worse, a thousand times worse, was the thought of leaving the children: Hartley, a naturally bright, spiritual child with a curiosity for life so like his own and a unique way of expressing himself, and Derwent, a fat, stolid, affectionate boy with simple pleasures. He loved his food. Every meal was a source of delight and a story that didn't mention pies or puddings wasn't worth reading. He was full of mischief. One day he thrust his grubby little hands into Samuel's face and lisped, "Clean, white hands!" then collapsed in giggles at his own joke.

Then there was baby Sara, the dearest little girl there ever was, a happy, gentle little soul with her mother's beautiful blue eyes. When she smiled it was as though she were bathed in sunlight. The journey Samuel had in mind would take him away from all of them for a very long time.

November brought heavy frosts, the lakes froze over and Samuel took Southey out walking.

"It's beautiful," Southey said, his face red and glowing from the cold.

"Watch," Samuel said. He picked up a flat stone from the shore and hurled it skimming across the ice. The sound it made was like birds singing.

These were the memories Samuel stored up to take with him when he had left.

Sara's innate dislike of Hazlitt turned out to be well-founded. He arrived one day in a dreadful state. "They're after me," he panted.

"What? Who?" Samuel asked.

"Hundreds of them. They say I did terrible things. It's not true. The girls wanted it. . ."

"I told you," Sara said sharply when he went to find her. "They say he was, well, violent."

"I don't believe it," Samuel said.

"Huh! Anyway, he can't stay here. It's the first place they'll look. We've got the children to think of."

"He'll have to, Sara. He's got nowhere else to go. Look, we'll smuggle him out when it's dark."

"I hope they catch him," she said. "He belongs in jail."

"They'd probably just duck him in the nearest pond," Samuel said. "To teach him a lesson."

But they managed to get him away and he arrived back at his father's house in Shrewsbury unharmed.

Samuel's nightmares were getting worse, with strange, vivid dreams that stayed with him long after he had woken up, making him ill at ease and on edge. One was like a story unfolding. There were two sons of a nobleman, a wealthy man with a large country house where he had enjoyed shooting and other country pursuits. One day the sons were brought out by the footman to face a crowd of people who said that the property didn't belong to them and they had to give it up. But the sons weren't about to be fooled and they fought the people who threatened them. Suddenly Samuel became one of the sons. The physical struggle was transported to his boarding school, scene of many of his nightmares. He begged them to have pity on the orphan of a nobleman but they carried him to bed. There, a woman started to masturbate him. The humiliation, the degradation, it was awful. He screamed and woke up to find Sara shaking him violently. "Samuel, you'll wake everyone up again!"

He was ashamed of his nightmares, so often going back to his time at school. Sometimes a boy was masturbating him, or maybe he was the one masturbating another boy. It made no difference; it was disgusting, abhorrent and he felt dirty, abused. He wrote his dreams down in his notebook, trying to make sense of them, but they were too bizarre.

When the Wordsworths told Samuel that Sarah Hutchinson was moving to Ullswater, where her brother had leased a farm, he almost changed his mind about going away. She would come to Grasmere more often. He would see her. But she hadn't wanted to see him last time she was there and she might do the same again. To have her so near and yet so far would be unbearable.

Anyway, he was going mainly for his health, he reminded himself, to cure his illness and his dependence on opium.

He decided to leave in January. Poole had told him he would be in London at that time, working with John Rickman, the Speaker's secretary, who had recently set up the census. Samuel wrote to him and asked him to find him some lodgings, somewhere central. He could earn some money writing newspaper articles while he decided where to go. The war with France meant travel to the continent was prohibited so he reckoned on Madeira, Sicily or Malta; he didn't mind where, as long as it was warm.

He also wrote to his friend Thelwall, who lived in Kendal, asking him to go to the best druggist in the town and buy him an ounce of crude opium and nine ounces of laudanum, packed in a stout bottle to withstand a long voyage.

The Wordsworths invited him to stay for a few days before he left. "Come for Christmas," Dorothy said. "Bring the boys." But Hartley didn't want to go so it was three-year-old Derwent who sat next to Samuel in the cart for the bumpy ride.

Sara had looked at him sceptically when he told her he would be gone at least a year. He had said it before. But this time he meant it.

"I'm never going back to her," he told Wordsworth and Dorothy. "Our marriage is over."

He hadn't had the courage to say it out loud to Sara. She would find out in due course. Much as he detested being married to her he had done his best to provide for her.

Like Derwent sitting placidly by his side, probably thinking of his next meal, baby Sara was too young to understand what was going on. For Hartley it was one in a long series of goodbyes. He looked up at Samuel with the closed expression he had when he didn't want to face something bad happening.

"Be a good boy for Mama," Samuel said, though Hartley was seldom naughty — Derwent was the mischievous one — and then he was gone.

Dorothy greeted him with delight when they arrived, looking behind him for Hartley, who was her special favourite.

"He's not here," Samuel said, unnecessarily.

"Never mind, never mind," she said gaily. "Come in and see my Johnny. He's grown since you saw him last."

He saw Mary hurry to cover her breast and looked away politely.

"I'll put our things upstairs," he said hurriedly.

"I'm hungry," Derwent predictably informed Dorothy.

"Well, let's see what we can find in the kitchen for you, shall we?" Dorothy said, taking his chubby little hand.

"Not as much as he'd find in Sara's kitchen," Samuel thought wryly. He thought Mary might introduce some changes but the diet was still as meagre. Maybe it would be different when Johnny was older and needed more variety.

The next morning Samuel woke with the excruciating pain and stiffness that signalled another attack of gout.

"It must have been the journey over," he said to Dorothy when she brought him a bowl of porridge. "I'm never very good sitting still in a cart in the damp air. I would have walked over if I hadn't had Derwent with me, and the luggage for the journey."

There was no question of him walking now. His bent knees would scarcely hold him up and he was so tired and weak all he wanted to do was sleep.

To save having to keep running up and downstairs Dorothy made a bed up in the parlour for him and she and Mary looked after him with such kindness and gentleness, bringing him tea, coffee and soup whenever he wanted it. Sara was a hopeless nurse in comparison, sighing impatiently and speaking harshly to him whenever he asked for anything.

Outside, the rain swept across the valley in curtains. Inside, the cottage was crowded and chaotic. The baby cried, Derwent ran around shrieking, Mary went down with a bad cold and the maid, Molly, fell ill.

It was impossible to rest during the day and by night-time he was exhausted, although he dreaded falling asleep. As he said his prayers, he begged to be delivered from the demons that came to him in his dreams. But it was no good and it was poor Mary in the downstairs room, afraid he would wake Johnny, and heavy with sleep and cold, who had to shake him awake and sit with him until he felt calm again.

The rain stopped as suddenly as it had started and in the last few days of December the weather turned unusually mild. Samuel woke one morning to see a wintry sun struggling through the white clouds. He stretched. For the first time in days he could straighten his arms and legs, flex his fingers. He felt a lightness of heart, a renewal of energy. Today he would get up. He would go for a walk.

Over the next few days he and Wordsworth visited his favourite places. Samuel sat and wrote notes on each one, descriptions to remind him of the places he loved so much when he was far away.

The mild weather couldn't last and quite suddenly an icy wind began to blow from the north. He and Wordsworth battled against it to reach the highest point above Grasmere. Here, while Samuel sat soaking in the scenery below him, Wordsworth took out his notebook and read aloud the next part of his autobiographic poem *The Prelude,* the epic poem Samuel was encouraging him to continue.

"Thou my friend was reared

In the great city 'mid far other scenes

But we, by different roads, at length have gained

The self-same bourne…"

Samuel was deeply moved. To be mentioned, almost by name, in such a great work, was an honour.

"I'd love to take some of your poems with me when I go away," he said.

"I'll ask Mary and Dorothy to write them out for you," Wordsworth said.

The icy wind brought snow the next day, great billowing flakes that quickly covered the ground and put paid to any thought of leaving yet.

But it gave Mary and Dorothy time to write out all Wordsworth's unpublished poems, more than Samuel had expected, over eight thousand lines, often working late into the night.

"It was the least we could do for you," Dorothy said. "We will miss you so much."

A few weeks later the snow in the lane had turned to a muddy slush and, although it still lay white and glistening on the mountain tops, Samuel decided it was time to go.

He left on 14th January, invigorated by the sharp frosty air and the bright wintry sunshine, and walked nineteen miles over the hills to Kendal in four hours. He could scarcely understand it himself. He could go from being unable to move and feeling nearly dead to bursting with energy and fitness overnight.

When he arrived in Kendal he wrote to Poole to say he should be in London by Friday 20th January and would meet him at the Saracen's Head at Snow Hill at six o'clock.

In Liverpool, however, he suddenly thought he could go and see Dr Crompton. It was over three years since he had last seen him, when he had brought Sara and Hartley up to Keswick. It seemed a shame not to pay a visit while he was here; he might never get another chance.

"Don't rush off," Dr Crompton urged. "Stay for a while."

He ended up staying nearly a week. Every day he meant to write to Poole to tell him he had been delayed, but every day he forgot and when he did remember, it didn't seem worth doing anything about when he would be seeing him in a few days.

The moment the coach arrived in London Samuel rushed to Poole's lodgings. "I waited until past midnight," Poole said. But he shook Samuel's hand warmly anyway and Samuel could see he was forgiven.

The man standing before him, dressed grandly for his stay in London, looked quite different from the working country man Samuel was used to seeing in Somerset.

"I've found you lodgings at Waghorns Coffee House," Poole was saying, "right next door to the House of Lords. I've made sure the bed is comfortable."

Waghorns was a homely little place run by a Mrs Segur. Every morning at half past eight Poole came over to have breakfast with him there before going off to his parliamentary office to work on his report. While he was out for the day Samuel decamped to the cosy parlour in Poole's rooms in Abingdon Street. He had an idea for a new piece of work: *Consolations and Comfort from the exercise and right application of the Reason, the Imagination and the moral Feelings, addressed specifically to those in Sickness, Adversity or Distress of Mind.* He reckoned he would need a fortnight's steady reading to do the necessary research and then he could get down to some concentrated writing.

He also had a series of essays on various subjects drafted in his mind, ready to be written down, and he thought he might write a study of Shakespeare.

But before he did anything else he must catch up with his correspondence; Sara in particular must know he had arrived safely. And she was the only one he could tell about his intimate health problems, the only one he trusted not to tell anyone else. Then he must write to Tom Wedgwood, the Beaumonts, the Wordsworths…

Next he must find a way to raise some money for his trip. He knew he could rely on support from his friends in this, his final chance to save his health. Sotheby had already lent him £100 (Wordsworth had agreed to stand security) and Samuel had written to the Beaumonts to tell them his plan; they would be sure to help out. Stuart had said he could borrow from him as long as he would write some newspaper articles.

Samuel duly dashed off six articles for Stuart's evening paper, *The Courier*, and promised to supply regular articles on British policy in the Mediterranean once he was there.

Meanwhile, it was good to be living the bachelor life again. He went out with Davy and Stuart, saw Godwin in Somers Town and Lamb in Pentonville. He was still trying to cut down on the opium but suffered dreadful withdrawal attacks. One evening while he was dining with Stuart he began to pour with sweat. The next thing he knew he was vomiting violently followed by an embarrassing attack of diarrhoea. After that he collapsed completely and had to be taken home and put to bed.

He was still undecided about his destination. Up until recently he had been favouring Madeira but lately he had been hearing a lot about Sicily. It had the right climate for him and was very beautiful and of course there was Mount Etna, featured in Homer's Odyssey and believed by the ancient Greeks to be the home of the Cyclops. Suddenly he made up his mind: he would go to Malta. From there he could visit Sicily; he would climb Mount Etna. Malta was an important naval base in the war in the Mediterranean so he would be in a perfect position to report on foreign news articles for Stuart's newspapers. The climate would cure him of his illness and addiction. He could keep a journal of his travels to write up for publication and write essays on art and politics.

He had enough money for the journey over and he was sure that he could find work when he arrived. If he couldn't find an administrative position with his friend John Stoddart, the king's advocate, he could ask Sotheby and Sir George Beaumont to give him letters of introduction to the Governor of Malta, Sir Alexander Ball. There might be a position on his staff.

The trouble was, with the wartime convoy system, it was hard to find a place on a ship.

In the meantime he got on with sorting out his financial situation. He made the entire Wedgwood annuity over to Sara, secured the life insurance he had taken out, paid off all the outstanding tradesmen's bills and co-opted Stuart as his banker in London.

On 21st February Samuel was dining at Rickman's house when a letter arrived for him. His heart leapt when he saw Sarah Hutchinson's handwriting and he tore it open impatiently.

His eyes scanned the words uncomprehendingly. She didn't want anything more to do with him. It had to end, she said. A great spasm of pain tore through his chest. His heart was breaking, he knew it.

The voices of his fellow guests receded. The room swam around him. He reached in his pocket for his notebook and pencil, scribbled a line, "Would you ask the maid to get me a Hackney coach?" and passed it to his host.

The journey home was a blur. Vague impressions of being helped into the coach, staggering into his room, throwing himself down on the bed. "Oh Asra, Asra," he sobbed. "Anything, anything but this…" He didn't need to see her again; if he could have gone on writing to her it would have been enough, the recipient of all his innermost thoughts. But that had been the problem. It was all his own fault. She had asked him time and again not to write so passionately. But he couldn't help himself. Now he had lost the one small crumb of comfort he had had.

The next few days passed in a sort of blind stupor. He couldn't eat, he couldn't sleep, he was exhausted but restless. Opium was his only comfort. It took the edge off his feelings, numbed the constant pain in his chest. He scribbled down an outline in his notebook for a poem: *Ode on a Suicide for Love.*

Now there was nothing to keep him in England any longer. He had hoped to find a place on a Royal Navy ship but in the end he found a merchant ship, the *Speedwell,* a 130-ton brig that was sailing in a Mediterranean convoy at the end of March for Trieste, stopping off at Malta. The journey would take about nine weeks, including a week at Gibraltar, and cost thirty-five guineas, not including wine or spirits. He would also have to pay extra for bedding but the captain said he could get that cheaply for him, except for a counterpane that he would have to provide himself.

Samuel wrote a list of other things he would need: a jacket with a hood; his green bag to sleep in; umbrella; pencils; portable soup and mustard. He would get a jacket and trousers in Malta and he needed a pair of strong boots, made large, for walking.

One evening he ran into a friend from the old days, George Burnett. Burnett had been one of the first advocates for his Pantisocratic scheme and had lived with him and Sara for some time when they were first married. He had been one of Samuel's staunchest allies, more of a hanger-on than an activist, but a loyal friend. Samuel was shocked at the sight of him. Burnett had always taken opium regularly but now he was clearly an addict. He was as thin as a rake, he trembled the whole time, his eyes were bloodshot and wildly staring. Desperate to help him, Samuel asked Rickman if he might find him some work.

In the middle of March, Samuel had a bad bout of diarrhoea that lasted two days. It was so much worse than he had ever had before that he wondered if he might have cholera. Hearing that he was ill, the Beaumonts invited him to stay in their splendid town house on Grosvenor Square for his last few days in England. When he arrived Sir George pressed an envelope into his hand. Inside, Samuel found £100.

Although he was feeling better now Samuel was sure that he was dying. All his symptoms pointed to it. There was a slim hope of recovery if he went abroad but he didn't imagine he would ever make it home again. He sat down and wrote long, emotional letters to all his friends. Since Sarah Hutchinson had forbidden him to write to her, he sent her a book instead, a copy of Sir Thomas Browne's *Pseudodoxia Epidemica*.

On 24th March he heard that the *Speedwell* had gone to Gravesend and was due in Portsmouth the following Tuesday. After months of waiting there was suddenly very little time left and he quickly booked his seat on the Portsmouth Mail. The following day he sat for a portrait by James Northcote, commissioned by Sir George, though he was sure it wouldn't be very good; he began to feel so ill and sleepy that he had to break off before Northcote felt he had finished.

When the time came for him to leave Grosvenor House, Sir George and Lady Beaumont presented him with gifts: wine, medicinal food and soups for the voyage and a specially handmade travelling desk for his writing, complete with an expensive concise dictionary and grammar book. Sir George's valet packed everything up for him and sent it off before accompanying Samuel to the Angel Inn in the Strand where the Portsmouth Mail coach was due to leave at seven in the evening.

When he arrived in Portsmouth, twelve and a half hours later, Samuel found that the *Speedwell* had been delayed due to the wind being against her. He spent a few days in a dirty, poky inn before looking for cheap lodgings in the town. Luckily, Stuart had given him a letter of introduction to a friend of his, Mr Mottley, a bookseller in the town, and Samuel took all his meals with him. Mottley was a friendly, generous man, who showed Samuel around the town, which was a jungle of bricks and mortar. From Mottley's comfortable parlour, Samuel wrote his farewell letters to Southey, Stuart, Sir George Beaumont and the Wordsworths.

He went shopping for a present for Hartley and Derwent and found a box of spillikins to send to them.

Finally he wrote to Sara, "My dear Sara, the mother, the attentive and excellent mother of my children must needs be always more than the word friend can express when applied to a woman. What we have been to each other, our understandings, will not permit our hearts to forget. God knows I weep tears of blood that so it is. For I greatly esteem and honour you. My very dear Sara, may God Almighty bless you."

The *Speedwell* eventually reached Portsmouth on the evening of 3rd April and Captain Findley presented himself to Samuel. "The wind is against us at the moment," he told him. "A southwesterly. We shall have to wait for it to change before we can leave."

It was a frustrating time. The wind swung first in one direction, then the other, then it was too strong. He was hurried on board, sent on shore again, told to re-embark, but finally on Monday 9th April they set sail.

Samuel stood on the deck and watched the white-flecked waves rolling below him, the thirty-five other ships of the convoy in full sail, the seagulls diving and swooping, the dim blue line of England getting ever more distant.

He was leaving everything he knew: his friends, his home, his family. He thought wistfully of the two Saras to whom his life had been bound for so long; the Sara he had married no longer loved him and the Sarah he loved didn't want him. There was no reason to stay.

As the ship ploughed on to the distant country and the unknown future he wondered if he would ever see either of them again.

Epilogue

Coleridge was away from home for nearly three years. He spent his time in Malta writing essays, reports and newspaper articles while working as acting public secretary of Malta under the Civil Commissioner, Alexander Ball.

Dorothy tells us he came back ‘utterly changed’. He had put on a lot of weight, his stay abroad had done nothing to cure him of his illness or his opium addiction and he now had to face up to the problems he had left behind when he went: his unhappy marriage and his impossible infatuation with Sarah Hutchinson.

His addiction coloured the rest of his life, affecting his relationships, his creative work and his reputation as a writer.

We will never know what either Sara felt for him. Sara Coleridge was staunchly loyal. History has shown her to be far from the ‘weakest, silliest woman’ that Dorothy portrayed. Intelligent, optimistic and fun-loving, Sara educated the children in mathematics, French and Italian.

Coleridge was convinced that Sarah Hutchinson loved him but we have no proof. She never married but continued to keep house for her brothers, transcribe Wordsworth's poetry and help look after the Wordsworth children.

Although he spent much of his life believing he was dying, Coleridge lived to the age of sixty-one, a respectable age for an opium addict. He spent the last eighteen years of his life in Highgate in London under the care of Dr Gillman, who tried to control his addiction, and died in 1834.

Sarah Hutchinson died a year later. Sara Coleridge wrote to Mary, "She was an excellent kind-hearted creature…her kindness to me I shall ever remember."

Sara herself survived her husband by eleven years, dying in 1845.

Bibliography

Juliet Barker: Wordsworth, A Life
John Cornwell: Coleridge
Hunter Davies: William Wordsworth
Stephen Gill: William Wordsworth, A Life
Richard Holmes: Coleridge: Early Visions
Kathleen Jones: A Passionate Sisterhood
Molly Lefebure: The Bondage of Love
Molly Lefebure: Samuel Taylor Coleridge: A Bondage of Opium
Adam Sisman: The Friendship: Wordsworth and Coleridge
Dorothy Wordsworth: The Grasmere Journals
John Worthen: The Gang

About the Author

Bethany Askew is the author of six other novels:

- *The Time Before*
- *The World Within*
- *Out of Step*
- *Counting the Days*
- *Poppy's Seed*
- *Three Extraordinary Years: The Coleridges at Stowey*

She has also written a short story, *The Night of the Storm*, and she writes poetry.

Future projects include a new short story, this one for the young adult market, and another full-length novel.

Bethany is married and lives in Somerset.

www.bethanyaskew.co.uk

Blue Poppy Publishing

Founded in 2016 in Ilfracombe, North Devon, Blue Poppy Publishing is a small but rapidly growing publisher. We always like to take this opportunity to ask you, please, to take a few moments to write a review of this book, either on Goodreads or on our own website, or even better if you host a book blog; and do let us know so we can point readers to it.

If you enjoyed this book, you might like Bethany's other books including *Three Extraordinary Years: The Coleridges at Stowey*, companion to this novel. You may also enjoy *Barefoot on the Cobbles* by Janet Few and *A Breath of Moonscent* by Allan Boxall, both published by Blue Poppy.